A Thing of Beauty

A Thing of Beauty

Michel Tremblay

Translated by
Sheila Fischman

TALONBOOKS 1998

Copyright © 1998 Michel Tremblay
Published with the assistance of the Canada Council.

Talonbooks
#104—3100 Production Way
Burnaby, British Columbia, Canada V5A 4R4

Typeset in Garamond and Gill Sans and printed and bound in Canada by Hignell Printing.

First Printing: September 1998

Talonbooks are distributed in Canada by General Distribution Services, 325 Humber College Blvd., Toronto, Ontario, Canada M9W 7C3; Tel.: (416) 213-1919; Fax: (416) 213-1917.

Talonbooks are distributed in the U.S.A. by General Distribution Services Inc., 85 Rock River Drive, Suite 202, Buffalo, New York, U.S.A. 14207-2170; Tel.: 1-800-805-1083; Fax: 1-800-481-6207.

Un objet de beauté was first published in 1997 by Lémeac Éditeur Inc., Montréal, Québec.

Canadian Cataloguing in Publication Data

Tremblay, Michel, 1942-
[Objet de beauté. English]
A Thing of Beauty

Translation of: Un objet de beauté.
ISBN 0-88922-390-4

I. Title. II. Title: Objet de beauté. English
PS8539.R4702413 1998   C843'.54   C98-910731-0
PQ3919.2.T7302413 1998

for Jimmy Théberge

"The hero, in the literary sense, is the protagonist who accomplishes a feat, one whose tragic weak point will bring about his ruin."

Dan Simmons
Endymion

"Anxiety, pain and pleasure and death are but one single way of existing."

Frida Kahlo
Journal

PART ONE

The Springtime of Every Promise

"The worst thing of all is knowing that you're right and
everybody else is wrong!"

—*The sayings of Victoire*

Number 410 Sherbrooke Street East was deep in the coma of a chilly early morning in late winter. The day before, the weatherman had announced the arrival of spring, a redemptive mild spell that would bring Montrealers out of their holes to breathe in the first breeze from the south, a pre-Easter Easter Sunday even though it wasn't Sunday, when the sidewalks would finally be bare, clear of any trace of slush or ice, where you could hear the click of the high heels of women on their way to do their morning errands.

A good foot of snow had fallen nonetheless, a fantastic storm that had blown up out of nowhere, driven by cruel gusts of wind that had howled all night as it beat at doors and windows, and the snow covered the city now like one last bad joke by the winter before it died.

All was calm. Hypocritically, nature was behaving as if nothing was wrong: no clouds were racing through the windless sky, no wind was making the snow swirl, the stars were disappearing one by one as a pallid light broke through in the east where the sun would rise at any moment; the storm hadn't happened, all was well, no one had anything to complain about. After all, a mere twelve or thirteen inches of snow weren't going to change the fact that March 21 was approaching, the crows would soon be cawing the news above the Côte des Neiges cemetery and Mount Royal would be awash in a multitude of little rivulets that would flood Park Avenue and Peel Street.

One of the tallest buildings in the neighbourhood—four storeys divided between two adjoining buildings, with one door, the one to 400, sealed off long ago—number 410 Sherbrooke East opened directly onto the sidewalk: no balconies, no paths lined with flowers in summer and scraped by snow-shovels in winter, no metal fence trying to define a semblance of a garden or a square of front lawn, unlike some other houses in the neighbourhood: the Club Saint-Denis for instance, or the Club Richelieu, its pretentious neighbours. No. When you opened the door, you were right in the heart of the action. Because action there was at the corner of Sherbrooke and Saint-Denis, especially since the beatniks, a mob that was loathed by the longtime residents of the neighbourhood, had discovered the ridiculously low rent for the apartments at 410 and taken over the premises in less than two years, leaving behind them the smell of unwashed, sweaty black sweaters and unfiltered Gitanes.

When she saw them walk past her apartment—the guys with long hair, the girls with skin-tight skirts and greasy hair—Madame Saint-Aubin, the janitor, always said: "If this keeps up pretty soon I'll be the only normal person around here! Which is when I'll get the hell out! And if the landlord hires some beatnik to replace me, there'll be filth running right into Sherbrooke Street!"

But at this indefinable time of day when it's neither day nor night, when the light is grey and none too clean, conferring a ghostly aura on everything, everyone was asleep, both those who'd retired early and those who would get up early, and at 410 Sherbrooke Street East, nothing was stirring.

The first rays of sunlight were falling slantwise onto the back of the house, leaving the front in shadow for another few minutes; the snow now had a bluish tinge, something like the colour of barely solid ice on a rink that was flooded during the night when the cold is at its most biting. For a brief moment it was no longer soft snow that creaked when you walked on it, but a stiff corset of ice, paralyzing, that would stifle the house from its foundations to its roof. In the time it would take the sun to make up its mind to gild the snow on the cornice, during that brief moment when it seemed that everything was touched by the grace of the light except it, simply because it was on the wrong side of the street, the apartment block became an image frozen in space and time. Immutable. It was impossible to imagine the building any other way: imprisoned in its coating of ice, it had stood forever at the top of the Sherbrooke hill, ostentatiously turning its back on what Montrealers called "the lower end of town," where the stores and businesses were, a dowager left behind in a working-class neighbourhood, strict but fair—to watch over Saint Denis Street as it climbed north, the twin steeples of the Saint-Jean-Baptiste church, the silhouette of Mount Royal that was beginning to reflect the first light of morning.

Nor could anyone ever have imagined that in a few months its inhabitants would be complaining about the heat because the apartments were so poorly ventilated: the July heatwave, the August mugginess, were still unthinkable because the cold seemed to be definitive, the very essence of the world.

The door of 410 opened abruptly and the notion of a cold eternity died suddenly when Madame Saint-Aubin appeared with her first garbage can. With one hand she dragged the big galvanized tin container filled with greasy, smelly things, while with the other she tried to keep the collar of her pink chenille housecoat closed. Shuddering when the door was wide open, she craned her neck, looked first to the left, then to the right, as if she were about to cross the street. Briefly, she gazed down at her fluffy slippers, shaking her head. Anyone going past just then would have heard her mutter between her teeth: "They'll never pick it up after a storm like that! Why should I kill myself taking out the garbage cans? And I didn't even put on my rainboots!" The door closed soundlessly, Sherbrooke Street fell back into its torpor, but it was as if the mere presence of a human being in this frozen tableau had given birth to the genuine light of day, to the true normal life of a busy street: an early morning bus drove through the intersection, sending up the day's first burst of slush, the front of 410 turned a degree paler because a window across the street had just sent back a ray of sunlight that you could describe, yes, you could, as spring-like.

Then the ploughs appeared. Lots of ploughs with lots to do, big and small, noisy and comical with their metal tracks and their curved blades, they pushed, towards the invisible gutters, snow already soiled by their mere presence. Droning cheerfully, they were clearing the way for the first car, the first pedestrian, the first dog brave enough to drop a turd into such an inhospitable environment. The snowbanks piling up along the sidewalks were already grimy and the gushes of icy mud splashed by passing cars would soon finish soiling them.

Men emerged from their houses with shovels and scrapers, trying to dig out cars buried under a foot of snow, a foot of snow for Christ's sake, after six goddamn months of the stuff; children toting schoolbags squealed and threw snowballs—dangerous, because they were too hard; the first accident occurred at the corner of Sherbrooke and Sanguinet. Shouts, raised fists, accompanied by son-of-a-bitches and bastards that rose into the air in a bluish mist.

All at once, as if at a signal, as if it had just been given permission to do so, the neighbourhood came to life.

***

It was the smell that finished waking her up, as usual. First, a breath on her cheek—she always slept on her back—she was only vaguely aware of, then the characteristic little morning snore, not as loud as the powerful operations of the middle of the night but just as insidious, that tugged her definitively from her dreams, then the odour, powerful and intrusive, of a man's breath first thing in the morning. She didn't open her eyes right away, she merely sighed. The first in a long series of sighs that would stretch out till evening, when she would collapse, exhausted, into her bed where she wouldn't sleep because she'd be too tired and above all too nervous.

The voice of Madame Saint-Aubin, heard the night before while she was dragging the garbage cans to the stairs: "I've just got one thing to tell you, my dear! There's two of them, the mother and her big lump of a son who's at least twenty, and there's just *one* bed!" The other woman adds her two cents' worth, the nasty remarks go back and forth and she, frozen in front of her apartment door, key in hand, not daring to move, holding her breath, but if she tries to put the key in the lock it will make a noise, Madame Saint-Aubin and the other woman will hear, they'll know that she's there, listening to them, that she knows that they know....

She mulled over that conversation all evening and part of the night. So that's what the others in the house are saying about them. And that's why nobody ever looks them in the eye, especially her son who too often haunts the corridors of 410 asking for his mother, because she's gone out to do her shopping or to take a walk or to visit her sister-in-law who's sick. A twenty-three-year-old son doesn't wander the corridors of a rooming house looking for his mother, she's told him that time and again, it makes people talk, it stirs up suspicions, it gives the goddamn janitor the idea of using her skeleton-key to come and stick her nose where it doesn't belong....

She was sure she'd guessed right. Madame Saint-Aubin had taken advantage of their absence to come and count the beds in the apartment and then hypocritically look away when she saw there was only one.

She opened her eyes, frowned.

"It's just because there's no room for another one, goddamnit!"

She turned her head slowly towards the left to peer at her son's big nose and his bulging forehead, as she did every morning. His eyes too, which were constantly moving beneath his lids. In the past, when he was little, the circles under them were rather attractive, they made him look different from the other children and they were always erased by the first meal of the day, as if in this child of hers who was unlike other children, they were a sign of hunger. Not any more. Now he always looked tired, surly, sick. Like her.

He started as if he'd been given a shock and hauled his big hand from under the covers to scratch his nose. Then he yawned and the smell was so strong she had to turn her head.

She gazed up at the moulding in the middle of the ceiling, the little cherubs that encircled the porcelain light fixture, holding up garlands mildewed and spotted from dampness.

Over the past thirty-five years there had been two men in this bed: first her husband who'd disappeared in the war—but he might be living with some Frenchwoman or an Englishwoman or a Greek or some kind of European who understood him, and then her son because she had no choice, because she couldn't afford an apartment with two bedrooms, because the two of them were fated to be this inseparable.

She could have committed him after his stay in the lunatics' wing at the Bordeaux jail a few years earlier. Brother Stanislas had told her she didn't have to put up with that, that her son was liable to become even more dangerous as he got older, that the government could take care of him, get rid of him, but she'd taken the term "get rid of" very badly and snapped that as long as she was alive, her son would never be locked up.

He had bent over her, his forehead creased, eyes filled with commiseration of a sort she'd never seen in all her life as a mother with an insane child.

"Even if he's dangerous!"

Today...this morning, at any rate, when she woke up, what wouldn't she have given to have said yes that time! She'd have been able to get up feeling light-hearted, fix herself toast and bacon and eggs, without worrying about disturbing someone who had nothing to do all day but stay in bed, who could only be moved by greed; she'd be able to go out when she felt like it, without having to drag behind her a ball and chain that weighed nearly two hundred pounds, she could get dolled up when she was in the mood, go out to the movies or shopping or even to look for a job.

Tears. She'd thought she didn't have any left and here they were, running down her neck and onto the pillow.

She threw off the blanket that also smelled of her big neglected child, placed her feet on the red rug and got up, stretching. At least her flannelette nightgown had kept her warm. She performed her morning tasks automatically, without thinking: coffee on the gas stove, slices of bread next to the toaster on the kitchen table, a loaf of the Château cheese with pimientos that she loved, the jar of strawberry jam, the butter, the sugar. While she waited for the coffee to perk she went back to the one and only bedroom, crossed it and looked up towards the basement window where the wall met the ceiling to see what kind of day it was.

She couldn't see a thing. It had snowed.

On fine summer days a light somewhere between yellow and grey descended to her place from the hole in the sidewalk; in winter, the light was brighter, clearer, she could practically make out the ultramarine sky over Montreal, the air colder than cold but dry, that froze your nose and ears. On the day after a snowstorm though, the layer of snow that covered the cement didn't allow any light to enter the basement of 410 and she felt more than ever as if she'd been buried alive.

Cursing, she went back to the kitchen and snapped on the overhead light.

"Not even a window to look out of! Not even a tiny little window so I can see people's feet walking on Sherbrooke Street, no, all I've got is a basement window, here I am in an apartment with a basement window that opens onto underneath the sidewalk!"

She went on cursing as she moved the coffee pot, which had started to gurgle; she liked her coffee strong and bitter, nearly burnt. A tea-drinker till the age of fifty, she had discovered the virtues of coffee here, in this apartment that was too small and too dark, because she'd needed a pick-me-up that was faster and more effective. She still wasn't crazy about the taste, sometimes she even missed her mother's green tea though she'd always criticized it as being weak and tasteless. But that burst of energy she felt after the first coffee of the day, the feverishness that forced her to move, to talk in a loud voice, to do something, anything, even if she wasn't in the mood, made up for the burnt taste and the thickness of the sickly sweet mixture.

She poured herself a cup and drank it standing by the stove, her head bent over the burners that still smelled a little of gas, even when they were turned off.

As her son still hadn't put in an appearance, despite the coffee aroma coming from the kitchen, she decided to wake him up with that of the scrambled eggs he was so fond of. She cooked up what she thought looked as good as it tasted: the delicious scrambled eggs, still just a bit runny, the perfect toast, the crisp bacon. And the kitchen smelled of life.

Imperiously declaring, "Does that ever smell good!" she sat at the table, convinced that at any moment she would hear her big son shuffling down the short hallway that separated the two rooms of the apartment. But there was nothing.

She heard someone walk furtively past her door and thought: The beatniks are up early this morning. Or coming home late.

She put down her knife and fork, grimaced as she got up because the dampness in the basement of this stone house was hard on her back.

He was still asleep, but not soundly. He was dreaming out loud as he did more and more often; she recognized the moans, the little cries, like those of a tormented animal or a frightened child, the abrupt shudders that made the bed shake. All at once, as she was gazing at her sick child, she was struck by the desolation of her life. This miserable little apartment, the one bed, the musty smell, the lack of light, the lack of money, the lack of encouragement, the lack of motivation. She rested her head on the door-post and folded her arms over her vast bosom.

"I've fallen too low. And I let it happen. I have to pull myself up before it's too late! Unless maybe it already is...."

She saw again her mother, Victoire, dignified and stiff in her rocking chair that used to dominate one corner of the dining room in the Fabre Street apartment. The old woman wore a cheap grey polka-dotted jersey dress with a lace collar she'd crocheted herself, concealing her mistakes with loops and bows of black ribbon. As usual, she wasn't speaking to anyone in particular but they all felt targeted and kept quiet. Her brother was playing solitaire on one side of the table, her sister-in-law was stirring her eternal soup with elbow macaroni, tasting without slurping so she wouldn't miss a word of what was being said, she herself was doing the ironing which left her with a sore right arm and an aching back, her daughter was putting on makeup and laughing, and her son.... Where was he, as a matter of fact? She made a mental tour of the apartment; everything was as clear as if she'd never left it. Because in spite of the anger, the shouting matches, the splits, the whole series of troubles and woes, it was the most wonderful period of her life; it was there that she'd been happiest, because at least she wasn't all alone in a cellar like a rat, with her crazy son, she was surrounded by people who, all right, so they didn't always understand her, but they.... Yes, they loved her. She saw him at the livingroom window, his nose pressed against the glass. He was too young to understand what his grandmother was saying and anyway, he was already off in his own world, not definitively, that would happen later, but still too wrapped up in his own difference to be considered normal. As she listened to her mother she took her son in her arms and began to rock him.

"You're never so low you can't pick yourself up, believe me. There's always something or somebody.... Take me, for instance...."

The speech would be long, the same one as always: courage in adversity, the importance of the family when things aren't going well, taking refuge in reading or knitting or crocheting, salvation through action or optimism at any cost, images of the countryside, stories of farmers who haven't yet experienced the inhumanity of the big city, the loneliness, the exile in the middle of the world.

But she listened right through to the end. If anyone had told her she was resurrecting her mother through the power of her imagination, that she was distilling into a single monologue everything Victoire had carried with her during her lifetime, she'd brush away the idea with a wave of her hand. Her mother really is there in front of her and she really is suggesting how to deal with her situation, even if she doesn't believe it. She is bringing back to life what her mother always used to tell her and she's managing not to believe it any more than she did twenty years earlier: what she needs now is not so much what her mother said as the resurrection of a memory. Of the comfort it represents.

But her son isn't three years old now and he isn't standing at a window lit by the morning sun. (Did her mother make those speeches of hers in the morning? And did her sister-in-law cook the soup before their evening meal? And did her brother play solitaire when he got up? What difference does it make, it's what she needs!) He's just wakened up and he's looking at her as if he doesn't recognize her. She knows that look in his eyes. A sign of the bad days. The bad days, dangerous ones even, when according to Brother Stanislas she ought to phone and tell him she can't take it any more, he can come and get Marcel, she wants him to come and get him. She walks over to the bed, sits in her place which has had time to cool down.

The big twenty-three-year-old child finally recognizes her, moans like a baby, hunches his shoulders.

"Have a bad night?"

He doesn't answer right away but gazes in turn at the plaster cherubs and the mildewed garlands.

"Tell Momma. Did you have a bad night?"

Finally he looks at her. Those eyes filled with tears will overwhelm her always, to the very depths of her soul, because she is the cause of them, because she is the one who produced this unhappy man, because it's all her fault that she was unable to give birth to normal children.

"It's worst of all at night, Momma! It hurts the most at night!"

Marcel is a little boy again and she holds out her arms to console him. To try, at any rate.

The scrambled eggs are cold now. The bacon is dry. The toast is soggy.

***

As soon as his mother told him it had snowed during the night he left his breakfast, which was too cold and probably indigestible anyway and pulled on his boots, parka, scarf, tuque and mitts. And after he'd sped across the kitchen on his way to the front door, Albertine thought once again about a huge two-hundred-pound child, a tiny brain imprisoned in a big body, and then she thought to herself:

"No, that's not true, his brain isn't little, no, he's just too intelligent in a lot of ways I don't understand, that's all...."

That was what Brother Stanislas tried to tell her.

"It's not that your child isn't intelligent, you mustn't think he's not intelligent, he's...."

He tried to find the words as he fiddled with the cross that hung down on his chest and rubbed against the fabric-covered buttons on his soutane till they shone, but she was the one who came up with the right word, with no hemming and hawing to gain time, with no euphemisms to sweeten the truth, because she's known it for a long time and because words, when she does think of them, have never scared her:

"He's crazy."

He didn't say yes, didn't even nod, he merely looked away and watched the skaters glide across the frozen lake.

She was furious, let down.

"You made me come all the way to l'Annonciation by bus to tell me something I've always known? It doesn't take a doctor, not even a Brother to see that he's crazy."

She looked at the dandruff on the shoulders of his soutane, the flakes numerous and surprisingly big, like snowflakes that haven't melted, and part of her wanted to laugh despite the gravity of the situation: up here, even the Brothers snowed!

"No, Madame. I brought you up here to tell you and to show you how happy Marcel would be if you'd leave him here with us for a while, till things settle down at any rate, because if I understood correctly his condition has been getting worse this past while. Look around you, Madame, isn't this a nicer environment than the one Marcel's in now?"

He was right, it was beautiful. Outdoors, at any rate. The Laurentians in winter, with the sky so blue and the snow that never gets dirty. The skaters playing hockey, the sounds, clearer than in the city, so clear you could have followed a conversation going on in the middle of the lake. And the wind, everywhere, always, that made everybody look healthy. As for the hospital itself (the asylum, actually, but Brother Stanislas insisted on calling it a hospital), it was an old greystone building not so different from the convents where she'd spent her own childhood, where she felt uncomfortable, not just because of the smell of cheap disinfectant that haunted her memory, but in particular because of the boarders—you weren't supposed to say patients—who were too quiet for her liking, who were zombies, in fact. All right, so they were playing hockey, but it was a slow, slack game, without energy, and the players looked as if they couldn't have cared less, as if they were movie extras, not people living a real life. That was what scared her the most: if she brought Marcel here they'd turn him into a zombie who would play hockey in slow motion— "Marcel, play hockey? Don't be ridiculous: he'd piss them all off, then he'd roll in the snow and scream bloody murder!"—and that was what she'd said to Brother Stanislas, who merely shook his head and smiled.

"You have to decide which is better: being a zombie and happy or hyperactive and unhappy—or even dangerous."

The reply had come too quickly, Albertine hadn't been able to hold it back:

"I can't imagine that you think what you said just now is intelligent. Aren't you supposed to be diplomatic with the patients' parents? You sure as heck won't cure him by drugging him!"

She saw the response in his eyes before he even opened his mouth.

"That's okay, don't say anything, I know he'll never be cured, he'll never get better like you want me to believe. And I also know everything you could tell me: that he'd be better off up here in the country, the country's so healthy, that you're better informed and better equipped than I am to look after him when he has his fits, that he'd be with other people like him.... As far as that's concerned, some mornings I look in the mirror and I think, he's pretty close to being with other people like him as it is, because I'm not that far from crazy myself. So maybe I'd be better off keeping him...."

"At least you could talk to him about it...."

"Sure I could talk to him, but what do you want him to say if I give him a choice between being locked up here in the country with lunatics that play hockey as if they haven't any idea what they're doing, or staying in town with his mother...."

"You could present it differently...."

"I don't want to promise him things I can't give him. I've never done that and I don't intend to start today, just to make you happy!"

"You're not helping him, you know."

She looked him squarely in the eyes before she got to her feet, taking her pale blue plastic purse trimmed with flowers of every colour in the rainbow, plastic too, a purse that made you think of Easter but that she carried all year because it was the only one she had.

"Anyway, there's one thing I know for sure: you aren't helping me one little bit."

And she'd taken the bus back to Montreal, an interminable trip that lasted nearly three hours, with stops, sometimes for nothing, in each of the small villages along the way, even those most deeply hidden in the folds of the mountains, even the most insignificant, even those that seemed to be totally deserted.

"I can't see myself taking that road every Sunday, good Lord no, that's the last thing I can see myself doing!"

With Marcel off capering in the snow like a pre-schooler— because she knows that any minute now she'll hear him come out with a loud "Yahoo!" when he gets a look at the snowbanks already piled up along Sherbrooke Street, just before he throws himself into one—she thinks about the wild ideas, the snatches of projects she's been thinking of lately, that she hasn't been able to reject altogether in spite of the guilt that torments her. Hope. Hope for another life. A better one. More peaceful. More gentle. Or wilder. With more life in it. But different. Different! If Marcel.... If only Marcel....

She gets up from the table, picks up everything that's sitting around, the good food they've barely touched—dammit she hates waste—throws out the leftovers, plunks the plates and cutlery in the sink, puts the kettle on to boil.

Stay busy. To keep from thinking.

She turns towards the telephone on the wall next to the front door. A note pinned to the flowered wallpaper. With a number scrawled under a name: Grocerie Papineau.

But it's not the number of the Grocerie Papineau. That grocery store doesn't even exist any more.

Through the stone wall, as if they've come from very far but so close that she shudders a little, she hears Marcel's first words. And what she hears him shout is: "Merry Christmas!"

**

Sherbrooke Street is so beautiful, he couldn't say anything at first. All the whiteness sparkling in the sun takes his breath away.

(It's Christmas morning, he's six years old, he's just opened his presents and he's decided to go outside and try his new shovel or his new skates....)

Two young girls walk by. He shouts "Merry Christmas!" and they laugh because they think he's kidding, this big man with the nice red cheeks who's all muffled up and wishing them Merry Christmas in the middle of March. But he didn't intend to make them laugh. He's decided it *is* Christmas because this day is worthy of the birthday of baby Jesus and he firmly believes that it is. Or rather, he's made himself believe that he believes it. It's a new game he's made up recently that rids him of any guilt, any doubt, even of the fear of being bawled out by his mother: once he realizes he's imagining things, even while he's acting as if he doesn't know, anything is possible.

This is a great discovery for Marcel. A beautiful day in March can be transformed into Christmas, his mother can become a Godfairy Mother (Marcel's mild dyslexia makes him distort certain names and he gets angry if anyone corrects him) he himself can become Tom Thumb and shrink so small he can go under doors, he's no longer afraid of being yelled at, no longer feels ashamed at not being like other people because he can only communicate through a network of imaginary worlds and characters taken from the books he's read, the movies he's seen, the TV shows he's watched; if worst came to worst he might tell his mother that he knows what he says to her isn't always true and may even sound dangerous to a down-to-earth woman like her, and she wouldn't be able to think of a thing to say.

If he tells her: "I know!" she can't do a thing to him!

Actually he keeps this last card for emergencies. He has often riffled through this scenario, improved it, polished it, he's on the nth version now, the one that's most complete, most precise. And this is it. He's still in bed, his mother has just got up, he doesn't feel like spending the day as Marcel-the-dummy....

No, not this morning. All this whiteness is too beautiful to ruin with a squabble, with slaps on the face, with someone's hair set on fire.

He frowns. Not because the snow is too white but because something's bugging him: more and more, his scenarios end with a vision of his mother's head in flames, he thinks it's strange but he hasn't tried to analyze it yet, so he stops himself from doing that for fear of what he might find.

He takes his dark glasses from his parka pocket. For ten years now he's always had them with him, even in the fall when it gets dark at four o'clock, even during storms or blizzards—whenever he has an urge to let loose, like the weather, to snow, to rain, to thunder. Of course the snow doesn't look as pretty through dark glasses, it's not white, but the luminous green of early evening, but it soothes him too in a way, he doesn't feel as much adrenaline racing through his body, he can breathe comfortably. And be absolutely sure that it's Christmas.

He walks in the direction of Berri Street, taking tiny little steps, his head raised towards the pale grey sky. And he wishes everyone he meets Merry Christmas. They laugh or at least they smile at this weird Santa Claus who's traded his bright red outfit for a navy blue nylon parka and a brown synthetic wool tuque without a pompom. A rather sad Santa Claus, who'd be scary if the day weren't so beautiful and so young. And if this wasn't Sherbrooke Street.

Marcel could ring the bell at the Club Canadien where his sister Thérèse has been working as a janitor for six months now, but he knows that she's still asleep and wouldn't be glad to see him. So he makes his way quite naturally towards Parc Lafontaine.

***

No one has trampled yet on the great expanse of white snow; Parc Lafontaine is innocent of footsteps except maybe the numerous families of squirrels that have always lived there and have already started capering here and there in search of their last stock of food, which they were surprised to find this morning covered with a sparkling crust of that cold substance they'd thought had finally gone for good; the Jacques Cartier Normal School, though it's an indescribable architectural horror, actually looks quite attractive, hidden by bouquets of trees that yesterday were covered with buds and now, this morning, weighed down by the heavy wet snow, form an obliging screen to hide its ugliness.

Will the buds freeze? Will the trees leaf out as usual? Yes, because the sun is there, already warm though it's still early morning. This blizzard will turn out to be just an accident, quickly rectified and even more quickly forgotten.

Marcel does not enter the park right away, doesn't even walk along the edge of it; for the time being he's content to admire it from across the street, as if he were reluctant to cross Sherbrooke Street and soil something that is clean. He walks past the municipal library without looking at it, crosses some more streets without saying Merry Christmas to the passersby he no longer sees: all his attention is focused on the smooth coating of snow, with no rough parts, no bumps or hollows, a little like the white sheet that served as snow in the crèche his Auntie Nana used to put up every Christmas when they were all still living in the apartment on Fabre Street, before the big battle, before the big split, in the good old days, the days when he and his mother weren't confined to an airless black hole that always smells of bacon fat or stale cigarette smoke, in that blessed time when, in spite of everything, his life was scattered with moments of joy and flashes of happiness.

Tears come to his eyes; afraid they'll freeze, he takes off his left mitt and rubs his cheeks.

Now, everybody has moved. All of them. The whole family. And nothing now is like it used to be. He saw his grandmother, Victoire, die, he thought he'd even seen her soul fly off to heaven; his mother is more and more pensive, withdrawn, and at the same time vindictive; his sister spends all day in a bath that's too hot despite the advice of the doctor who claims that boiling herself like a lobster that way is weakening her dangerously; his cousins hardly talk to him any more because they're afraid of him—at least that's what he senses whenever he finds himself in their presence by chance, because they never ask for him; his uncle Édouard, his mother's younger brother, still claims he's a duchess in a world where every person can become what he wants to be; and his uncle Gabriel drinks because....

Because his Auntie Nana is going to die.

Whenever he thinks about it he bites his lips to keep from howling at the unfairness. When his aunt, his only ally, his only friend, is gone, he will be quite hopelessly alone in the world and he's afraid he won't be able to fight the evil elements that have begun showing up in his mother ever since her recent trip to l'Annonciation. Because he doesn't really understand, his Auntie Nana has always protected him against Albertine's rages and his cousins' jeers. Oh sure, there's Thérèse who adores him, he knows that, but Thérèse, he also knows, has her own problems and she hasn't been looking after him so much since she moved in nearby, because something very ugly is hounding her, something that she knows she can't escape from.

And in any case, the relations between Albertine and Thérèse have been steadily worsening for years.

So what will happen to him when his Auntie Nana isn't there to encourage him to go on living when he's discouraged with life?

Forget all that. Concentrate on the beauty of Parc Lafontaine in the morning sun. The whiteness. Especially that, it's so important: the whiteness.

Without really planning it, almost without realizing it—one second he's on the south side of Sherbrooke Street, the next second he's in the park, at the corner of Calixa-Lavallée—Marcel crosses Sherbrooke to the sound of blaring horns and squealing tires. Drivers are afraid they won't be able to brake in time to avoid him because of the thin coating of ice that hasn't had time to melt completely, and they're expressing their anger: windows are hastily rolled down, words of abuse rise above the traffic sounds, but Marcel doesn't hear a thing. He is already deep inside the silence of the park.

As he walks he makes the characteristic sound he loves— somewhere between the crunch of the hard crust giving way under the walker's weight and the swish of cotton batting being squeezed between a thumb and index finger—of the last snowfall as winter nears its end, a reminder of what has been, a promise of what is to come: everything may be white today but tomorrow morning it could well be green again. The snow is young and won't have time to grow old, it will evaporate under the springtime sun or it might even be swallowed by the grass that has already started growing.

Crows greet him with their ugly croaking when he walks beneath the vault of the trees, but aside from that there is silence. The traffic noises from Sherbrooke Street are wiped out all at once and the only sound that reaches his ears is that of his own heartbeats, rapid and heavy, and of his boots as they clear a path towards the middle of the park. He runs past the Plateau Hall without looking at it so he'll arrive as quickly as possible on the gentle slope that goes down to the snow-covered lake, the goal of his walk.

He stops briefly to catch his breath, takes a few steps, smiles.

Here it is at the bottom, imprisoned between two small rises, perfectly flat: the giant screen for his winter dreams stretching out between the restaurant that's closed for the season and the row of green wooden benches no one remembered to put away for the winter, where he has spent so many fascinating hours, so many intoxicating afternoons.

His lake.

He pulls down the zipper of his parka, puts his hand over his heart.

"It's true I'm too fat. I ought to be careful. Not run like that. It's bad for me."

It would never occur to him to eat less, less fat in particular, no; he tells himself that exercise is bad for his heart and he promises himself to do as little as possible.

Then, very slowly, he descends the gentle slope, watching carefully where he places his feet, turning around several times to gaze at his footsteps meandering behind him, a double line of bluish holes he sees as very threatening because they're following him so closely. But he knows he mustn't embark on this kind of game if he doesn't want to spoil the wonders that are forthcoming on the snow-covered surface of the lake. He tumbles more quickly down the last section of the slope, braces himself against the back of a bench, then walks around it to sit down. When he comes to the front of the bench he brushes off the snow with his mitts, makes a nest for himself just wide enough for his buttocks, sits down, folds his arms, crosses his legs.

Right away he feels the twinge, the warmth in his solar plexus—in his own mind he pronounces it "scholar plexus" and tells himself it's legitimate because he's sitting on a bench, even if it's not a school bench—and then the projection begins.

This time, it's the beginning of everything, his own genesis, which he has spent so much time constructing and perfecting, the nucleus of all the stories he tells himself here in the winter and hidden in the bushes in the summer, the beginning of the great novel of which he is the hero, the first chapter, no, the introduction, the preamble.

He's very excited, he's shivering a little but not from the cold; he's fidgeting with excitement on his bench.

It takes up the full width of the lake, it's in colour, CinemaScope, Technirama, VistaVision, Todd-AO and Cinerama. Is the sound too loud? That's good! Is the picture too big to fit inside his field of vision? Too bad! It's gigantic. It's epic. It's a period piece. And the title is....

The Birth of the Hero

At the sign of The Sucking Sow, a disreputable pub on the fringe of Soho, pints of bitter and gut-searing gin flow freely at high tea-time. Suspect shadows, ghostly apparitions out of Dickens, women of easy virtue and men of questionable character pass beneath the corbelled balcony, then step inside the door whose panes of glass are decorated with pale blue and white glass cabochons, shaking their umbrellas as only Londoners can do.

The sign itself—a metal sow in gold and red sucking at a mug of ale, nailed to a wooden plaque in the shape of a knight's shield, once pale blue and white now long since faded—creaks and moans in the wind and rain. Because in CinemaScope colour movies set in Soho, it's always windy and raining; it looks more beautiful, more disturbing, more picturesque that way.

When the door opens, pushed by a drinker going out for a piss or by a customer on his way in, sounds of all kinds rush into the dark street: cries, laughter, singing, beer glasses clinking, mugs being plunked down on the bar, its wood polished by time, while the smell of badly digested drink drives away the rare passersby who don't drink and attracts those who are in search of instant, simple-minded pleasure and temporary oblivion. Once the door is shut, the sounds of the pub are muffled, the wind and rain are back in the foreground on the soundtrack, the street is sad again—a dingy street in postwar London enhanced by some little medieval and Victorian touches to make it really look like London. The camera climbs slowly in a sudden gust of wind, stays on the sign which creaks as it sways. We see then that the sow is laughing too, she has her tongue out and she's winking, and the combination gives her an indecent look.

The little boy in a man's body is hidden by a porte-cochere on the other side of the street. What street? Let's say it's called Watkins, or Hutchkins, some English-sounding name. Under the porte-cochere at 13 Hutchkins Street, in the Soho district of postwar London, a little boy in a man's body, chilled to the bone in spite of his parka, his boots, his tuque and his mitts has been standing and waiting for hours. He is waiting for somebody. Waiting for somebody to come out. Somebody he has followed here and who must be fairly sloshed now, given the number of hours that have passed since he first went inside The Sucking Sow.

A woman walks by, laughing; she's wearing a very turn-of-the-century long gown, high-heeled boots, a dead rat boa, a reticule that slaps her thigh, and an incredible hat complete with plumes, birds, cherries, flowers—the works. The little boy in the man's body is well aware that this prostitute is an anachronism in postwar London, she'd be too old, a hundred at least, but he likes her curvaceous silhouette and her coarse laugh so he lets her walk all the way down the street without chasing her off the screen. The camera follows her, because the little boy in a man's body needs some diversion before he goes inside the pub. She disappears down a street that's even darker, an alley actually, a foul lane that smells of piss and garbage, and the little boy in a man's body thinks of Jack the Ripper with his doctor's bag, his black cape and his vampire smile. He'd like to warn her (in another film, in another episode of his adventurous life, an immortal masterpiece of world literature he himself had brilliantly adapted for the screen, he was running behind her, he would save her just in time, at the very moment when Jack the Ripper held up his knife, already stained with the blood of his other victims, then he'd trample him underfoot, trample the greatest murderer in history, the cruellest too, he would plunge the monster's own weapon into his throat, he'd cut him into little pieces to give him a taste of his own medicine, the goddamn crazy doctor, goddamn maniac, goddamn Brother Stanislas, goddamn groping Brother Stanislas, then he'd turn towards the prostitute who would already be trying to lure him with her...with her what: her charms, her harms, her farms, her arms?) but he doesn't have time to worry about such things, about a supporting actor, a mere passerby, an extra, because inside The Sucking Sow awaits....

He turns his head abruptly. Someone has come out. But not *him*. And so he'll have to go inside to find him. Like last time. The time when he didn't have time to finish because some children came and threw snowballs at his screen and ruined it.

He pulls up the collar of his parka, tugs his tuque over his ears, races across the street. His parka becomes heavier right away and darker, almost black. It's not merely rain, it's a downpour falling from the dirty London sky. He was under it for no more than four or five seconds and already he's soaked to the bones. He sneezes three times, murmurs "God bless you," smiling despite the gravity of the situation, climbs the single step that leads to the little balcony smelling of rotten wood and the stale beer that never dries.

Before pushing open the door, he runs his mitts over the blue and white glass cabochons. It's beautiful. It's warm and wet. And it's actually vibrating from all the noise inside the Sucking Sow. For a while now musical notes have been streaming from a honky-tonk piano while a woman—who must be fat, to judge by her powerful voice—bellows some old English popular song about love that's flown away and an urge to jump into the Thames. He knows the song is entitled "The River Thames" because he's just decided that it is. (Is that possible though, a honky-tonk piano in London? Isn't that an instrument from the American West? Doesn't matter, he brushes the thought away, brings the camera in close on the door-handle and his hand, which is still imprisoned in his wet mitt....)

The smell is so strong it surprises him. (You can't smell smells in a movie, not even in American movies, he ought to know that...but that doesn't matter either, he just has to make a face or hold his nose and everybody in the theatre will understand.... He has to keep going now or he's liable to lose the thread....) Liquor of all sorts, unwashed clothing and bodies, sawdust that's lain on the floor for generations, sticky from spit, unhealthy dampness that sticks to your skin right away and stirs around in your stomach, nausea that's hard to contain. Sweat and filth, the worst mixture. The Sucking Sow smells like a pig sty (till quite recently he used to say pig's tie.) This time he really does make a face, but it's not for the camera, it's involuntary, and he shudders, disgusted.

He doesn't like it when something doesn't smell good, because there are times when that means a fit is on the way. This time though there's no smell of burnt caramel and he's relieved. But he has automatically tried to find a wooden spoon, looking quickly all around the room.... He spotted one on a table where four men sit drinking. The spoon sits in an empty soup bowl, it's probably disgusting, but easy to reach. Just in case.

He walks up to the polished walnut bar with its gleaming brass railing that glows red in the light from the big fireplace, leans on it as he's seen so many American actors in so many westerns do, each one worse than the one before. He doesn't like westerns but right now he needs an image from one to help him put on a good front, to impose on the other customers in this disreputable pub in the London slums an image of a man instead of that of the child in a man's body which he is.

"Is there anybody here that saw my father?"

He knows he's speaking English because he's in an English movie or an American one shot in London, but he hears himself speaking the weird kind of language he knows from dubbed versions of foreign films, that sound funny because the tonic accents have been switched around to follow the actors' lips, with an improbable choice of words, especially when the film has a country or working-class setting and the original dialogue was in slang or cockney. He still laughs about it, which may be why he can't take westerns or some cops-and-robbers films seriously:

The cowboy with the accent of a beret-wearing, baguette-toting, bicycle-riding Frenchman comes out with the equivalent of: "I say, chappy, do watch out for the firecracker, won't you?"

Or the black man from the southern US who speaks with an improbable West Indian accent.

For love stories it doesn't matter so much. Kisses and declarations of love are more universal than run-ins between members of the underworld or card-playing cowboys.

He hears himself then speaking a French more elegant than his everyday *joual*, but distorted by his lack of vocabulary and his inability to imitate foreign accents. To him, anyone who doesn't speak like his mother has an accent and he often has trouble following Frenchmen in the movies or on TV. They talk fast and loud and they use five-dollar words whose meaning he has no idea of.

The barman wipes up a trace of something sticky and vaguely sickening just beside the elbow of the child in a man's body who jumps and immediately wishes he hadn't.

"And who's your father, you pigheaded lout?" (He'll definitely have to find another expression, they can't keep saying pigheaded lout every five minutes! "Milk drinker?" Okay, he'll try that.)

"And who's your father, milk-drinker?"

He puts on the voice of a grown man, a policeman, a wrestler, even a lumberjack who hasn't been to town for six months and is dying for a drink:

"First of all, you're gonna bring me a gin and tonic, and don't stint on the gin, with...with ummm...." (Blocked already.... He's not going to order a slice of lemon pie for heaven's sake, even if that's what he's been craving ever since he thought up "milk drinker!")

"With umm...how'm I supposed to know, eh?... Some Scotchman's soda?"

(Nope, that won't do either, he'll work on it later: for the time being what matters isn't so much the dialogue, it's finding *him*, the man he's followed all the way here, the one he wants to confront at last, after so much futile searching and so many incredible adventures through so many movies, all of them unsuccessful, never finished, always interrupted....)

He waves his hand, the English soundtrack comes back, but this time he fixes things so he hears it in his own kind of French.

"My father's name is Paul, he came here for the war, with the Canadian army, a few years ago, twenty years actually, and my mother and my sister and me, we've never laid eyes on him since, so I was wondering if maybe he was here! He's the kind of guy that spends his time in the tavern. And I seem to remember it didn't matter to him how clean it was."

A slight prickling sensation on the nape of his neck, the same one gets every time he arrives at this line. Someone is looking at him from the back of the pub. He turns around as fast as he can, just in time to see the end of a sleeve, the heel of a shoe, the bottom of a trouser-cuff. This time he's got him.

The man who will tell him about his birth.

At last.

"Just a gin. And bring it to me over there, at the back, I think I just spotted him."

But he can't move. After so many misadventures, so much dejection, so many false hopes and dubious trails, is the meeting going to happen right here, right now, at the back of an English pub that reeks of booze and slovenly humans? Is it no more complicated than that? Or is a trap waiting for him along the way, as usual, and will he see his father escape at the last moment, he's used to that, it's happened so often....

He unbuttons his parka (actually he pulls down the zipper, he'd forgotten that his coat doesn't have buttons) after peeling off his mitts. Then he stuffs his tuque into a pocket. When you're meeting your father for the first time in twenty years, it's important to look not like a child in a man's body but like an all-round man, a real man, one who lives like a man and thinks like a man. He hesitates. Won't his father realize at first glance that he isn't really a man?

(No, not rejection! Please, not rejection! Not today! The snow is too beautiful, the screen is too perfect, and the time has come for the real confrontation!)

A silhouette is lurking in the shadows. A man hunched over a stein of beer, his back bent, not as if he's ashamed or afraid, but rather ready at the first sign to pounce on his potential assailant or rush towards the small door on his right that seems to open onto the backyard or the alley. Only his eyes shine when he focuses on the child in a man's body; the rest, his clothes, his limbs, even his head form darker spots, shifting, because he moves a lot for someone who wants to hide. Nerves. He has them too.

"Can I sit down?"

The voice that rises in the dark is cracked, burnt by alcohol and tobacco.

"This is a pub, anybody can go wherever they want."

A weird thought springs to his mind then, one that has nothing to do with the film itself, and it distracts him for a few moments: when the film is shown on TV in a few years, after his triumph on the big screen, maybe they'll have to cut this scene because it's too dark. You wouldn't see anything on the small screen and the audience would switch to see what was showing on Channel 10. He's seen so many French movies, set during the Occupation, that were unbearable on TV because half the sequences were so dark you had no idea what was going on.... Bourvil crossing Paris with his suitcase full of pork, the Resistance members setting bombs under the tracks of Nazi trains, Eric von Stroheim himself urging the torture of men already half-dead.... You could lean forward, stick your nose against the set, brighten the picture....

(But this isn't a real movie. The screen isn't a real one either. It's all in his head. And it doesn't matter if it's dark inside his head, it's perfectly normal in fact.... So he goes back to The Sucking Sow, to the small smoky room—why not, the man's probably a chain-smoker—to the disgusting smell of booze and unwashed bodies. The most important thing is not to lose the thread, things are going well today, he may even be able to take the sequence all the way to its conclusion....)

Immediately, the child in a man's body looks to his left.

Yes, that's it.

There's a whip hanging on the wall. It probably belongs to a coachman who's come here to get smashed between deliveries, either that or it was left behind ages ago, back when little Oliver Twists were beaten till they bled if they ever made the mistake of asking for a second bowl of porridge.

(He is smiling now in spite of himself. If his mother had whipped him every time he asked for a second bowl of oatmeal he wouldn't have much skin left! No, he mustn't smile, mustn't let himself be distracted by stupid ideas, he knows, he knows he always has a tendency to stall when he gets to this scene, that he lets himself drift towards lighter segments in the story of the hero's birth, because he's afraid of what may happen if he lets these two characters talk for too long. He's afraid he'll enjoy too much what he's come to do here at The Sucking Sow, in the heart of London.)

This time, he'll have to get to the point without letting himself be distracted. To the birth. The avenging hero's birth.

He takes the sequence from the top again, adding a little light this time so people can see what's going on. And why not make it a black-and-white film? No. It will be so beautiful a while from now to see the blood welling up or flowing.

"Can I come in?"

"This is a pub, anybody can go wherever they want. You want the toilet? It's over there."

The child in a man's body looks where the silhouette is pointing, spots the whip. Takes it down.

(That's a good touch, the victim himself, unbeknownst to him, showing his torturer the instrument he'll use. And the whip, that's a lot better than a rifle or a sword or a good old American fist.)

The man brings a cigarette to his mouth. Briefly, a will-o'-the-wisp floats in the dark.

"That yours, that whip up there?"

"Nope."

"So how come you took it down?"

"You never know. Might come in handy some time."

The silhouette hunches over a little more, huddles over the stein of beer, seems to cling to it like a lifeline. Now it is not a man holding a stein of beer, it's a pint of beer holding onto a man to keep him from collapsing under the table, from spreading like a puddle of piss.

(That's a good touch. It's the best sequence he's imagined in a long time. That's because it's spring. Ideas are fresh in the spring. He smiles again, gets annoyed at himself, goes back to concentrating on his film.)

"Mind if I don't ask you to sit down? I gotta be getting the hell out of here...."

"Not till we talk."

"Why would we do that? We don't know each other."

"Yes we do."

The hero pulls up a wooden bench, sits down, brings his head close to the other man's, which doesn't move or tremble.

"You knew it was me, eh?"

No answer. All at once the air seems even more overheated. The child in a man's body would like to pull off his parka but he'd have to stand up, make some ungainly moves, contort himself, put himself in a position of weakness next to this man who's staring at him now as if to provoke him. Who even smiles. A nasty smile.

"Sure. I knew who you were right away. The spitting image of your mother."

"But everybody in the family always says you and me we're like two peas in a pod. Especially Momma."

"Your mother always comes out with the stupidest things."

The child in a man's body lays the whip on the table. The man laughs this time, a very ugly laugh from far away that comes out crooked and full of rotten teeth.

"You don't think you can scare me with that?"

Just then the owner of this dive comes over with the gin, a very tiny glass if you compare it with the man's huge stein of beer. He goes on laughing, rubbing his eyes because he's having so much fun.

"It's dark in here. How about some light?"

(He wonders if this is a useful sequence, wonders about the timing of the owner's arrival; but the hero has ordered gin and surely the prospective viewer will expect the drink to be served before the end of the scene, which will be a fairly long one. And the owner's sudden arrival will create a diversion, it will lighten the atmosphere in this rather harrowing sequence. But is it really harrowing? Or is it only harrowing for him? And is the film.... No, no, it's going so well now! The film is good, he mustn't doubt that! He has to go on!)

Without taking his eyes off the child in a man's body, the man replies:

"We don't need any lights for what we've got to say to each other. Angus, let me introduce my son.... I haven't laid eyes on him for twenty years, but the kid hasn't changed one iota! Still as ridiculous as ever!"

(It's no good, that line, it's too flabby, not aggressive enough.... Let's take it from the top.)

"We don't need any fucking lights to say what we've got to say.... Angus m'boy, this is my.... I can't call him a kid for Christ's sake, he's too big, so let's say this is something me and my wife had.... The one before, I mean, the hysterical one over there that I dumped, the goddamn lunatic.... A real lunatic, like all of them on her side.... The whole gang of them from top of the ladder to the bottom and I'm not shitting you, a bunch of fucking lunatics, and my daughter's the worst of them all.... Christ almighty, when you think that a guy goes missing in the middle of a war so he can dump his family, he's gotta hate them all, right? And believe you me, I hated them! Especially that...that fat lump dressed up for playing in the snow in Parc Lafontaine, the big tub of lard that turns up after a donkey's years and thinks he's going to scare me with his little coachman's whip. What the hell are you doing here anyway? Eh? Trying to scare me? Eh? Or punish me maybe? For what? For abandoning you? The whole goddamn disgusting bunch of you? I got a good life now, I got a wife with a brain in her head and kids I don't have to be ashamed of, so get the fuck out of here and let me live my life!"

(That's too long, the man says too much, too fast, the child in a man's body is afraid that he can't react—even more, that he can't act. He's afraid of the man getting up and leaving like he did last time, and disappearing forever. He has to tell about the birth of the hero today, the screen is so beautiful, the sun's so warm, and his need to shit, that divine need to shit that comes over him whenever he has one of these waking dreams, it's a sign that everything's going well, that he's on the right track, that he can see it through to the end if he doesn't lose control.... So he'll have to skip his own reply which would be even longer, he can feel it, the rest of the scene too, the cries, the tears, the recriminations, he can always say them to himself tonight before he falls asleep.... Right now, though, he has to act...has to swing into action! Especially now that he's found the right weapon!)

The owner has disappeared, the sequence has taken a leap forward, terrible things have been said, biting criticisms have been dished out, vile replies stammered as the other, the man, the father, became aware of the son's fury and his tremendous need to...to strike out!

It happens so suddenly, he jumps on the park bench that's freezing his ass.

He is standing over his father who is still huddling over his pint of beer, he actually has the impression that he's standing on the table, that's how big he feels, his shoulder and wrist ache, he hears cries of panic, sobs, howls of pain. Someone is begging him for pity and pardon—and he refuses! The whip is everywhere at once, in the air and on his father's body, all over his father's body; fleshy pulp, dusty flakes of skin fly through the stale air in the pub. He can't see the flakes of skin because it's too dark, but he can smell them! He smells, sniffs, inhales, he revels in his father's skin as he reduces it to dust with his whip that bites, cuts, splits, mutilates, retaliates and punishes for long minutes, maybe even hours.

Violence! At last! He has achieved violence!

Violence—so good, so luminous, a new consolation, a new remedy for an old wound rendered incurable by too many ineffectual remedies and poultices, a dreamlike state, a state of grace, nirvana, the absolute serenity he's been seeking for so long.

His father is nothing but an amorphous pulp that reeks of liquor and cheating, but he keeps lashing out at him time and again. The drinkers have gathered around him, the room has grown bigger till it's the size of the Montreal Forum on Wednesday night. A man cries into a microphone: "Welcome to Wrestling Night at the Forum!" Ten thousand people get to their feet to applaud him: the avenging son, the vengeful son, the hero who this time didn't fail in his duty, the hero who has conquered and punished! The hero, who has finally been born!

When he stops, all that remains of his father is a little pile of shit. He's been reduced to what he has always been.

He's exhausted but happy.

He's breathing at last.

The end of the film is imprecise, wreathed in the vagueness we assign to things we don't want to end because they're so good or so helpful. He knows vaguely that someone is carried off in triumph, that a mother who is grateful because she's been avenged is waiting for her son in a dress white with snow at the heart of a buried city.

The End appears on the screen in Gothic letters—to look more English—against a background of the hero in majesty wielding his whip.

For a few moments he stays there suspended over the frozen lake.

It's over now.

He has succeeded.

Is it as good as he'd hoped it would be?

He can't say, but he feels tremendously relieved.

Then he gives a little squeal of surprise, tears come to his eyes, he gets off his bench, puts his hand on his big behind.

He has soiled his pants.

"You're twenty-three! You're twenty-three years old, Marcel, you aren't a baby!"

"I know I'm not a baby! Anyway, this hasn't happened for a long time!"

"A good thing! It's all I need!"

Albertine helps Marcel out of his clothes. First the parka, then the boots, pants, shirt.

"After this, though, you can finish by yourself."

"Sure, I know, I can do it."

"Are you going to clean everything properly?"

"Sure."

"You have to make it clean, clean, clean...."

"Godalmighty, Momma! I don't want to go around all day smelling like this!"

Albertine shudders. It's been years since she's seen her child undressed like this: the hair, the pink flesh—too much flesh, because Marcel has put on a lot of weight this last while—the vulnerability too, of a naked man who has no pockets where he can hide his discomfort, and then that appendage she can make out under his shorts, which she has always found slightly disgusting, especially her husband's—all of it embarrasses her. She looks away.

When it comes time to go to bed at night, they undress in the dark or in the bathroom; he puts on pajamas, she dons one of her two nighties, the winter one or the summer one. They don't look at one another; they turn their backs as they say goodnight, and if Albertine wakes up in the middle of the night and sees her child's back, she shuts her eyes right away. Because it isn't proper for a woman to watch her big twenty-three-year-old son sleep, even if he's wearing pajamas. And also because for so many years she so loathed the back she saw when she woke up at night. Back then. Before the war.

But now they're in the same bed, she and her son, and how can she avoid it? Fate has thrown them into this bed with no concern for propriety, for decency, for common sense, and she's helpless. She rented this dark apartment because it's cheap, she tried to persuade Marcel to sleep on the old sofa by the front door, but he was afraid of burglars and it was too cramped, and she....

She rolls up the trousers to take them to the cleaner, smooths the parka as if to brush off non-existent dust, then picks up the boots in one hand and leaves the bedroom.

Yes, she did what she could. Would life have preferred something different? Then let life take care of them: she has no more strength, she's abdicating. She has abandoned any vague urge to struggle because fate, goddamn fate, goddamn life, goddamn existence gets in her way, they always have, they give her a hard time, they trip her up, make her fall. She has fallen once again, a little lower, a little deeper inside the deepest wave of her existence; she's drowning, she's well aware of that, she accepts it, she's waiting for the day when resistance will be impossible, when the very notion of resistance will no longer be an option and she'll be able at last to collapse. Along with her child. Because she's convinced that her child will die along with her. In a great fire.

So, the image of fire has come back. She sits on the sofa in the hallway, clutching Marcel's clothes.

For weeks now, she has been haunted by the vision of a great fire. Not one that she's looking at but a fire that is consuming her. Consuming everything, her entire life, and that makes up for everything, for all her mistakes. At first she thought it was a dream, that she had dreamed about the great fire that was devouring them, both her and Marcel, then she realized that the great fire was inside her even when she was awake, that it appeared at any time and more and more often, that it sprang to her mind like an end that was possible if not probable, a relief unlike that other dream she had knowingly made up to get through the unbearable days she is living deep in this dark hole, a dream in which they are happy, she and her son, because she's found a solution to their intolerable life and she, at least, is happy because....

Once again her confused mind sends her skidding, she can't think straight, too many contradictory ideas come to her at the same time and she can't find her way. Above all, she doesn't want to lose her mind. Like her child. A shudder, a brief dizzy spell. She puts her hand on her head. She knows that in a few seconds a pin, thin but long, will stab her brain, just behind her left eye, and that she'll have to take to her bed with a cold washcloth on her forehead. The doctor she went to one day talked about migraines, but she calls them "bilious attacks" because she's convinced it's what she eats that makes her sick, not her wandering mind.

No. The attack won't come. It will be a while yet, when she comes back from the dry cleaner's.

"Okay Momma, you can come in, I'm all clean now!"

She sets her bundle on the sofa and cranes her neck towards the door, as if that way Marcel might be able to hear her better.

"You know you have to be punished, don't you?"

Brief silence. He has probably crossed his arms and dropped his head the way he used to do when he was three. Who knows, maybe the twenty years since then haven't really existed!

"Yes. But not too much, I didn't do it on purpose."

She leans against the unstitched cushion she's been planning to mend for so long, a faded peacock that's losing its insides in a great foam of upholstery stuffing.

"No. Not too much. You're just going to stay inside all day."

Right away he's beside her, moving at surprising speed for a man his size.

"That's too much, Momma, I wanted to go back to Parc Lafontaine and play in the snow!"

"You're too old to play in the snow, Marcel."

"Nobody's too old to play in the snow, Momma. It's so much fun!"

(The CinemaScope screen and what is projected onto it isn't a game for children, after all, but he can't tell his mother about that.)

"You ought to come with me some time, you'd like it! We could roll in the snow! We could lie on our backs and make snow angels!"

The thought of his mother rolling in the snow or moving her arms to make angels' wings makes him smile despite the punishment that's in store for him.

"It's not going to happen, my boy, I didn't even play in the snow when I was little! I never liked the snow, never!"

She stands, looks him up and down without blinking to make him understand that she's serious and that he must obey.

"That's it for today, you're staying in. You can read a book or watch TV, but you aren't walking through that door! Not even the apartment door! Understand? And I'm going to tell Madame Saint-Aubin to keep an eye on you and to bring you back by the scruff of your neck if she sees you wandering the corridors like a lost soul!"

She leaves him standing there beside the battered sofa as she goes to put on her coat.

"Get me my rainboots from the closet."

***

On the door of the janitor's apartment is a sheet of paper on which someone has scrawled: "I'm in the tub. Come on in, it's open, money on telephone table." Albertine recognizes Thérèse's writing.

"She's a trusting soul!"

She pushes open the door. The livingroom is dark with shadows, but a splash of sunlight coming from the kitchen extends to the runner in the hall. And yes, there's a ten-dollar bill on the table next to the phone. The bathroom door is ajar and she can hear water running.

"Thérèse?"

No reply.

Albertine walks down the hallway, Marcel's trousers rolled up under her arm. There's a smell of coffee and burnt toast.

"She still burns everything.... She'll never learn."

Thérèse is stretched out in the huge, deep bathtub, a washcloth over her eyes and all the lights out. The hot water is running and steam is filling the already suffocating room. It's as humid as a night in July. Thérèse has always liked humidity and hated the cold.

"Another migraine?"

Thérèse isn't startled. She only stiffens her neck as she turns her head towards the door.

"It came on me while I was burning my toast."

"You mean you haven't eaten?"

"That's right. The pain was so bad I had to get into the tub. It's still on the plate. If you want it...."

"I can make my own breakfast, for heaven's sake! Anyway, it's nearly time for lunch."

Albertine has walked into the room which is amazingly large for a bathroom—but this is no ordinary house, it's a private club, reserved for the rich, who need more room for getting washed, she supposes—and taken a seat on the toilet. Her daughter, despite her drinking, smoking, and generally wild life still has a magnificent body, not that of a young girl, she weighs more than she did ten years ago and wrinkles have begun to trace their hypocritical network around her eyes, but the very firmness of her flesh, the roundness of her body, the weight which the experience of living bestows on a gaze already beautiful and on a generous mouth, wreathe her in an undeniable sensuality that the members of the Club Canadien try to exploit and that she shamelessly makes use of, with an inviting burst of laughter that is already famous even though it's new.

Thérèse has to be the best-paid, best-tipped janitor in the city of Montreal. In fact, Madame Saint-Aubin, who doesn't know that she's Albertine's daughter, doesn't mind spreading the most incredible tales about her, which Thérèse's mother listens to in silence, with her forehead creased and her mouth agape. She finds it hard to picture her daughter as the heroine of these hair-raising accounts of debauchery, of late-night visits and orgies of all kinds with whatever wealthy men and passing strangers Montreal can muster.

One day when Madame Saint-Aubin was in particularly dazzling form, Albertine said in a barely audible little voice:

"I think you're going a bit far, Madame Saint-Aubin. She doesn't seem like such a bad girl...."

To which the janitor of 410 replied, enunciating clearly:

"She's not a bad girl, she's a demon from hell who does her housework stark naked and spreads her legs for any man she meets!"

Albertine didn't push it, she really didn't want Madame Saint-Aubin to add any details to what was already too precise, or to arouse her suspicions by defending Thérèse too staunchly.

"You just got here and you're already off in the clouds?"

Albertine looks up. She had actually just been thinking that there's no such thing as chance, there must be some reason for her to have seen both her children naked in less than half an hour, her big twenty-three-year son and her big daughter who is...how old is Thérèse anyway? Thirty-five? More? No, less, she was born in 1931. She's thirty-two. These two bodies, so strange to her now, came out of her, she made them, it was she who had made those hands, the globular breasts, the stubborn, domed forehead, the eyes that are too round, and frightening when Thérèse gets angry, and the vagina through which another human being has emerged in turn.... She has always thought and often told her family, who have never understood her: every day is a new beginning.

"You're right, I was daydreaming."

She bends over the steaming tub.

"Shall I turn off the water for you?"

Thérèse brings up her knees, as if she's afraid her mother will look at her sex.

"No. I like it hot."

"I can see that, but you don't have to scald yourself!"

"Don't start that again...."

"The doctor told you it's dangerous.... Look, you're all red."

"Keep looking, I'll be even redder.... Stick around for a while and I'll look like a shrimp...."

She replaces the washcloth over her eyes.

"Did you come here for anything special?"

"No. I was just walking by. I'm taking your brother's pants to the cleaner."

"Shut the door on your way out. I was expecting the kid from the grocery store, that's why I left it open. But I'm getting out of the tub now...."

"You'd have let him in while you were in the tub?"

"Sure, why not?"

"He'd have seen you on his way to the kitchen...."

"I'd have told him to leave his bags in the hallway. I put his money next to the phone. For pete's sake, Momma, it's not 1919! Now leave, I have to go out too.... See? You made me mad and now my headache's worse."

She picks up the washcloth which has landed on the floor with a little plop, soaks it in water that's practically boiling.

Albertine is back in the hallway, surrounded by the aroma of coffee and eggs. She goes to the kitchen, pours herself a big cup of coffee. Strange. Her daughter seems to have got the migraine that was intended for her.

All at once the sound of running water stops and the resulting silence seems heavy, nearly threatening. Either she or Thérèse has to say something, she senses that this silence could be dangerous.

"I wouldn't want to see your hydro bill!"

"What? Speak up, I can't hear you!"

"I said, I wouldn't want to see your hydro bill! All that hot water...."

"Are you nuts? You think I'm the one that pays it? It's the club's water, I don't pay the hydro here, I'm the janitor! I don't pay a thing myself, but you better believe I'm well paid!"

Thérèse stands there, hardly covered, rather half-wrapped in a blue chenille bathrobe that brings out the red of her skin and the Hollywood blonde recently inflicted on her auburn hair.

"You're lucky! I wish somebody else paid my hydro bill!"

Thérèse looks at her mother for a few moments, then goes to the gas stove for the coffee-pot. She could say something bitchy, make some vicious remark, but is it because of the fatigue that shows in the circles under her eyes, or the migraine that's pounding her head? Whatever it is, she remains silent. She refrains from saying anything about the money she gives her mother, money she's worked hard to earn—taking out garbage, scrubbing floors, cleaning disgusting toilets, sweeping all the rooms with their old carpets that smell of dust and stale cigar smoke; she doesn't feel like launching into that, it would take too long. And her mother wouldn't understand that she costs even more than a big electricity bill.

But Thérèse does not refrain from telling her, abruptly and bluntly, the news she's been keeping to herself for days, news that will shut up her mother for quite a while because it's going to turn their lives, all their lives, upside down—her own, Albertine's and Marcel's. She says, very loud, without turning around, as she pours her coffee:

"By the way, that reminds me, I'm leaving here."

Still not turning, she takes her first sip.

Albertine reels from the punch. She collapses onto the chair by the wall, under the second telephone—two phones in the same house! What a waste!—and she feels like plugging her ears. What kind of mess is Thérèse in this time, what rubbish is going to come out of her mouth, what horror, even—like the time when she told her she was going to marry Gérard, who'd nearly raped her when she was a child....

"Nothing to say?"

"What do you want me to say? I'm waiting for you to say something! Maybe you'll tell me you're going to the North Pole to sell drinks to the Eskimos. I just want to prepare myself mentally."

"I'm not going that far. Actually, you'll be surprised when I tell you where. Aren't you curious? Even a little?"

"What's wrong with it here? You can take as many baths as you want, you don't even have to pay the hydro! And you like men so much, here you can see them all day long! Late at night too, most likely...."

"You know perfectly well, a janitor isn't what I want to be. I did it because I thought it'd be easy, and now I'm getting the hell out because it's hard! You've said it yourself, you've spent your whole life cleaning other people's dirt and you're fed up with it. Well I'm fed up too! Even if they pay me well for doing it!"

Albertine lowers her head, starts fiddling with Marcel's pants, which are giving off a smell that's too insistent to be ignored.

"So that's it. You're going back to St. Lawrence Boulevard. You won't be selling drinks to Eskimos, but you'll still be selling drinks. I thought you were through with that. You said so yourself. You said you were sick of drunk men and the women that hang around to rob them...."

Thérèse turns, leans against the stove, takes another sip of coffee—still hot and a little too strong, the way she likes it.

"We'll talk about St. Lawrence Boulevard later on. Right now, I want to see the look on your face when I tell you the rest. Because there's more. So listen: I'm getting back together with Gérard...."

Her mother is on her feet at once, holding her purse and Marcel's pants against her chest. She's about to raise her arm, and Thérèse knows Albertine is going to point at her while she's talking, like she does when she's really angry, like when she rails against life and uses her index finger as a rapier or a rifle, and Thérèse decides to make her move quickly, to cut her off by telling her everything right away, because she hasn't finished, far from it, and the rest of what she has to say is liable to humiliate her mother completely, to crush her like a bug.

"And I've rented the old apartment on Fabre Street. And since I won't be able to afford to pay your rent anymore because I'll have a lot of responsibilities—the rent, the phone, the hydro and all that—I've decided you'll come too. You and Marcel. Back to the house where both of us were born."

Albertine hasn't sat down again as Thérèse expected. She's leaning against the kitchen table after dropping the pants there, which smell really terrible. She has lowered her head. That's so rare, Thérèse feels a joy that's more than nasty or cruel, an amazingly warm fluid travels through her nervous system; she shudders as she tells herself that even so, her mother mustn't see her quivering with joy. She takes down a sweater hanging by the stove and wraps it around herself.

"Why'd you do that?"

It's a thin little voice, it doesn't seem to have come from this small dejected woman of whom Thérèse can only see the greying hair and the ridiculous black felt hat, but from the other end of the apartment, from even farther away, as if already Albertine was no longer in the room with her but was running away to hide in her hole and lick her wounds.

"If you think I did it just to be mean you can think again. Listen, sit down, do you want another coffee? I can heat it up, it won't take long. I know you like it strong. And when we're back together like we used to be, you'll make my strong coffee for me, won't you, Momma?"

Her mother looks up so quickly Thérèse can't help being startled and humiliated as a result, because Albertine has seen it.

"Are you making fun of me?"

Thérèse takes a package of cigarettes from her bathrobe pocket, lights one, picks an imaginary shred of tobacco from the tip of her tongue.

"Nope."

"It's all true?"

"It's all true."

"I ought to...I ought to...."

"Spank me? Like a child? Come off it. Hear me out, maybe then you'll understand. Maybe."

"There's nothing to understand. Just to put up with. As usual."

She knows the story that's coming will probably be long and, even more, full of revelations that will be at the very least unpleasant, especially for her, so she sits down again, though she doesn't pick up Marcel's pants.

Thérèse wrinkles her nose, glances at the soiled clothing.

"Was he sick again?"

"If that was it I wouldn't be so worried. He shit his pants."

"How come? Where?"

"Never mind, Thérèse, I can take care of your brother by myself! Just say what you've got to say and if it doesn't kill me, we'll talk about Marcel afterwards."

"What I've got to say won't kill you."

"You must be sorry."

Thérèse chortles, letting out a cloud of grey smoke that drifts straight up to the ceiling.

"You know me too well!"

"Not well enough, you mean! Even now, there's times when I can't see you coming, when you take me by surprise. Like this morning. I just ask how you're doing and out comes one of your big fat announcements!"

"I know. I like doing that!"

"Okay, now let's quit wasting time. Go on, say it, I'm ready!"

Thérèse will stand there leaning against the stove during the entire account; she'll have time to sip her coffee while she watches out for every one of her mother's reactions, anticipating them, let down when she misses an effect, so excited she can feel her heart beating when Albertine looks away or brings her hand to her throat to rub her double chin with thumb and index finger, a sign that she's overwhelmed and is trying to regain her composure. But in the end Thérèse will be caught in her own trap and her monologue will end with a sincerity she hasn't intended, as she pleads her case to her mother who will straighten up on her chair and brace herself while she watches Thérèse being deflated.

"I've been thinking for a while now about getting back together with Gérard. Don't say anything! Let me finish, you can give me your comments after that! Not because I love him, as you might imagine.... You know how I feel about him, I've blown up about him often enough.... It's partly because I miss Johanne: I hardly ever see her anymore since she decided to stay with her father...and partly because *he* still loves me and besides, it'd be convenient. That's right, convenient! I've told you before, I'm sick of being here; you're right, I want to go back to the Main. I've made new connections, maybe I'll go back to the Coconut or the French.... Nights, which is what I want, so I won't have to put up with my gallant spouse coming on to me.... Besides...I don't know.... Look...I ran into Lise Allard a while ago.... She's married now, she isn't Allard any more, but anyway...and she told me she'd heard from Madame Rouleau that our old apartment's available. The Lavoies went back to Gaspé because they couldn't get work here. Can you imagine how I felt when I heard that? Fabre Street, Momma! The forties and fifties when twelve of us were living in those seven rooms, three families, all related and all mixed up! We were all unhappy there, but it was still the most wonderful period of our lives, I know it was! For all of us! Maybe we had to live in each other's pockets too much, and we used to bitch and complain all day long, but it wasn't as bad as now, with the family shattered and we don't even see each other! I told myself...I know you'll think this is stupid, but anyway...I told myself, maybe it's a sign.... Why not go back there—me and Momma and Johanne and Gérard? That's right, even Gérard! If everything goes back to what it was before, at least it will be unhappiness we already know, that we've lived with before! I'm sick of living from day to day, Momma, I'm sick of not knowing what's ahead of me, and reacting by sitting in a scalding tub till I look like a lobster! If we go back there, if I go back to work at the French Casino, I'll know what's coming, there won't be any surprises, I won't be scared any more! Oh, I'll swear, for sure I'll swear, and I'll kick and I'll yell and I might even go back to drinking now and then because I'll be working around liquor, but it'll be a situation I know! And we won't be as poor as when we all have our own places, you and Marcel in your hole, Gérard and Johanne on Dorion Street, and me here in a janitor's apartment where anybody can call on me any time and ask me for anything they want! With the money from Gérard's accident, and the fortune I'm liable to make on the Main, we'll live better, Momma! And don't tell me you won't be better off in the house where your children were born than buried in a damp basement under Sherbrooke Street with just one bed for you and Marcel! I'll take Auntie Nana's old room, you'll take Grandma's, Marcel can sleep where Uncle Édouard used to, and Johanne can have your old room! It'll be fun, Momma! It'll be fun with all of us in the same house, but not sleeping in the same places! And...you never know...maybe we won't be happy because we don't know how to be happy, but at least life will be more bearable!"

After starting out cutting and vindictive, she becomes pleading, conciliatory. Tears have welled in her eyes and she hates that, but there's nothing she can do to hold them back: she can't control the tears or the flood of words, everything's getting away from her, the fine self-confidence she had at the beginning of the conversation, even her certainty that she was right. By depicting the life that lies ahead of them on Fabre Street, the beautiful picture she'd drawn of it is being radically transformed and she can feel anxiety taking hold of her, she can feel a knot forming in her stomach, a hand closing around her heart—and she's choking.

She goes blank for a moment, feels faint as she always does when she stays too long in a bath that's too hot; she feels some coffee scald her hand. When she comes back to herself, barely a second or two have passed, but her mother is already beside her.

Albertine takes the cup from her daughter's hands and sets it on the stove.

"What about the neighbours, remember how they all came out on their balconies and applauded like lunatics because they were so glad we were leaving, what do you think about that, Thérèse? Are they going to come out on their balconies again and throw stones at us because we're coming back? Are they? You want to go back and live in the midst of people who've insulted you all your life?"

Thérèse crosses the kitchen nearly at a run.

"I suppose you're getting back in the tub so you won't hear what I've got to say, aren't you? As usual?"

She follows her, watches her undress, throw herself into the still-steaming tub. Thérèse disappears under the water for a few seconds, then reappears, dripping wet, glistening, so beautiful.

She leans against the rim of the tub.

"Turn on the tap, Momma, it isn't hot enough!"

Albertine bends over, turns on the hot water.

"When you break out in blisters you can turn on the cold."

Thérèse's perverse smile is a sure sign that something bad is about to come and Albertine resumes her seat on the toilet to await the parting shot.

"Don't think you've won, Momma. It's too late to turn back. I've signed the lease. And I've cancelled yours at 410. Like it or not, we're going back to Fabre Street on the first of May."

Before leaving, Albertine turns towards her daughter.

"There's no point, Thérèse. Because no matter where you are, you're never happy. You'll be no better off there than you are here. And the rest of us will be the ones that pay. As usual."

***

This time he didn't take any chances, he decided to go to his Auntie Nana's by bus. First, because he didn't want to walk across Parc Lafontaine again, there would be too great a risk of surrendering to the CinemaScope screen a second time; and because he was afraid he'd be seen by his mother or his sister when he walked past the Club Canadien, and one of them would run after him and bring him home.

He boards the northbound Amherst trolley-bus, then the number 47 Mont-Royal going east. Both are nearly empty and Marcel feels important the way he did as a child when he played hooky and rode buses all over Montreal. He got lost every time, and every time the police brought him back to his mother, advising her to keep a closer eye on her weird child in the future. She would punish him then and, in tears, he would think about all the wonders he had seen.

Being disobedient is bad, he knows that. When his mother punishes him for doing something serious, like this morning, he has to obey her. Even though he's been an adult for ages and could make all his own decisions if he wanted, because the law says that after people turn twenty-one, they can do whatever they want. But Brother Stanislas explained to him one day, gently but firmly, that his mind was different from other people's—he knew that, everyone was always telling him so—that it didn't always work the way it was supposed to, that it sometimes suggested he do things he shouldn't because they were dangerous, and if he was ever in doubt, obeying his mother was his only refuge.

But he's pretty sick of obeying his mother, and his need to get away from her is more and more frequent. And urgent. He even takes perverse pleasure in doing the very opposite of what she asks. He can see that it bugs her, that she often becomes impatient, promising him the worst punishment, of which the most terrifying—in fact the only one that really scares him and keeps him from going too far—takes the form of an institution for people like him who are different and can't control themselves. But his need to follow his instincts, to obey his own mind and not somebody else's, to let himself dream out loud or to live his dreams, the pleasure he takes in flying away where others, those who think they're normal, are glued to the ground, or to dive into non-existent water, or to make movies for himself, more beautiful than real ones, in which he is always a hero braver than the real heroes, anxious to experience his different way of seeing things instead of repressing it, all that has become so pressing, so urgent lately that he's started planning his escapes to accomplish exploits that may be imaginary, yes, it's true, but so gratifying. From now on he will hide so he can dream.

The heat in the Mont-Royal bus isn't working and Marcel is shivering slightly. To see outside, he does what he used to do when he was little: he puts his hand on the frost-covered window, grimacing while he waits for the ice to melt because it stings, then he puts his face against the watery magnifying glass that has formed and has started to drip onto the metal window-frame. Everything is distorted, as if he were looking at the street through a big marble that gives curves to things that don't have them. Marcel presses his nose against the glass to see the name of the next street. De Lanaudière. He's nearly there. He gets up, pulls the bell three times because he likes the tinkling sound. The conductor, thinking he has an impatient passenger on his hands, looks at him in the rear-view mirror, frowning. Marcel gives him a friendly wave and pushes the barrier that opens the back door.

As soon as he steps off the bus, he starts to feel seriously cold. The pants he changed into are too light for the season, an old pair his mother had set aside to make dusters. The cold comes in through the holes in the knees and the fabric of the seat that's worn thin. And as always when his mother isn't there to keep an eye on him, he hasn't done up his boots, preferring to risk arriving at Auntie Nana's with wet feet rather than make the effort of bending over, feeling his fat belly being squeezed, his head filling with blood, for a task as banal as tying laces.

By the time he gets to the corner of Papineau and Mont-Royal, where there wasn't time to spread sand before it melted in the warm

March sun, the snow is already turning to heavy grey slush. Cold water gushes up from under the wheels of cars, crossing the street has become a difficult operation—and Marcel has to cross twice! First Mont-Royal, because the light is green, which he manages without mishap because there are no vehicles, in particular no buses, heading south just then but—and he should have expected this—as he's about to cross Papineau he gets generously splashed by a little red truck that speeds by just a few feet away. The water is cold, it's dirty, it fills his boots and plasters his clothes to his skin. Even his tuque is wet and the wool feels heavier now. Just as he is breaking into a run to get there faster, Marcel wonders if he'll have to get undressed for the second time this morning—and not even in his own house. Of the three men who live with Auntie Nana in the apartment on Cartier Street—her husband Gabriel and their two sons—only Uncle Gabriel is as corpulent as he is; and so Marcel is imagining himself dressed up like an old man over sixty, smiles at the image of himself (hunched over, with no hair, with wooden false teeth that he calls a bridge and that shifts around in his mouth, his breath always smells of beer, he's more experienced and brags about it too much, especially when he's been drinking, he makes a lot of noise when he blows his nose with oversized handkerchiefs that form a lump in the back pocket of his pants), then he reminds himself that a fair amount of what he's wearing now comes from Uncle Gabriel because his mother never has money to buy him clothes, so he stops smiling as he thinks that, for the rest of the day, he'll be wearing clothes that will be his eventually, when they're worn out.

But would these clothes still smell of Uncle Gabriel? If so, he won't be able to insist, as he does when his mother brings them home, that they be dry-cleaned before he wears them, and he'll have to endure the assaults of his Auntie Nana's husband's personality. He wonders if he'll be able to.

Marcel is very sensitive to odours, especially those of bodies, which he always takes to be an outline of the person he is smelling, a summary of his personality, his flaws and his good qualities. He always smells people when he meets them, discreetly ever since the time his mother asked why he was always sniffing when she stopped for a chat with the neighbours, but certainly, he's convinced, with a perceptiveness that only he can master to this degree. Beneath the heavy perfumes women wear—his mother: "When you go out you gotta smell good and you gotta smell strong!"—and the cologne that men sprinkle on their handkerchiefs, he can flush out the genuine odour, the one distilled by the glands, that contains everything about a human being, a confession that doesn't need to be expressed, an involuntary confession that's more eloquent than any grand declaration, knowing winks or apparently sincere handshakes.

For a long time now he has been dividing human beings into two categories, those who smell good and those who stink. He allows the first to approach him and keeps his distance from the others. Those who don't smell good are sometimes perfectly nice people who don't wish him any harm—his cousin Richard, for instance, Auntie Nana's oldest son, a gentle man who's sincere in everything he does—but something about their odour tells him to watch out, and any signs of affection or interest from them get a cold reception.

His mother smells good. His aunt too. And his sister. No one in the world smells as good as they do. Theirs are the most fragrant, the most intoxicating odours that he knows, and he could inhale them endlessly. (Even when she's angry, even when she's punishing him, at night too, when he can sense that he himself stinks, his mother always smells good.)

On his way across Cartier Street, just as he turns in the direction of number 4505, he has a brief vision, a revelation rather, because for the first time he can put into words something he has suspected for a while now, and it slows him down, nearly brings him to a halt in the middle of the street: when his mother becomes a living torch, on the day or the night when she catches fire, it will be because she doesn't smell good any more.

***

"Your mother just called. She's coming to get you."

"How'd she know I was here?"

"When you run away, Marcel, you always come here. Or to St. Lawrence Boulevard. But right now, with all the snow we've had, St. Lawrence must be pretty well dead."

"She could've just told you to send me home...."

"She said she has something to tell me.... And she said you should wait here and not run away like a burglar that's caught with his pants down."

Marcel chortles.

"Come on, burglars don't drop their pants to do their robberies!"

"It's an expression, Marcel."

"I know. I only wanted to make you laugh."

The fat woman has been losing weight recently. Not a lot, but enough to be noticeable. In the family, they say in veiled terms that she has a woman's sickness. Marcel would like to know just what that is—he suspects it's cancer, but what exactly is a woman's cancer?—he listens to the conversations between his sister and his mother, the ones that go on here at his aunt's house when everyone is together; the only details he's been able to get so far are that it's in the lower part of the body, that it's terribly painful and, worst of all, that it's fatal.

His Auntie Nana is going to die. Though he repeats it to himself dozens of times a day, he still can't believe it.

"As far as that's concerned, making me laugh nowadays isn't easy, is it?"

The kiss she gives him is dry because her lips are cracked; it feels as if someone is rubbing his forehead with steel wool and he tries not to shudder. Not that it's unpleasant, nothing his aunt says or does is ever unpleasant, but because it's happening to her, because it's unfair, because he wants to protest, to wave his fist and insult God, like they do in French movies. Hey, that's an interesting image, he'll have to remember it for his next screening in Cinerama or VistaVision.... During a blizzard, maybe.... The hero is looking for...for something. Unable to find it, he waves his fist at heaven....

"You're all wet! Did you get splashed? Those damn streetcars, they've got no respect for anybody! There's a clean towel in the bathroom, you can take a bath if you want."

"No, that's okay, I'll dry up."

"Dry *off*, Marcel."

"Dry up. Off. I can't ever get that straight."

"Your sister too. She's over thirty and she still says dry up. At least go and wipe off the slush...."

She isn't looking him in the eye as she usually does. She's looking away, her gaze lighting everywhere on him except in the most important place, the eyes, to let him understand that everything's fine, that the disease hasn't gotten any worse, that she's not all that sick, she's not going to die right away, she's not going to die at all, she is eternal. But her gaze, which moves around too much, is a glaring confession that he can't ignore.

The iris in her right eye is too big, his mother says that happens when the fat woman *has to* take drugs. She emphasizes the phrase so people will understand that her sister-in-law isn't some kind of addict, that she takes drugs because she needs them, because otherwise the pain would be too bad and she'd have to go back to the hospital—she who has always asked to die at home, surrounded by her things and by her family.

Does she realize Marcel is watching her? Whether she does or not, she gives him a slap on the rump the way she used to when he was a child.

"Go wash your hands, young man, we're going to eat."

He watches her go to the sink where she begins to stir something that makes a nasty plopping sound.

"Auntie Nana...."

"Don't ask me any of those questions, sweetie. We don't talk about things like that. We just wait for them to happen."

How did she know he wanted to talk about that, about the disgusting thing that's growing in her pelvic area like a poisonous flower, that's eating away at her bit by bit?

Walking past her on his way to the bathroom, he notices that she's fiddling with something flabby and brown and slightly sickening to look at that's swimming in a whitish liquid, and another image, not as beautiful as the first one, forces itself on him: Nana lying in her bed, holding her belly in both hands and...insulting God. Again! He looks up at the ceiling, he can't help himself. Something he used to wonder about when he was little comes back to him now and he can't help smiling at how naïve he used to be: can the good Lord really see all the way through the ceiling of the second storey, the floor of the third storey, the ceiling of the third storey and the roof of the house?

He has stopped beside his aunt, abruptly, still peering up at the ceiling.

To divert him, and also to determine whether he's going to have a seizure, if he's still with her or has just taken off for one of his other worlds, as she calls them, she speaks to him as if nothing were amiss, merely an aunt talking to her nephew who's dropped in for a visit. If he replies normally, everything's fine. If not....

"I'm soaking pork kidneys for tonight. Nobody else likes them but they aren't expensive and...and I like them!"

Immediately he turns his head towards her. She sighs with relief. She won't have to go looking for a wooden spoon, root around in his mouth to withdraw his tongue, to control him, keep him from moving so he won't hurt himself.... And would she even have the strength to do that?

"I like them too, Auntie! I love kidneys, especially the way you cook them!"

She gets the message, hides her smile by lowering her head to her work.

"Know what, Marcel? I've got an idea. Why don't I cook them right now just for you and me, for our lunch?"

Marcel looks down at the fat woman's hands. Guts. It really looks as if she's playing with her own guts.

She senses his distaste and intervenes before he turns down her offer.

"Looks disgusting, doesn't it?"

He swallows before he replies.

"I guess so."

"You'll see though, they taste good."

"I know. I've eaten them lots of times. But this is the first time I ever saw them before they were cooked...."

"I'm going to cut away the nerves and slice them up nice and thin, then I'll fry them in butter with onions, and when they're nearly ready I'll pour in a little tea and they won't look anything like they look now. They'll be golden and just a little crisp...."

"What's that white stuff they're sitting in?"

"That? I'm soaking them in milk."

"Yuck! Why?"

"I'd better not tell you what part of the body they come from, Marcel, or you won't want to eat them. That's why your uncle and your cousins don't like them. Let's just say, if I didn't soak them they'd taste like pee."

"What? And we eat them!"

"Don't think about that...."

"Now that you've told me...."

"I'm sorry. Anyway, I didn't really tell you. You can always pretend I didn't say anything, you're so good at pretending...."

She gives him a beautiful smile just like when she was still healthy. Marcel's heart melts, he forgets where kidneys come from, he pretends—it's true, he's good at that—she hasn't said anything about them, and he heads for the bathroom, exclaiming just a little too loud to sound really sincere:

"I can't wait to taste those kidneys!"

He stops before going into the bathroom, turns towards his aunt, of whom all he can see is one elbow jutting out from the sink.

"Do we have to wait till Momma gets here?"

His aunt's voice is tinged with good humour, all is not lost, all isn't lost for today, another day has been saved, she's not going to fall to the floor, holding on to her guts...holding on to...to her kidneys?

"Marcel, don't ask questions when you know the answer!"

***

Albertine looks the way she looks on her bad days. Her black eyes hold the surrounding light, weak though it is, and they glow from within, as if a fire were smouldering behind her pupils, a storm that's just waiting for a chance to show itself, that is even looking for her. As soon as the fat woman opened the door, Albertine strode past her after barely saying hello and went to look for her son.

"He's in the bathroom, Bartine."

"What's he doing there?"

"Well, he was wet when he got here, he'd got splashed, so I told him to clean up a little...."

"Has he been here long?"

"Now that I think of it, yes, he's been here a while.... I was starting to cook my lunch when he turned up."

"I hope he didn't tell you he was going to wash his feet!"

"No, but what difference would it make if he had?"

"Never mind, I know what I mean.... When he says he's going to wash his feet he turns on the water full blast and he can stay there for half an hour."

"Bartine! He isn't thirteen any more, he's twenty-three! He's a consenting adult, he can 'wash his feet' as much as he wants and it's none of your business!"

Albertine is already pounding on the bathroom door.

"That's what you think! I have to keep an eye on his morals too, you know! The Brother said so! He's irresponsible, I have to watch every single thing he does. If I don't, it's a sin for me too! Marcel? It's Momma! Wipe your feet and come out, we're going home!"

"Can't you at least stay for lunch?"

"I guess he didn't tell you he's being punished. He's supposed to stay inside all day!"

"Be that as it may, he still has to eat! You know how he likes his food!"

Albertine goes to the kitchen, runs herself a glass of cold water and drinks it noisily, like a very thirsty child. Then she sets her glass in the sink, wiping her mouth with the other hand.

"What are you having for lunch?"

Nana opens the frigidaire and takes out the dish of kidneys, cleaned and thinly sliced and already floured.

"These kidneys and some potatoes and carrots from yesterday."

Albertine bends over the big white bowl. Nana can make out a brief battle between greed and what Albertine calls her own morality, which consists of always doing exactly what she wants and never listening to others. And of course greed wins hands down.

"Kidneys for lunch! That's for supper! What came over you, cooking kidneys for lunch?"

"If I told you it was a treat for Marcel I imagine you'd scream bloody murder!"

"He shits his pants and you reward him by feeding him one of his favourite things?"

From the stunned look on her sister-in-law she realizes she's just committed an indiscretion, that she had no reason to mention Marcel's accident, and all at once she turns red as if she were on the verge of apoplexy.

The fat woman lifts each slice of kidney and adds it to the sizzling hot pan where she has already sautéed some onions.

"In his pajama pants? In bed?"

Albertine sits on the straight-back chair she has just pulled out from under the kitchen table.

"No, no...in his real pants. Outside. In Parc Lafontaine, of all places. I'll tell you the whole story, maybe I'll feel better...."

In the time it takes her to recount Marcel's misadventures in Parc Lafontaine, then his flight, probably by bus, to avoid a harsher punishment, the kidneys are nearly ready and the kitchen is filled with the delicious aroma of browned onions and fried pork. Marcel himself is leaning against the sink now, behind the back of his mother who hasn't heard him come in.

Her tale finished now, Albertine turns abruptly in the direction of the hallway that goes to the bathroom.

"Where is he, as a matter of fact? His feet're going to shine, that's for sure!"

Then, noticing him, she jumps up, her hand ready to strike. Marcel has automatically covered his face with both hands, not so much from fear of being hit—his mother threatens and yells but her bark's a lot worse than her bite—as from shame at being humiliated in front of his aunt yet again.

"Just you wait till we get home...."

He interrupts before she goes too far.

"Auntie Nana just told you, you aren't supposed to treat me like a child!"

"No back talk or you won't get any kidneys! You'll have to watch me eat them and hear me smack my lips, even if I'm not all that crazy about them. I can do that, you know. You know I could do that, don't you? So you better watch out."

The steaming plates are on the table, the kidneys glistening beside the potatoes and carrots covered with the sauce—the fat woman's famous tea sauce—and some number one canned peas.

"Bartine, for heaven's sake! You're a bigger baby than he is!"

End of discussion. Albertine hangs her head like a child who's been scolded and Marcel sits down to eat his lunch with a look of triumph.

Albertine mutters as she picks up her fork:

"Just you wait till we get home! At home it's me that rules, not common sense. It's my common sense that matters and you know what that means!"

The fat woman smiles faintly, then she winks at her nephew who can't believe what he's seeing: never, ever, in his entire life, has he seen his aunt wink. She's better. She's cured! She isn't going to die!

"Haven't you forgotten something, Bartine?"

"What? Now what is it?"

"You forgot to take off your coat, dearie!"

The two women can't have guessed it, but the laughter that explodes from Marcel in the diningroom is a ball of emotion that rises to his throat and comes out in great waves of delight, of dismay too, because his aunt has just used a word that comes from so long ago, from the far-off Duhamel his grandparents had left to settle in town, she'd said "dearie" in that typical way his grandmother Victoire was always saying it, she'd pronounced it the same way, she'd spoken exactly like her mother-in-law, with the same intonation, the same, exactly the same music; for a blink of an eye, Marcel thought he was hearing and seeing Victoire, sitting in her rocking chair in the corner of the diningroom of the Fabre Street apartment, he thought that he could smell the old woman's odour of camphor that she gave off from November to May, that he could hear her voice, broken but cheerful; for a fraction of a second he was listening to his entire childhood and a mixture of joy and pain bursts from him in a cascade of childlike laughter.

His mother looks at him with a silly expression on her face.

"Come on, Marcel, it isn't that funny!"

Nana wipes her mouth with her napkin, brushes a tear of laughter from her left cheek.

"You're wrong, Bartine, it is so! You should see the look on your face!"

Albertine knows that for the rest of her days—they're numbered, it's true, but still!—her sister-in-law will gleefully tell about that time when she, Albertine, sat down at the table to eat kidneys for lunch without taking off her winter coat. Because greed is stronger than common sense. She's humiliated in advance because she has no sense of humour, and a horrible thought, a monstrous wish that she dismisses at once, that she attributes to her rage, springs to her mind: she sees Nana lying in her coffin, wearing her best dress. At any other time, before the fat woman took sick that is, she would have dreamed of this wish, knowing it was harmless, she'd have delighted in this waking dream which would have soothed her, but now, sitting opposite this woman who soon will die and whom she has always loved and deeply respected, she is filled with a searing sense of guilt and she has to put down her fork.

"Come on, Bartine, it's nothing to cry about! It's just funny, that's all."

Marcel has stopped laughing. He heaves a long sigh, picks up his cutlery, dives into his meal. He gives little grunts of satisfaction that are worth all the compliments he wouldn't know how to formulate.

Nana brings her hand closer to her sister-in-law's.

"Are you going to take off that damn coat, Bartine?"

***

The incident occurs while Nana and Albertine are doing the dishes. With her arms in dish-water up to the elbow, the fat woman swishes the plates in hot water while Albertine finishes drying the glasses, hurriedly because she dislikes housework. Whenever she tells this story later on, Albertine will say it was at this very moment that she realized it was all over, that the fat woman was truly nearing the end of her too brief time here below, that the few jolts of energy she'd shown since getting out of the hospital came more from a desire to conceal her condition than from that fine vitality Nana had always possessed, despite her corpulence.

Albertine is in mid-confession when it happens; while her sister-in-law's back is turned so she can't see her unless she stands up at the sink, which is too low, and tilts her whole body in Albertine's direction, she recounts how this disastrous day got under way: the snow this morning that sucked any light from the apartment, Marcel's strange awakening, his departure—too hasty not to be suspect—his return with...with *that* in his pants, her own visit to her daughter who is killing herself by degrees by scalding herself and above all.... After beating around the bush for far too long, she finally starts talking about Fabre Street, about their imminent return to the apartment she doesn't want to go back to, that place she knows all too well, where she's spent too much time, where too much has happened, in particular she doesn't want to live there with *him*, with the lackluster Gérard who's been wandering from one chair to another for nearly two years now, exaggerating the limp that's due to an accident nobody's convinced really was one, about her own unhappiness at the prospect of this backwards step, this snake that's biting its own tail, this eternal new beginning; she has just asked the question that she hopes will trigger in Nana the sensible advice that has been her specialty for so long, that's been so beneficial to the whole family: "What do you think about it?" when, not getting an answer, she turns towards her sister-in-law.

The other woman is half-collapsed in front of the sink, her hair, always so carefully combed, drooping onto her face, she can barely stand on her feet and Albertine, bending over to her to ask naïvely what's wrong, realizes that Nana is trying to say something, that she's moving her lips but nothing is coming out because she doesn't have the strength to produce sounds. At any moment now she will fall to the floor, she's slowly slipping down, her arms are already beginning to emerge from the greasy water. Albertine cries out:

"Marcel, come and help me, hurry up, Auntie Nana's going to faint!"

Marcel, who was watching television while stoically awaiting his second punishment of the day, comes running.

"My God, what should we do?"

"You hold her under the arms, I'll take her legs...."

"What'll we do then?"

"Put her in her bed, idiot! Hurry up now, before she lands on the floor...."

It's hard because she is so heavy, it's ridiculous because they are awkward and can't support her properly; Albertine starts to cry.

"Don't take her like this, God, don't take her like this, she can't die like this, on the hall floor, just because we aren't strong enough to carry her to her bed! Wait! Wait till she's lying between her own clean sheets, give me time to pull up her covers, wait till she's had time to ask forgiveness for sins I'm sure she hasn't committed...."

She realizes that she is praying—she who for so long has cursed God and reviled Him because He refused to let her live a normal, decent life, instead sending her an imbecile for a husband and two crazy children.

"Forget everything I just told you and listen to me, for once!"

She won't receive any response, there isn't one, she knows that.

She shrugs, picking up her dying sister-in-law's legs. No, she's not dying, it's just a fainting spell, she'll get over it quickly and they'll be able to laugh about it in a few weeks when she's better, when she'll want to cook up her famous pork kidneys with tea sauce and she'll tell her: "Bartine, go buy me some pork kidneys, I'll cook them up with onions in my tea sauce...."

Marcel, red-faced, sweating and panting for breath, is crying too, a child's sobs, half-cries, half-howls, surprising in his big flushed face; his mother encourages him as best she can but she doesn't want to waste the small amount of breath and strength she still has. She would take Nana in her arms if she could, lift her up like a feather, hold her against her heart, she would kiss her, yes, she'd kiss her, weeping and pleading with her not to go, not to leave her all alone in the world. With Nana gone, the small amount of common sense this family has ever known will be gone forever and all that will remain.... Ah, at last, the bedroom, the bed.

***

With the covers pulled up under her arms, a cold washcloth on her forehead, her skin so pale it's nearly translucent, Nana is resting in her bed with the blue-and-lilac striped sheets.

Marcel holds his aunt's hand while Albertine bustles about in the kitchen finishing the dishes, putting things away to keep herself busy while they wait for the ambulance. She tries to be as quiet as possible, but now and then the clink of a plate or a glass, the sound of a saucepan in the background reaches the fat woman's bedroom and Marcel sighs impatiently.

"Can you hear me, Auntie Nana?"

A slight nod. She can hear. But her eyes stay shut, her hand cold, her breathing laboured.

"Does it hurt?"

Another nod.

"A lot?"

She finally opens her eyes.

"Just now. It hurt a lot. You'd think...."

She frowns, closes her eyes again. A wave of pain crosses her face, Marcel can see it being born, growing, he feels the horrendous groundswell of suffering, the unspeakable torture that is swooping down on Nana, whose hands, with no concern for modesty, have taken refuge in the region of her crotch.

"Is it bad again?"

She moans a little, bites her lips.

"It's worse...."

"Have you got any medicine, any pills I can give you?"

She shakes her head.

"I...I threw them all away. I thought...I was better. There's nothing you can do, Marcel, don't look, it's ugly. Go back to your mother. Go help her."

"No, I want to stay with you. The ambulance is coming, it won't be long. They'll give you something."

She turns her head towards him.

"Why did you do that?"

"We had to do something! We thought...."

"You thought I was going to die?"

"Momma did. She ran to the phone. But I think she did the right thing."

She brings her hand to her forehead, removes the washcloth that already is not so cool, holds it out to Marcel who grabs hold of it like a viaticum.

"Did you tell your Uncle Gabriel?"

"He's on his way, Nana. He just had to shut down his machine, then he was coming."

His mother's voice has startled Marcel. He didn't hear her coming, hadn't even noticed there were no more sounds from the kitchen.

The fat woman frowns, her mouth is slightly twisted, her lower lip quivers.

"I'm scared they'll keep me, Bartine!"

Her sister-in-law looks down.

"That might be the best."

Sighing deeply, Nana lifts her hand as if she wanted to touch the ceiling or to call for help through the plaster and wood.

"I want to die here, in my bed. Beside my husband. Is that really too much to ask?"

Albertine has not raised her head.

"Maybe. Because your husband and your children are worried when they leave for work in the morning. Because we're all worried, the whole family. It doesn't make sense for you to be here all alone all day long. If you were in the hospital...."

The fat woman cuts her off.

"My whole life I worried about everybody else, but I never wanted to put all of you in the hospital to get rid of you!"

Albertine cannot respond to the sick woman's unfairness—she is convinced that her sister-in-law is being unfair when she accuses them of wanting to get rid of her—but she also knows that it would be pointless to begin an argument that Nana is too weak to carry through. She contents herself with crossing her arms and leaning against the doorway.

The fat woman's eyes are closed now.

Marcel, who has gotten up during the exchange between the two women, is bending over his aunt.

"Is it starting again?"

"No. It hasn't stopped."

He is bent over her, he sees her as if he were stuck to the ceiling and she were lying on the ground; he is very close to her face though he feels far away; he is light all at once and nearly happy, his heart tells him that something important which he ought to understand has just happened, but he searches Nana's face in vain, trying to read there pain as he did a while ago, or relief if the wave of pain has passed, and he still can't see what is making her so feverish.

"Let her sleep, Marcel. She needs to sleep."

His mother disappears into the hallway that goes to the kitchen.

"All right, Momma, I'm coming."

Then all at once, it's there. He finally understands. It's so simple. The smell. It's the smell. His aunt's smell hasn't changed. She doesn't smell of death, whatever death may smell like. She smells the same as ever. True, it's a variation of her odour that is rising from her bed, probably because of the pain, but the fundamental essence, the original source of it is the same. The fat woman isn't going to die. Not this time.

He straightens up, holding back a cry of joy.

And his old dream of saving his aunt comes to him while he sits on the foot of the bed, looking himself straight in the eyes in the big mirror on the red-stained fake mahogany chest of drawers, a great source of pride to his aunt.

He is going to save her. He's going to stop her from dying. He's absolutely convinced of it.

He quickly rejects the movies however, despite the mirror shaped like a CinemaScope screen, it's not a movie that he needs this time....

What he invents this time is a novel, a short story rather; a beautiful short story by Madame Gabrielle Roy, his Auntie Nana's favourite writer, who like her came from the Canadian west and like her, left to settle in Montreal. The fat woman has read everything by Madame Gabrielle Roy, for ages now she's even tried to share her admiration with the rest of the family, she made them all read *The Tin Flute*, *Where Nests the Water Hen*, and *Street of Riches*. He himself has read *The Hidden Mountain*, but he didn't understand very much because he has trouble concentrating on a book.

His short story is all about Saskatchewan where the fat woman spent her childhood, instead of Madame Gabrielle Roy's native Manitoba, but that's not important, the two neighbouring provinces look so much alike. It's a story filled with fields of wheat, with indescribable horizons, with fire, water and, in particular, with our hero, who once again will conquer Fate and its Evil Spells to flourish high and proud the flag of Justice and Right.

It is brief, it smells of brush fire and stagnant water, it takes place under a starry sky veiled by smoke, it's beautiful and it's mostly about him, Marcel, because in the end, as always, it's to himself that he wants to do good.

And the title is:

The Prairie That Fills My Heart

In Saskatchewan, according to legend, God Himself drew the horizon line, using a lump of coal or a scrap of charcoal. Kneeling in the middle of the vast prairie, He drew the nearly perfect line which marks the limit between the lid of the sky set down on the plateau of the land and the end of what is visible to us of the great sea of wheat. Some maintain that He also sketched the outlines of the first silos, while others argue that, after all, God invented the horizon before there were silos.

The bountiful, generous prairie is a source of happiness because it provides man with work to be done and the fruits of that labour, it provides the material with which to build his house, to marry, raise children, see them leave to repeat what he himself has accomplished, and finally to die, at peace with himself as much as possible and with the respect of his peers; but the land is also the source of what are known as the great terrors of the prairie, that is the twin fears that strike young children and intelligent women. Fear of the day and fear of the night, fear of their inordinate beauty, of their unfathomable vastness.

By day, the fear is horizontal, it propels you forward, pushing you first towards the boundary of your own land, because even if you stand on tiptoe you cannot see the full expanse of it, and then ever farther, past the near neighbours, past the more distant ones, beyond the towns big and small, and in the end crushing your heart in your chest when the revelation finally comes to you that the perspective which begins at point zero, represented by your front stoop, has no real, verifiable limit. The children clamber onto the roofs of the houses, the women shout at them to come down while they intently watch the wind, the violent prairie wind, born of the horizon that does not exist, that can in a single gust take them away forever, scatter them to the four corners of the world. The mothers themselves dare not look too far beyond the fields of wheat waving endlessly like a woman's hair in front of their houses and behind and all around them. They fear the sickness. The prairie sickness. They never speak of madness, they say "sickness" as they wipe their hands on their white aprons before making a vague sign of the cross, just as their sisters in the eastern part of the country prefer to say "cabin fever" to describe the strange malady that takes hold of them in the middle of winter. For even when winter is at its worst, when they've been shut inside for weeks because there is so much snow and even the outhouses are hard to get to, they hardly dare venture a glance outside the kitchen window because they fear they'll start howling with terror before this whiteness that is too white, that seems to be endless too. They wait for the sun to set, for night to fall, bringing with it the other fear.

At night it's different, the fear is vertical, it pulls you upwards, no, it makes you fall upwards, because you have the impression that you're a drop of water born on the surface of the earth that must fall so as to lose itself somewhere in the Milky Way, a meaningless drop of rain like all the others, yet different because you've been taught that no one drop of water resembles another. With snowflakes it's easier to verify, you've done that all through your childhood, but a drop of rain! On those too humid nights during the too brief summer, the women settle in rocking chairs on their front porches and often they are surprised to catch themselves gripping the armrests when they peer too long at the sky. Life may be harsh here in the middle of the wheat fields that make you dizzy, even seasick, but there's no reason to lose your head because of those countless stars that call to you, that attract you and draw you up to them! You must resist the silent song of those faraway sirens. Then the women go inside to sleep in their damp beds, beside husbands who are swollen with dampness too. Though they do not sleep, they dream all the same, eyes fixed on the ceiling, on the plaster moulding, on the plump cherubs and the garlands of fruit and flowers. They dream about the mythic mountains that are said to rise up further west, at the boundary of Alberta and British Columbia, the appropriately named Rockies, gigantic blocks of granite thrown down there perhaps by God Himself, to check the assault of the inappropriately named Pacific. High beautiful mountains, crowned with snow and ice, whose purpose is to limit the horizon, to cut it up, break it into a thousand sparkling pieces, subject it to laws that have nothing to do with the straight line, a vast picture you wish you could draw—nearby, there, at the end of the wheat field—to kill off once and for all the twin fears of those who live on the prairies.

(The introduction is a little long, it's time to introduce the heroine, to hint at the coming catastrophe, the threat that weighs on her and her family. The setting is almost too well established, it's time for action. Still, he has to take the time for a good description of the heroine....)

It's these mountains that the ten-year-old Nana is thinking of as she rocks herself in the middle of the night while she looks out at the wheat field shimmering in the moonlight. She is the pride of her mother, Maria, who came back to Saskatchewan a short while ago, after wasting some time in the cotton mills of Providence, Rhode Island, on the east coast of the United States. Maria does not regret her journey however and she knows she never will. Because she brought two children back from there, two daughters who quickly became the centre of her life, the apple of her eye, her very reason for living.

Unlike her older sister, Maria's younger daughter has inherited none of the features of her father, a French master mariner who early on had disappeared into the mist and drizzle of the Gulf Stream. No, she's the spitting image of her mother, with her high Amerindian cheekbones, the square forehead, the narrow mouth and determined chin. And the coppery skin. And the thick black hair which she subdues into tight braids that flap merrily against her back when she plays hide-and-seek or skips rope with her sister and their girlfriends.

She undid her braids before she went to bed and now her hair falls onto her shoulders, too heavy in this oppressive heat. A few minutes ago she tossed her hair over the back of her chair in an attempt to expose her neck to a little of the warm wind that sometimes blows over the fields on summer nights, but it pulled, even pinched and in any case, Nana doesn't like to feel the damp painted wood on her nape, so she lowered her head and felt the weight of her hair down her back. It's too hot, drops of sweat are running down her spine, her hair is sticking to her skin, but she feels enveloped, protected by its weighty mass.

She gives the rocking chair a good push and watches the world shift on its axis, watches the steps move away, then come back towards her, the field of wheat rise and descend, the sky sway. Yet nothing is moving in this vast setting crucified by the heat, except her.

The front door creaks on its hinges and Nana turns around.

"You know Momma doesn't want us sitting on the porch at night!"

But immediately, Béa is at her side; she has pushed her aside in the big chair to make room for herself, then slipped in next to her sister and grabbed hold of her shoulders.

"Were you too hot?"

"Way too hot. I couldn't sleep."

The French they speak is very strange, different not only from that spoken in France, as is only natural, but also different from that of their cousins in Quebec: their French is almost too careful, learned in school, the French the nuns speak, with Rs not only rolled but sounding doubled, as if that letter were the hinge, the central feature of the words they speak. Their accent is Québécois as are some of the words they use, because that is the general flavour of the French spoken in Saskatchewan, where for more than twenty years now have swarmed the jobless from Quebec or Francophones from the United States who had been promised heaven and earth if they came and settled in the west, first in Manitoba and later on here, in Dollard, in the neighbouring province, but they also have a way of clearly enunciating every word that sometimes twists their mouths, giving them a comical look that brings laughter from their less conscientious classmates who are content to jabber a few words of French, a language required at school but totally unimportant in the society they're growing up and in which they may never use again.

At home, their mother has gotten in the habit of speaking English to them after all those years in the United States, even though she is a French-speaking Cree from northern Saskatchewan. After all, she earns her living in English and French has become both difficult and superfluous because she speaks it less and less. Between themselves, however, the sisters have adopted French, as if to set themselves apart from the world around them, to stand up to it, provoke it.

One is ten years old, the other twelve.

(Okay. The time has come. It has to happen now. It has to start with the smell, but not too fast, it has to make the reader sense the fear sneaking in, first a vague doubt, which the sisters will push aside, then terror, the real thing, when they realize that disaster has really landed on them and that everything may be lost already. And then introduce.... But wait, we'll see about that later on.)

"Look up there, there's no clouds but there's heat lighting...."

Béa has spoken in a whisper, her brow furrowed. She gives the impression that she's covering over what she really wants to say, as if she were using a euphemism to express something more troubling that she doesn't want to see yet or, even less, to understand. Her sister, more pragmatic and younger, supports herself on Béa's shoulder as she climbs onto a chair.

"That's not heat lightning, heat lightning isn't that colour, it's more like white. This is red...."

"Sit down, you're rocking the chair, we're going to fall!"

"I'm telling you, it isn't heat lightning! Go wake up Momma!"

"Are you nuts? You know how much she hates it when we bother her in the middle of the night!"

"She'll hate it even more if she finds herself in a house that's on fire and her two daughters burning like torches!"

"God, Nana, you really lay it on thick!"

Béa gets out of the chair, holding her sister by the waist. She lifts Nana, then sets her down.

"You sure are heavy!"

"I'm not a baby! I'm ten years old!"

Béa laughs, hopping up and down the way she does whenever she catches her sister out.

"Maybe not, but you're still a child!"

Nana is standing on tiptoe. She's even jumping in place, trying to see farther away.

"And you, you little brat, you'll be a baby till you die!"

(Careful with the dialogue! In the novels by Madame Gabrielle Roy people speak differently, they don't use everyday expressions, they talk like people talk in books.)

"And you'll be a baby till your dying day!"

Béa's head is crowned by an orange-coloured glow and she turns around abruptly.

"Did you see that?"

"What is it?"

"How come you asked? You know perfectly well what it is...."

Nana opens the door and shouts:

"Mama! Mama! Fire!"

Béa pulls her by the arm, clamps her hand over her mouth.

"Wait till we're sure! If there isn't a fire she'll scold us!"

Just then they smell something all too familiar, the dreaded odour, the third fear, the worst, of the inhabitants of the prairie, the uncontrollable terror that drives horses crazy, that makes animals run away and fills men with terror: the acrid smell of smoke that stings eyes and irritates throats—the hideous smell of fire. Nana is right, there is a fire somewhere.

They turn their heads towards the horizon at the same time, like watchful animals. If it were a few hours later they would think it was daybreak approaching, the sun preparing to emerge at the end of the fields to the east, so beautiful is the light. A halo glowing red hovers above the motionless wheat fields, giving them the late-summer tint that announces the hardest and longest days of the year: ox carts, pitchforks, boots that are too hot, big straw hats, clothes stained with sweat, impressive checkered handkerchiefs, silos that must be filled before the rains come, the sun that refuses to set and the night, too short, when sleep, dreamless and too brief, resembles death a little. But it's July now and in July the wheat fields don't yet have that beautiful golden colour, they are still growing, they have not yet reached maturity, till very recently they were still green and the heads have not yet started to bow under the weight of the ears. Nana knows that this stupendous spectacle shouldn't be taking place at this time of night, that it's an act of aggression against men and strictly gratuitous on nature's part, and she brings her hands to her heart, which is beating too hard.

Suddenly a flame, only one but broad and high, rises above the land of their second neighbour, Léo Robichaud, wrenching from both sisters at once a cry of recognition, surprise and defeat. The horror has come. The greatest horror, the most devastating, the most unfair, inevitable, implacable.

Galvanized by terror, Béa starts running around in circles on the porch, crying: "Fire! Fire!" as if the mere fact of naming the evil could make it disappear. Nana is already inside. Speeding through the house, she shakes her mother who is fast asleep, open-mouthed, snoring loudly. From their bedroom upstairs they can sometimes hear their mother's snoring through the floor and it makes them laugh, but this time Nana is in no laughing mood, she shakes her mother like a bundle of rags, shouting into her ear that she has to wake up, there's a fire, a bush fire coming faster than a galloping horse, a fire that kills everything so quickly, that they'll all be dead if they don't take flight right now.

Maria wakes up, quickly realizes something serious is going on even if her daughter's words are more and more incomprehensible.

"Where's your sister?"

"On the porch! She's waiting for us!"

"Did you collect your belongings?"

"There's no time, Mama, the fire's already just two farms away!"

Fire. At last Maria understands what the disaster is.

"Hurry, wet your clothes and your sister's at the pump, I'll meet you there...."

"Come on Mama, right away!"

"All right, all right, I'm coming.... I have to get a few things before I go...."

"No! We have to leave right now! Hurry! Hurry!"

(No, this dialogue isn't working. When Madame Gabrielle Roy writes dialogue it sounds perfectly natural, but this is totally false. In future, he'll have to concentrate on the descriptions as much as possible and avoid having the characters talk too much. Unless he goes back to the other way of writing dialogue. But then it wouldn't be a novel by Madame Gabrielle Roy! Writing movies is a lot easier!)

They find Béa on the balcony, crying and still racing around like a headless chicken. Maria takes both her daughters by the shoulders and pushes them towards the four steps that go down to the little garden where the blue and pink petunias already seem to be suffocating.

All at once the horizon exists, resplendent in its apocalyptic cloak. A wall of flames crowned with sparks is advancing towards them from all sides at once, maybe not at the speed of a galloping horse as Nana maintained, but pitiless in its thirst for destruction, if you can say that fire is thirsty. Acrid smoke from ears of wheat that aren't fully ripe, that are taking some time to burst into flames, rise into the sky in coils that are blacker than the sky. The fire's glow is so intense you can't see the stars.

The three women look around them and on all sides, they see nothing but flames and smoke. Maria thinks to herself that she mustn't give in to panic, that's the first thing prairie children are taught: keep calm in the face of a brush fire. Good God! A brush fire! She has inherited her parents' fear of them, she imparted it to her daughters as soon as they were living in Providence, even though brush fires don't exist in the east, all her life she has feared this catastrophe, but this is the first time she has witnessed one. It's just as terrible as she's been told, but far more beautiful as well. She is fascinated by the frightening spectacle that is unfurling before her eyes and she's annoyed with herself.

Because she knows very well that there's nothing she can do to oppose this catastrophe, there is a strong temptation to give in right away instead of fighting, to kneel before all this beauty and horror, to allow the flames to lick her—apparently people are often suffocated by smoke before they're burned by the fire—let them devour her and...and wait for her head to burst into flames, for her hair to catch fire....

(Careful with that image. It's dangerous. And too valuable. He has to hang on to it. For later. And for another character.)

Now the fire is encircling their land and there's no way out. They stand there in the middle of the road, motionless, hands over their mouths, throats already tingling unpleasantly. In a few seconds, a minute at the most, they will start coughing.... Béa has stopped crying and she gazes, fascinated, at the wall of flames as it crackles louder and louder. Nana yells to her mother that her sister has been "hympotized" by the fire, but with the crackling sounds of fences going up in flames and of wheat devoured standing in the fields in just seconds, she's not certain Maria has heard her.

Almost simultaneously they look up at the sky, in search of air a little less contaminated, yes, but mainly to try to gaze at one last star before they die. Maria is perfectly aware of it, unlike her two daughters, who wonder why they're raising their heads to the sky like this while the devastating fire is advancing towards them.

Maria thinks she should kill her two daughters before the flames reach them, so she won't have to see them writhe and hear them scream, but knowing she wouldn't be brave enough she reproaches herself for her cowardice; Béa isn't thinking about anything, she's in a near-catatonic state, at this precise moment the inside of her head is an exact replica of what is happening outside; Nana, though, wants at all costs to save the three of them. There is no question of giving in to the warning she's been hearing ever since she was a small child, which claims that it's those who don't take the necessary measures who are the quickest to leave and the first to die. She knows she should have thrown herself under the pump, dragging Maria and Béa along and wetting their clothes as her mother had told her to do, but it all happened so quickly, the pump is out of reach now, her sister has nearly lost her sense of reality and her mother.... She looks at Maria, thinking this cannot be the last time, because she loves her too much. Her mother's neck is craned towards the star, the last one, just above them, which they can't be sure really is one because there are others, billions of them, dancing around it, playing at hiding it and then setting it free, as if to mock them, the three women who each will die if a single one lands on her head.

(Now is the time. It has to happen now, the hero has to appear. But it's hard, it may be too late, the fire may be too near for their rescue to be credible. But credibility doesn't matter, what does matter here is...is for Nana to be saved, isn't that right? At all costs! Even at the cost of credibility!)

Nana slaps at her skirt as she squeezes her legs together. She feels something burn her left thigh. That's it, it's going to happen now. She is powerless against the force of fate, against the will of something that's immeasurably stronger than she is. She feels herself being crushed under God's thumb like an insect. She brandishes at the sky a little fist on which the nascent hairs are standing up. She takes the time to curse God, unequivocally, so

He'll understand, formulating in the clearest possible terms the very opposite of an act of contrition, and after that she takes her sister's hand and then her mother's. She tells them, for what she thinks is the last time, that she loves them, then she forces them to their knees—not to submit, but in a final hope that the fire will pass over them, forgetting them. All three stand there, rooted to the spot in front of their house which is not yet in flames, awaiting an atrocious death they don't deserve. But no one deserves death, thinks Nana, just before she passes out, no one has ever *deserved* death.

She doesn't have time to pass out though. There is a strange eddy forming in front of the three women; a shadow jumps through a kind of hole that has appeared in the atmosphere, a man's voice rises through the brush fire.

Where has he come from? From where has he sprung up with all those big wet towels that feel so cool on their skin, and his voice, at once authoritarian and gentle, from what fantastic dream, what secret desire? And who called him, who has made him loom out of nowhere to come to their rescue because no one else could do anything for them? Was it Maria, who during most of her lifetime has in fact got along without men? Was it the delicate Béa with her fire dance on the front stoop and her incomprehensible incantations of a fear-crazed child? Or was it Nana, the resourceful, dynamic Nana who through her will alone has called to her a hero who would be born in fifteen or twenty years and who would not reach maturity till the 1960s? Did she call upon for help the only human being who could twice save her from death, first now, in 1912, and then at the other end of her life, in 1963, when a hideous disease would be gnawing away at her?

(He mustn't explain where the hero has come from in too much detail; that would destroy a mystery, it would be trying to explain something that must remain secret and obscure. Since the hero always intervenes to save a desperate situation, he has no need of a pedigree, a birth certificate or a history attesting to the fact that he is well-born and that he has lived well too. The hero is there to act, so let him act! In any event, Madame Gabrielle Roy has never gone in for fantasy. Let's say that he's a brave and compassionate neighbour. Secretly in love with Maria despite the age difference, right, that's more plausible.)

He is a young man in his early twenties, fairly tall, somewhat corpulent—some would say downright fat, but in a pleasing, attractive way; his intelligence makes up for his ordinary face with its ordinary features, and the fire of determination can be seen in his eyes. One can feel it strongly, but his strength is that of moral conviction rather than tremendous physical power. He wastes no time introducing himself or explaining his presence; he immediately throws towels over the three women, tells them to breathe through their mouths, to throw themselves to the ground where the smoke is not so thick and to crawl after him as quickly as they can.

"The little pond behind the house—it's our only chance!"

It hadn't occurred to Maria and she chides herself as she follows the hero, who moves at astonishing speed for a man of his corporence. She says "corporence" in her head, as she would have said it out loud; she doesn't know the word "corpulence" in French. In English, she would have thought "corpulence" because she knows the word in the language she speaks every day, but surprisingly, if she's in trouble she thinks in French and the word that comes to her is "corporence."

The little girls are moving too slowly for his liking and the hero tells them to climb onto his back and lie flat on their stomachs; it looks as if he's playing horsy with them, bear, actually, because he has a bear's waddling gait and good-natured manner. He looks like a big mother bear trying to save her cubs from the fire. If the situation weren't so tragic, Maria would laugh at the sight of her daughters on the back of a fat man who is agile if not elegant, who is heading for the only body of water on their property. But why didn't she think of it? Water is the only thing that can fight fire, everybody knows that! Then she remembers. Because of the leeches, that's why! Because Béa panics at the mere thought of leeches. Béa would never, ever dive into that pond, even at the cost of her life!

While the four of them go around the house on the right side on their way to the pond that she hopes won't have been sucked up by the disaster, from the corner of her eye Maria sees the front steps catch fire all at once, like a pile of dead wood that has been tossed onto the embers in the fireplace. In a few minutes the house where she was born will no longer exist. She can't stop herself from turning around one last time. Now the house is at the very heart of the inferno, but it's not burning yet. Maria thinks about her bed, so cozy, that will go up in flames, about the dishes she inherited from her own mother, good solid dishes of enameled graniteware, which will twist and melt in the blaze, and, oddly enough, about her daughters' dolls. No one has the right to sacrifice little girls' dolls.

Sparks rain down on their bodies, they shudder, the women slap themselves; not the hero though, he doesn't have time. He has just smelled the odour of water, of stagnant water; he can hear the laments of frogs and toads, and bigger animals run past him, nearly trampling him; they've thought the same thing he has, not in words but through an atavistic instinct, and they are seeking the same refuge.

Béa cries out when she spies the water.

"Leeches! Leeches! Not leeches!"

She struggles, she kicks, but the hero, who has no time to devote to the fears of a hysterical little girl, virtually throws her into the dark water head first.

"Farther! Go out as far as you can, right to the middle of the pond!"

All four splash about in the muddy water, which stinks but to them seems divine; even Béa seems to have forgotten about the leeches. No, her eyes are wild, she is looking all around her, slapping her legs, churning the water, hopping up and down, but she is advancing. They are amazed to find so many animals there with them, little prairie creatures of which you usually see only the rear end when the creature bolts after inadvertently stepping on a dead branch; somewhat bigger creatures the prairie dwellers have learned to hate because of the danger they represent to the cattle that are moaning now, tails between their legs; and even a few familiar cows, not quite as dumb as the others, who have found their way to safety while they go on chewing their cud. Placid now, they stare at everything vacantly, while minutes before they were scurrying and mooing.

All this fine company, animal and human, is in the middle of the pond. The four humans are enjoying the coolness of the water; they feel their burns less keenly now, they bathe their faces so they'll stay wet, they are crying with gratitude and relief.

Time passes in the midst of the inferno. The sky is ablaze. There is a rain of sparks they must avoid. They don't dare let themselves give in to their drowsiness.

The hero seems ill at ease here, in water up to his neck and doing nothing. His task accomplished, he feels as if he has nothing to do and seems bored. Nana comes up to him to show her gratitude; he holds her in his arms very tight, confessing that he must set off now for other adventures. She understands. At least she says she does.

Just before taking off, because he's no longer needed, the hero says as gently as possible so as not to frighten the three women:

"Stay here till somebody comes to get you. Don't on any account leave the pond. You may feel cold, but remember, it's infinitely better than what could happen if you got out."

The three women kiss him, hug him, thank him from the bottom of their hearts—especially Nana, who, without knowing it, senses who he is and, without saying so, makes a date with him for another time, another place.

The hole in the night re-opens and the hero makes his way to it, waving one last goodbye. The women sense that he doesn't want to go but that other tasks, perhaps even more gigantic, await him at a time beyond their era and their understanding.

The women will stay there for the rest of the night, surrounded by animals sometimes dozing, sometimes reeling from the pandemonium around them; they will watch their house burn into a black and red silhouette before daybreak, the smoke rising from the devastated fields at dawn as the sun climbs over this merciless devastation, they will see for themselves their irreparable losses, their broken lives, and the fourth fear of the prairies will land on them. The fear of not surviving the cruelty of fire, of not being able to fend off despair.

Nana often looks in the direction of the hole in space, the knot in time. Did she really see that hero come from elsewhere, did she travel on his bear's back, did she kiss him in gratitude for saving her life and the lives of her mother and her sister?

When they leave the pond some hours later, along with the animals with singed fur, they will avoid talking about him, about his wet towels and his inspired idea.

When he regains consciousness—or as he'd say, when he wakes up, because he'd rather see this spaced-out interlude of numbness as a light sleep than admit to himself that it's another manifestation, a benign one, of his illness—he is still in the same position, facing the mirror above his aunt's chest of drawers, but his eyes have drifted from his own face to that, pale and emaciated, of the sick woman.

She is asleep. Her breathing is regular. Only her eyes, fluttering under her eyelids, testify to the pain that pursues the fat woman even in her dreams. She has left one hand in the place where the pain is, a great flower of flesh on top of those sculpted into the chenille bedspread.

Marcel realizes that his face is covered with tears. So that fire in Saskatchewan didn't dry them! He gets up as carefully as he can; Nana senses the movement on the mattress and moans faintly, bringing her hand to her forehead to check that the cool cloth is still there. She doesn't find it. In her nervousness, Albertine has forgotten about it. Just as he's about to leave the bedroom to tell his mother, the whine of the ambulance siren rises in the springtime air over Mont-Royal Street and the fat woman wakes with a start.

She gives Marcel an accusing glance he'll remember for the rest of his life. In it can be read not only her disappointment at having been betrayed but reproach as well, and maybe even—but that's not so certain—contempt. He could put up with anything from his aunt except that. She is the only one who has never looked down on him—even his mother and his sister sometimes show their contempt when he makes a particularly serious gaffe—and he couldn't bear it if she started now, especially when she's about to leave him, perhaps for ever.

"Momma had no choice, Auntie. You're too sick."

He turns red immediately. Do you tell a sick person she's too sick? Shouldn't you instead encourage sick people, downplay their pain, act as if everything is fine and all's for the best, the way his mother does when he wakes up in her arms with a wooden spoon in his mouth and foam on his lips, when he comes back from one of his profound journeys that aren't always unpleasant, no matter what other people may think?

But his aunt is sicker than he is, she's going to die, he can't make her think that all is well and life is beautiful!

His mother bursts into the bedroom, wearing her coat and rainboots.

"They're on their way, Nana. Everything's going to be fine, you'll see. They'll look after you better than we can. It's their job, they know what to do!"

The fat woman moves her hand from between her legs up to her heart.

"I don't want to be looked after, Bartine, what I want is to die here, with my own things, is that too much to ask?"

"But you're in such terrible pain!"

"I can deal with pain...."

"No you can't! Maybe you could last week or even yesterday, but not now. If we hadn't been here, Marcel and me...."

"If you hadn't been here just now I'd've managed by myself and you'd never have known!"

At this inadvertent confession Nana, ashamed, turns her head towards the window.

"You mean this has happened before?"

Albertine approaches the bed and bends over her sister-in-law.

"Answer me at least!"

Nana has closed her eyes.

"I know this isn't the time, Nana, but I've got something to tell you: if it *was* the time, I'd tell you off, I'd yell at you for not letting us know...that...that...."

The words don't come, her thoughts are all confused, she's tangled up in her own sentence, bits of thoughts cross her mind which she can't put into words and she stands there, bending over Nana, powerless as usual to clearly express what she's feeling. Frustration makes her tremble and Marcel, thinking he sees one of those rages of hers that leave him so shaken-up for the rest of the day, grabs her shoulders to make her straighten up.

"You shouldn't yell at her now, Momma, she's going to the hospital."

The doorbell rings; all three start, as if an unexpected full stop had just put an end to this conversation in which, however, nothing has yet been said.

"It's never the right time to tell her off! It never has been! The rest of you always protected her."

Albertine is desperate; she's not going to say that! Not now! It would be pointless and, even more, cruel! But her need is too strong, now when she ought to be silent the words form and she ends her sentence already annoyed with herself for delivering the final blow to someone she has loved so much.

"You've always loved her too much, the rest of you! You always loved her more than me and you never hid it!"

The doorbell again. Albertine leaves the bedroom. Runs out, rather, holding her coat closed over her vast bosom, her purse flapping against her leg, her rainboots dragging across the gleaming linoleum.

Marcel stands in his mother's place as if, for once, he were trying to replace Albertine in the role of the fat woman's confidant that had always been reserved for her.

"Don't listen to her, Auntie. She doesn't know what she's saying. She's too upset."

Nana raises her hand and gently takes her nephew's.

"We don't have much time. They'll be here in a few seconds. I just want to tell you.... Somebody has to know it.... I just want to tell you that it's worse, it's a lot worse than you think. Dying, I mean. Slowly dying. Rotting away. That's what's the hardest to take, Marcel. The rotting away. From inside. To know that you're rotting away from inside and there's nothing you can do about it. I've seen enough spoiled meat in my life to know what it looks like. I feel...I feel...."

Her chest heaves, the words come out of her mouth all wrong because she's trembling and Marcel is surprised to find himself sobbing over his aunt.

"I feel like an old steak that's hung around too long! I know that isn't a beautiful image, I wish I could find a better one, but what I'm feeling is ugly, Marcel, and that image...."

Sounds in the house. Voices.

"She's in the bedroom...."

"We know where it is, we're the ones that got her last time...."

"Be careful with her, okay?"

"We're careful with everybody, lady."

"I know, but she...she's different. If you only knew."

The fat woman has tightened her grip, her nails are leaving marks in Marcel's skin.

"That image is the closest I can come to what I'm thinking. I'm sorry you're the one I said it to, Marcel, I know how sensitive you are and I know how it's going to upset you. But I had to say it. Can you understand? Can you understand that?"

Marcel, who doesn't understand a thing, who is at once both proud and appalled to be his aunt's confidant, nods his head, saying yes, he understands, he understands everything, the image is clear, she was right to say it, to say it to him.

All at once, as if fate has willed it, there are five people in the bedroom which consequently becomes too small; they bump into one another, apologize, change positions; they execute some dance steps that in any other circumstances would be ridiculous, but that the tragedy of their situation magnifies; they are magnificently ridiculous because they are executing the dance of death.

***

He stood motionless for a few minutes outside the drugstore at the corner of Cartier and Mont-Royal, just below his Auntie Nana's apartment; he looked towards the left, where the ambulance disappeared as it turned down Papineau. He could have flown into a rage as he does when someone or something resists him for too long; he could have torn his clothes, kicked the brick wall, thrown himself to the ground while hammering it with his fists; instead, he stood there frozen in his outraged vulnerability, gloved hands thrust into the pockets of his parka, tuque stiff on his head, boots still not fastened. He has put on his dark glasses because the snow is too white, but also because he can feel the approach of a headache brought on by his disappointment.

He thought he could save his aunt; now he is watching, dismayed as she leaves for the hospital.

The beautiful story by Madame Gabrielle Roy didn't work. Usually, though.... Usually, it's to save himself that he makes up his stories, that he projects imaginary films onto the frozen surface of the lake in Parc Lafontaine in winter or the south wall of the Church of the Immaculate Conception in summer, that he writes epic novels or paints fabulous frescoes; it's to resolve his own problems that he uses his imagination: to extirpate the pain he feels deep in his heart, to express his disgust at injustice, to rise up against what is none of his business, to determine the fate of those he believes are his enemies and then emerge from it with increased stature, relieved and victorious. And it works. Always. This time, though, he focussed his energy on someone else, on one of the people he loves most in the world, and it didn't work.

He truly believed that a kind of miracle would come about through him, an act of generosity by the good Lord, for once. His calculations were off, the hero missed his chance, now he has to be punished. Not one of those ridiculous punishments his mother hands out when he drops a cup or comes home late, but a big fat one like those he imposes on himself when he decides that he's an idiot for getting caught. Now he's been caught in a state of helplessness and he must pay the price.

Physical suffering leaves him rather cold; he has punished himself physically often enough to know that it doesn't do any good, that he doesn't come out of it relieved, that a bruised thumb, a scratched face or a skinned knee only makes his rage worse, fueling it and exasperating him. No, the worst punishment he can inflict on himself....

He turns abruptly towards the drugstore window, walks up to his own reflection, tries to find the eyes of the transparent silhouette that in the end shows him nothing but cardboard cutouts advertising Palmolive soap and Colgate smiles leaning against a fragile wall, cardboard too, that serves as a display unit.

He can see the space he occupies himself, its width, its height, but everything that is really him—his features and his limbs, his clothes too—all of that disappears into the transparency of the glass, as if he has only two dimensions and no thickness. He takes off his glasses. That's worse, now he can hardly see anything. So he won't be able to look himself in the eye when he makes his wish. His vow of chastity. His vow to keep his imagination chaste.

Because the worst punishment he can inflict on himself is to not use his imagination for the rest of the day. He does that only in cases of extreme necessity, after a particularly serious gaffe or when he decides that his daydreams lead to nothing but an even deeper depression—which has happened often when he starts the scenario for his film and can't find his father, neither in a western nor in a horror film nor in the adaptation of Jules Verne's *Les Enfants du capitaine Grant*. It is an exemplary punishment that sometimes does him as much good as his wildest daydreams, because fasting, as he was taught during insanely strict Lents, cleanses the soul as well as the body. That, too he believes. But he's still apprehensive about the nearly insurmountable difficulty of it.

And so he is looking in the direction of his own eyes to convince himself, as usual, that he's made the right decision. Behind the little cardboard wall he spies the racks of medicine, the rows of bottles of Aspirin, cough syrup and mouthwash. He won't be able to make his wish under these conditions; after all, he can't take a bottle of Listerine seriously! He needs a mirror. A real one. To...to hypnotize himself.

Where can he find a mirror? His aunt's apartment is empty but he doesn't have the key. And he doesn't want to wait till he's back home, he'd have time to change his mind twenty times along the way.

He thinks about the barbecued chicken place just next door where his sister worked a few years ago, where he often went to gorge himself on chips and gravy. But will they recognize him, will they let him cross the big room and slip into the toilet to hypnotize himself? He has no choice, it's the only means available. Without thinking about it any more, he walks around the drugstore, heads east and opens the door of the restaurant.

***

Albertine has crossed her arms over her winter coat which she didn't have time to button before she left. Her black felt hat sits on her head askew. She dares not look at the sick woman lying on that ridiculous stretcher which is obviously too small for her. When the ambulance swerves on the ice that's not yet fully melted, the fat woman moans faintly. You can tell that she's holding back, that she doesn't want to complain, doesn't want to disturb anyone, as usual, but the pain is too severe and she utters little cries in spite of herself. Is she even conscious? Albertine decides she isn't because that's more convenient.

Papineau Street streams by through the rear door of the ambulance. Snow everywhere. Cars skidding. Passersby bent double as they watch where they place their feet. Dazzling sunshine. All of it—the last snowfall, the approaching spring— would be so joyous if.... Albertine starts rummaging for a handkerchief in her purse where anarchy reigns because she never takes the time to tidy it. Digging around, she finds chewing gum, crumpled papers that once were wrapped around something sweet and sticky, a lipstick she's spent weeks looking for (yes, she checked in her purse, several times, but she didn't find it!) and then, just as she was about to give in to exasperation, the white cotton hanky she keeps there, just in case.

She would like to believe that she's blowing her nose to express her sorrow or because she's crying, but she realizes it's an automatic act that has meaning only as social behaviour: a woman who's taking her dying sister-in-law to the hospital is *supposed* to cry; it's normal, it goes without saying, but Albertine ran out of tears a long time ago and, in spite of her immense sadness at the prospect of losing her beloved sister-in-law, she has no desire to cry and thinks her action is ridiculous. Why blow an empty nose? Why wipe away non-existent tears?

And why, above all, why pour out a heart you've done everything to disavow?

"It's just to put on a brave front. Till the ambulance crosses Parc Lafontaine."

She looks around. Did she say that out loud? And if so, did Nana hear her?

The fat woman looks at her.

"You're awake? For a long time?"

"I wasn't asleep. It hasn't been five minutes since we left the house, Bartine!"

"Did the shot they gave you help any?"

"Yes, shots always help. Even though I don't like taking that stuff."

Nana takes one arm out from under the blanket, places it on Albertine's knee.

"Hold my hand, Bartine. It's normal for you to do that for me, don't you think?"

They haven't touched one another for so long—a dry kiss at Christmas or birthdays, that's about all—and they're both so reluctant to show any emotion that Albertine looks at her sister-in-law's hand with something close to disgust. She has automatically folded her arms on her chest again and the white hanky is jutting out from her right armpit like the stuffing from a battered chair.

"Don't you want to hold my hand? I think it would be good for me."

"We're nearly there.... We're nearly at the end of Parc Lafontaine."

"Hold my hand anyway, Bartine!"

Albertine hesitates, plays for time, pretends to blow her nose again. What will they look like, holding hands like two crazy old women? She didn't even hold her own mother's hand when she was dying! She thinks:

"Those are things you see in the movies, not things you do in real life! Life isn't all cuddles and hand-holding, life is cold and it's rough!"

A dry hand slips into hers, takes the handkerchief, lets it fall. Albertine is so astonished at the feeling of that skin against her own, she starts to shake. And in the end it's her sister-in-law who consoles *her* while the ambulance is crossing Sherbrooke Street on the way to the Emergency.

"It's okay, Bartine, nobody can see us! Though if you ask me this could be as good for you as for me. Hold tight. Don't be shy, if it hurts, just tell yourself it doesn't hurt as much as what's burning inside me! I like you, Bartine, but you have to learn how to not be so crabby. Let yourself go a little, it makes no sense going stiff like that! And promise me something. Please. Promise you'll take my hand without arguing if I ask you to, in the hospital, when it gets worse."

The ambulance has turned left towards the Emergency entrance. Albertine is flung against her sister-in-law and they let go of each other's hands.

"We're nearly there, Bartine, in a minute it'll be too late. Promise. Promise me now."

Nana has picked up Albertine's hand and now she is holding it even tighter than before.

Albertine can't open her mouth. Of course she could say yes to her sister-in-law, she could pat her arm, console her, reassure her, make her think that she'll hold her hand whenever she wants; but she knows she isn't capable of doing that, not even at the final moment if she is there for Nana's final moment; she doesn't want to lie, she refuses to make a promise for the wrong reasons, one she would never be able to keep, and so she stiffens, purses her lips, retreats into herself something like the way her son does when she scolds him. She has become a knot of nerves and muscles, a concrete wall, smooth and hard; the fat woman, sensing it, doesn't insist and meekly puts her hand back under the blanket.

The ambulance doors open with a clatter that makes both women start. An orderly climbs up, slips between them.

"I was supposed to stay in the back here with you, but I figured you'd have things you wanted to say to each other...."

***

Madeleine recognized him right away with his stiff tuque and his dark glasses. She greeted him effusively because she'd become attached to him back in the days when Thérèse used to make her life hell every day from eleven till seven, the terror of shy customers who dared not confront her and an awe-inspiring partner in countless insults and endless run-ins with those who intended to be respected and dared to stand up to her. Complaints had piled up and even Monsieur Dubuc, the manager, who was afraid of her, had hesitated for a long time before he spoke to her. Thérèse hadn't left many pleasant memories at this quiet restaurant patronized by regulars. After she left on a sudden impulse, no one asked about her; some customers were even seen to heave a sigh of relief. Some employees too. Including Madeleine.

Marcel didn't take a seat in the last booth at the back as he did when his sister worked there; Madeleine thought he'd just come in to say hello. After two sloppy kisses on his plump cheeks, she took off his tuque to ruffle his hair.

"God, have you ever grown! I can hardly reach the top of your head! And I can't say you've slimmed down either!"

He didn't laugh, didn't even smile, which worried her a little.

"Say, you didn't come here with bad news, did you? Is something wrong with your sister? How come you're wearing those glasses?"

Marcel looked towards the door of the men's washroom.

"I just came in to ask if I could use the toilet."

Madeleine laughed and smacked him on the rear through his parka.

"You mean you gotta go, kiddo? But doesn't your aunt live right next door?"

Before she had time to finish her question, Marcel was already heading for the men's room.

"I'll fix you a big plate of chips and gravy just the way you like!"

But he had already disappeared.

Madeleine smoothes her beehive, her pride and joy but the butt of jokes by all of Plateau Mont-Royal, who think that beehive-shaped half-wig sitting on top of her head weighs her down, because of her tiny size, though she thinks it makes her look taller. Since she's been wearing it, she has held herself straighter, a regal bearing, and some malicious gossips claim that she really thinks she's somebody. A queen. A queen bee. That nobody wants anything to do with because she's never been known to have any friends.

She frowns. Marcel really was very strange with those dark glasses he's been wearing for ten years—she recognized them because, back then, they were already a constant source of argument between brother and sister—and the nearly palpable nervousness she'd sensed when she kissed him. She also remembers that he was often sick, suffering from some mysterious illness Thérèse had always refused to give a name to, that the restaurant employees had been quick to interpret as a shameful disease, one of those abnormalities that families hide, something fatally wrong with the lungs for instance, or a weakness in the head (a euphemism for *insanity*, a word no one would dare to use because every family has at least one lunatic), or quite simply c-a-n-c-e-r (another word no one dared to say out loud). They had never been able to learn anything, except that Marcel was strange and had to be constantly watched. And protected.

She also thinks it's odd that his shape is exactly the same at twenty-three as at thirteen, only fatter. She didn't feel that she was speaking to a man. As if Marcel, as he got older, had merely swelled up. Worried now, she swept into the kitchen where the chef was chatting with the dishwasher, smoking though it was against the rules.

In the men's room, Marcel stood in front of the little mirror. He pulled off his dark glasses, leaned across the sink, splashed some very cold water on his face. And he was still dripping when he confronted himself in the grimy mirror.

It's always very hard for him to punish himself because he knows that he's weak and inclined towards the easy relief his imagination offers. When something doesn't suit him, he can simply escape into his dreams to forget it all or to deal with his problems, and reality becomes completely incidental. In the present circumstances, for example, he could simply go back to Saskatchewan to save his aunt from a hideous death, but that's precisely what he wants to avoid, it's because he couldn't save her the first time that he wants to punish himself now. For him, the wall between dream and reality is made of coloured crepe paper; he tears it several times a day, he passes from one side of it to the other with ever greater ease—except when he decides that he has to be punished. And then the price to pay is unbearable because he forces himself to face up to reality for one whole day, with no forays into the redeeming world of wonders, with no hope of being able to embellish that which he thinks is ugly, or to exalt to the point of madness that which he thinks is beautiful. This is the way he always punishes himself for his failures. Which are rare.

He leans towards the mirror, looks himself straight in the eyes, exactly as he did an hour earlier when he began the story by Madame Gabrielle Roy. This time, though, it's so he can talk to himself. Out loud. He knows that he'll have to speak loudly, maybe even bawl himself out to be convincing, so he does what he does at home when his mother is listening at the door, he turns the taps on full blast. Hot and cold water swirl in the sink, making gurgling, sucking noises, and steam ascends in the tiny washroom. Heat rises, he should take off his parka. But it's too late now, Marcel has started his monologue.

It's childish and repetitive, the very opposite of his plunges into literature and film; it's insistent, enveloping and, above all, hypnotic. He lulls himself with words repeated infinitely which little by little (as he interprets it) finally subdue his imagination.

"Okay. Now listen to me. And listen good. You're gonna listen to me good. You're gonna pay attention. And not think about anything else and not look at anything else. You gotta listen to me good. All right? You hear that? Did you hear that? Did you hear me good?"

Something deep inside him is resisting, struggling. It is taking the form of the little voice of a child who is squealing and crying so as not to hear. That too he has to subjugate. He mustn't hear that little voice any more. And so he digs very deep, he plunges into the inky darkness where the voice has taken refuge, he holds out an imaginary hand—no, no imagination! but he has to, he has to so he can kill the little voice that's keeping him from concentrating!—in search of the little child who wants to dream. It's long, it's hard and during the whole time he has to keep talking to himself. Talking. Talking good.

After a very long period, minutes that seemed to him like hours, after an endless litany of talking and talking good, just as he thinks he's about to pass out, his knees weak and eyes fluttering, a tiny bell goes off far away inside him, not so much a bell as a kind of regular humming, and he knows that it worked. His imagination is gone. He has killed it. For today. When he wants to go back to normal, all he has to do is turn off the humming. He's ready, at least he thinks he is, to face up to the rest of the day without using.... He doesn't want to think the word "imagination" again, it's too dangerous, so he quite unequivocally thinks "madness."

When he comes out of the men's room, Madeleine, the chef and the dishwasher are waiting for him with strange smiles in which he sees fear, and a plate of chips swimming in gravy.

The emergency ward at Notre Dame Hospital is packed. They've left Nana's stretcher in the corridor. Doctors and nurses walk by without seeing her, hurrying to bandage a cut, clean a burn, disinfect a wound. Or profoundly upset as they were a while ago at having to tell parents sobbing in the waiting room that unfortunately, their son's car accident was fatal, they'd done all they could....

They had given the fat woman another injection and asked her to be patient, to try and sleep while her room was being made ready. Because her doctor had given the order to keep her here. That was three hours ago; at first Nana dozed off, then the surrounding noise had wakened her. She was surprised to see Albertine standing beside her, lips pursed and frowning. Nana wanted to send her home, but her sister-in-law wouldn't hear of it, she even ventured some black humour, saying the emergency room at Notre Dame wasn't nearly as depressing as her basement apartment on Sherbrooke Street. Nana smiled, but Albertine wasn't fooled.

"I shouldn't try to cheer you up with jokes, eh?"

"At least you try."

Long minutes have passed; when Nana asked why her husband wasn't there, Albertine merely shrugged and said a little too loudly:

"You should know, he likely stopped at the tavern for some courage and then lost it from drinking too much."

Nana gave Albertine's hand a friendly slap.

"Don't say things like that about my husband!"

"He's my brother, I've known him longer than you.... You'll see, he'll come staggering in here stinking of beer, he'll come and bawl in your arms so we'll feel sorry for him and you'll have to console him. Men are all alike. We know them inside out. It isn't that he's bad, he's just a man."

Nana does not reply. To her amazement she doesn't feel like defending her husband, though she has spent her life protecting him.

More long quarter-hours passed; finding nothing more to say to each other, the women were silent. Albertine fiddled with her purse, took off her coat, put it on again as if she was going to leave, then apparently changed her mind and took it off again. Stretchers rushed past them at an insane speed and what they saw sometimes made them want to howl in horror.

Then all at once there was a bustling around Nana's stretcher. Her room was ready. They straightened her top sheet and adjusted the bottom one as best they could, and a nurse even fluffed up her pillow. They asked if she was in pain, if she wanted an aspirin, something stronger, another injection even. She said no to everything, merely shaking her head. Her doctor paid a flying visit to tell her he'd got a private room and she didn't thank him because she immediately thought he was preparing her for death.

And it was at that moment, just before they took her up to her room, that she decided to confide in her sister-in-law.

"There's something I want you to understand, Bartine. About the hospital. This hospital. You know I had my five children here, the three that are left and the two I lost during the war.... Which means.... I really don't know how to say this so it won't sound silly.... You see, for me this hospital represents life. I gave birth to five babies here. Babies I wanted and loved as if I was demented. For me, this hospital represents life and I don't want to die here, do you understand, I don't want to die here! I'm prepared to die if it's my time, even if I think I'm way too young and I haven't lived enough yet; but not here, not in this place where I was so happy—five times! I want to die at home, I think it makes more sense! Because I wasn't always happy at home, while here.... Sorry, I'm repeating myself. But I want to be clear! I want to hear you tell me you understand what I'm trying to say!"

Albertine lowers her head.

"There's other hospitals!"

"The others are worse, I don't even know them!"

"At home you won't get your shots...."

"I'm not talking about shots!"

"But I am. I understand what you just said, I'm not a moron! But if I had a choice between passing away in a hospital unconscious and drugged to the eyeballs, and dying at home in indescribable pain, believe me, I'd forget my principles and it wouldn't take me long to make my choice! What good are those principles anyway, will you tell me? Oh sure, you were happy here, sure, you gave birth to five babies. So what? Think about yourself a little, for God's sake! And...maybe I shouldn't say this, but think about other people too, who're watching you die inch by inch and can't do anything for you. Do you think it's easy for them? You won't take shots even at home. They'll watch you.... Are you going to let them watch you die?"

This time she hit home. The fat woman closed her eyes.

"Are you telling me I'm being selfish?"

"You've never been selfish, it's true, but now...."

Nana turns her head towards the wall.

"See, I thought the very opposite. I thought I'd be selfish if I let them drug me and I died without suffering."

"Surely you don't think a person absolutely has to suffer when they die!"

The fat woman turns her head abruptly towards her sister-in-law.

"Did you ever see anybody die happy?"

Albertine starts rummaging in her purse, again to put on a bold front.

"Don't talk about that. Please don't talk about that. It scares me. I can't think about that, whenever I think about it I want to scream. I often wonder where I'll be when it happens, and what it'll be from and how old I'll be.... I can't do it. I can't even think about it. It's agony. It puts me in a terrible state.... Now where are my nerve pills? I had some! I'm sure I still had some, in the bottom here!"

Nana in her rage has raised her head a little. She's shouting now too. Heads turn in their direction, someone even heaves an exasperated sigh because this fat woman gesticulating on her stretcher isn't behaving properly at all.

"You're just like your brother, aren't you? You're the one we're supposed to feel sorry for, right? Is that it? Do I have to console you? Like I'll have to console him? Never mind, Bartine. Pretend I didn't say a word. Go home. Don't think about death. Specially not yours. Specially when you're healthy as a horse!

And don't come to my room with me, I don't need you. There's people paid for that."

Albertine sets her purse on the stretcher, buttons her coat crooked without realizing it, straightens the black felt hat which had fallen over her ear a while ago...

"If you're going to take it like that..."

...and leaves the emergency ward without saying goodbye to her sister-in-law.

The fat woman sighs, exasperated.

"Good riddance to bad rubbish!"

That was one of the favourite expressions of her sister Béa when they were children in Saskatchewan. She can hear her high-pitched voice, she can see again the black grade-school uniform, the white apron for their home economics classes (yes, even at that tender age women had to be prepared for their role as wife and mother!), the nun they'd detested so much, Sister Rose of Lima, whom they called Rose Lima Bean because they hated that dry, tasteless vegetable. Again, her sister's voice when Sister Rose of Lima left the classroom: "Good riddance to bad rubbish!" and she starts to cry unrestrainedly, huge sobs she's kept inside for too long. It relieves her and exhausts her. Automatically she puts her hands between her legs. And just as the pain comes back she remembers what she dreamed when Marcel was in her bedroom.

Fire. Fire all around. Not just in her belly, everywhere, outside. The stifling smoke. The apocalyptic splendour of the flaming prairie. Her mother, her sister and herself prisoners on their porch. And then.... Who was he? Who was the fat man? The hero who'd burst on the scene out of nowhere? The man who'd made them get down on their hands and knees, crawl through the mud and dive into the pond behind the house, surrounded by the wild creatures of the prairies and their own animals? It was someone she knew, a familiar silhouette, she's sure of that. But whose?

"Your room's ready now, dear.... I'm going to push you to the elevator. Now, don't cry. Blow your nose. Everything's going to be fine, you'll see."

She didn't even open her eyes, merely hid her face in her hands as the stretcher set off down the corridor of the emergency ward at Notre Dame Hospital.

***

The first hour is always amazingly easy. Thérèse has often said the same thing about her numerous attempts to stop smoking. The first hour's easy, you feel fine, relieved, you're still excited by your resolution (especially if it's January first and you're bombed), you feel as if the world belongs to you and there's no smoke in the future.

That's exactly what Marcel tells himself as he boards the Mont-Royal bus later that afternoon. The world belongs to him and there's no smoke in the future. He's not taken in though by the momentary sense of exaltation brought on by his brand-new decision to stop using his imagination: he has tried so often and it has never lasted very long. But as he does every time, he tells himself that this time is the right time, even though he knows he's made his decision on a day that will only last a few hours.

Of course the world looks different through that end of the telescope. Things simply are what they are, everything is small and gloomy, the passersby are not bearers of fabulous stories or lethal viruses, store windows aren't inhabited by malevolent creatures or celestial beings, the bus won't be hijacked to Alice's Wonderland or to the Neverland of Peter Pan. Stripped of any transposition, of the grace of fabrication with which Marcel colours everything that goes on in his life, the world carries on at its own little pace, chronological and linear and desperately down to earth.

If all that is to remain in place, however, if he is to be able to follow everything and not be tempted to interfere and make everything either more beautiful or ugly, Marcel has had to do an odd kind of housecleaning inside himself. He feels a little as if he's been deflated, or as if he's applied the brakes a bit too quickly during an exciting race. He's experiencing a slight dizziness, not unpleasant but rather surprising; a void has been created where usually incredible, often terrifying stories vie for space. Since nothing lends itself to interpretation now, everything becomes smooth and slippery. This world is slipping out of Marcel's grasp while the other one, the one he's been improvising for so long now, as he lives his life, complex though it may be, is easier to control. Because it stops and starts existing when Marcel wants it to. Whereas this one....

That woman coming out of the bakery with her big paper bag, for instance: he can't do anything for her, he simply can't, to take her out of her monotonous life, to turn her into some diabolical creature or a saint en route to adventures whose importance for the future of humankind she's not yet aware of (no, no, don't think about that, he mustn't set out on that road, he mustn't), or that man who is too tall in an overcoat that's too big, he could fly away, carried off by a gust of wind (no, be quiet, look somewhere else, don't let yourself drift....) It would be so much fun though!

Marcel has rested his forehead against the cold surface of the window in the hope of freezing his brain. That's precisely the image he has: his frozen brain sitting in the freezer section of the frigidaire with the peas and the leftover ice cream. And that's where he should keep it till tonight, till he goes to bed, till he closes his eyes....

But then, once his eyes are closed, he knows very well that all his defences will be down and the real world—his world, the one he invents, the only viable one, the only one he wants to live in—will come back in all its terrible force.

Marcel smiles. Because starting now, he won't be responsible for what goes on inside his head.... Because he'll be asleep. He tells himself he can't wait to be asleep, but for the time being, he is forcing himself to stay awake while he looks out the window at the passing parade of the lives of everyone else.

***

When he arrives at Sherbrooke Street he has no desire to go home, of course. His mother probably won't be back from the hospital, he'll be all alone in the small apartment, the temptation to escape through the plaster mouldings on the ceiling will be too great, with the plump cherubs and the garlands of fruit, and he won't resist for very long. He can't lie down in the bed he shares with his mother or on the sofa in the hallway, without experiencing the anguish that has come to join the other feelings since they moved here: the lump in his throat, the weight on his heart, the dizziness that's the opposite of dizziness, that comes from confinement rather than from fear of the void, that sometimes keeps him awake till the early hours of morning, feverish and trembling.

Over the months he has learned to use the plaster mouldings to break away from that dizziness, to throw himself into the ceiling the way you throw yourself into the void, to plunge into the plaster and become part of a world that's more bearable, where sons sleep with their mothers, not from necessity but from vice. Not that he's ever gone in for that kind of dream; no, his mother's presence in the bed is too negative, her rage, her spite are too tangible, even when she's asleep, for him to have the slightest urge to succumb to an incestuous dream. But in his wildest dreams, in the depths of the most harrowing nights, as he follows suspect roads reputed to be dangerous in the heart of his hero's blackest adventures, he has met some of those dark horsemen with flamboyant armour whose cruel gaze betrayed their depravity (a word Marcel loves the sound of, it makes him think of something deep, like water) and an inclination to seduce and profane whatever stirs, even their own mothers.

His hero, though, is not inclined to depravity. Sometimes he tells himself: "Okay, today I have to have a dirty dream," but he can never put one together that really suits him, with the right partner, in the right situation; his dirty dreams only turn up during his real sleep and they have an aftertaste of the incomplete, of frustration, because, of course, he always wakes up at the best part. As for his masturbation, his foot-washing sessions as he calls them, thinking his mother is fooled, those take place on the toilet or over the bathroom sink and there's nothing about them of the daydream or the romantic; they're performed at top speed, in response to a purely animal need, and they're followed by attacks of guilt so powerful that they leave Marcel exhausted and gnawed by remorse. Not only certain of being punished but also convinced, as the teaching brothers always told him, that one day he'd end up deaf.

And so he walks right past 410 Sherbrooke Street East, not even glancing at the door to see if Madame Saint-Aubin was chatting with one of the tenants or yelling at a beatnik, a sight he always adores. He likes the fact that Madame Saint-Aubin doesn't mince words—except of course when she talks to him—and sometimes he even hides behind the basement door to spy on her outbursts or her temper tantrums. Not today. He speeds up, lowering his head, and heads for the Club Canadien where his sister works.

That overly ornate, pretentious building is the closest thing Marcel has seen to a castle, to his idea of what a castle looks like: the stone staircase, the impressive balcony, the gallery below with its slits you could fire a cannon through, the oak door with its wrought-iron hinges and ornamental scrolls, the huge entrance that's always fragrant with polish and beeswax, the many salons you can glimpse if you crane your neck.... He's never had a chance to visit these salons or the other rooms in the Club Canadien because his sister,furious at him for using the front door instead of the side door that's reserved for the staff, always grabs him by the hand and tugs him down into the lower depths, the guts of the grand residence. Like their mother, Thérèse rules over the basement of a huge house, but hers is a vast and mysterious basement that excites Marcel's imagination. In fact it's here that a good many of his Hero's adventures take place; it has become the fortified castle of Ivanhoe or King Arthur, it was from here that Maid Marian fled to meet up with Robin Hood, it was here on the front steps that Juliet Capulet first met him in the guise of Romeo Montague, and it was on the stairway over there, just in back, that he first spied the silhouette of his father.

He stops just as he's about to press the bell. He knows he has to avoid his sister's big apartment if he doesn't want to provoke his imagination, but the temptation to kiss Thérèse is too strong, her skin that's always fragrant with Chénard's Tulipe Noire perfume, like their Auntie Nana's. With his head resting against the hard wooden door, he listens to the far-off echo of the chiming bell.

***

"I've told you a hundred times, use the side door, it opens right into my apartment!"

"I thought you were vacuuming...."

"Who ever heard of vacuuming at five in the afternoon! Okay, come on in before somebody sees you...."

"Have the rich men started coming yet?"

"Of course the rich men have started coming.... But the rich men have a key so I thought you were somebody's guest...."

"Is it you that opens the door for guests?"

"No, it isn't me that opens the door for guests, I'm just the janitor. But when you rang three times and nobody answered...."

"Good thing, I wouldn't've known what to say...."

Marcel cranes his neck, sees two crossed legs jutting out from an easy chair, a folded newspaper, swirls of pipe smoke rising in the stuffy air of one of the salons. Then a man walks into his field of vision, a glass of something brown in his hand; Marcel tells himself it must be liquor and thinks that maybe his Hero could belong to a private club like this.... He sees David Niven or Gary Cooper or (what's his name, oh that's right!) Paul Meurisse in the role of the Hero, anyway, someone with a lot of class, who can impose it on everyone else; and then he bumps his head on his way down the stairs to the basement.

Tomorrow for daydreams.

But that one he puts aside.... A wonderful spy story with exotic settings, his sister held prisoner by a modern-day pirate.... But when he gets to the bottom of the stairs, he thinks his sister wouldn't mind at all being kidnapped by a modern-day pirate and that he'd be better off with a less willing victim. His mother, maybe.... He chuckles at the thought of his mother tied to a coconut palm on some desert island in the Pacific, with a gag around her mouth and a torn skirt like Dorothy Lamour; Thérèse turns her head.

"What's so funny, are my seams crooked?"

"Nothing, I just thought about something funny."

As soon as they're inside his sister's apartment, he smells Kellogg's All Bran muffins, his Auntie Nana's recipe, and his mouth waters.

"Muffins like Auntie Nana's!"

Thérèse smiles in spite of herself at her brother's childlike enthusiasm.

"My friend Harelip came over for tea.... I think there's a few left.... They aren't hot, but they probably still taste all right."

In the corridor, Marcel stops in his tracks. He even shrinks back, as if Thérèse had just given him some bad news. He looks behind him, nearly panicking, but his sister isn't aware of it. He hears her talking to Harelip.

"It's just my kid brother. Speak of the devil...."

Another voice rises in the kitchen, lower than that of Thérèse, hoarser too; you can hear in it her abuse of alcohol and strong cigarettes.

"My God, I haven't seen him for ages! Where the hell is he?"

"He was right behind me...."

A chair is pushed, someone crosses the kitchen, a shadow emerges in the doorway.

"If it isn't my favourite Marcel!"

The sight of Simone Côté—a.k.a. Harelip to the crowd of the Main, from Sherbrooke down to Viger and on both sides of St. Lawrence, from Fat Minoune's on Dorchester all the way to Betty Bird's brothel on Sanguinet near Ontario—always makes Marcel feel uncomfortable, because he never knows if he's talking to a woman or a man, if he ought to call her "Monsieur" or "Madame." Actually, he knows that Simone Côté is a woman; he knew her as a child, she's been his sister's friend forever—his sister who *really* looks like a girl and not just any girl either—but for a while now Simone has looked so much like a man that he wonders if she's been mistaken all that time, if when all's said and done she's always been a guy but didn't know it. Already as a child who attended the École des Saints-Anges with Thérèse, and later on when the three of them, Thérèse, Pierrette and Simone, went out together dressed to kill in their dresses and crinolines and flying-saucer-shaped hats, maybe she was a guy then but didn't know it. Maybe one morning when she was washing between her legs like you're supposed to, she got a surprise.... Marcel turned red at this vision and Harelip noticed.

"It's true, you still squirm when you're around other people. Here, let's have a kiss."

She goes up to him, stands on tiptoe because she's far from tall, and plants a kiss on his left cheek, the softness of her lips surprising Marcel once again. Because there's no beard, of course, but mainly because of the harelip that splits Simone Côté's upper lip in half and always makes her look as if she's sneering. Every time she gives him a kiss he's afraid he'll feel her tooth scrape his skin. In fact, when she smiles as she's doing now, one of her incisors is bared, which always makes Marcel thinks about Christopher Lee who was so terrifying in *Horror of Dracula* a few years earlier, and he expects to see Simone's teeth growing longer, her upper lip curling back—though it already is curled back, too much for his liking—her eyes rolling back and a guttural voice inviting him to bare his neck....

Everything about Simone Côté makes Marcel think of a man, a real one: the Hollywood haircut carefully brushed back, the total absence of makeup, the fairly good quality three-piece gabardine suit, the white shirt with pale blue pinstripes, the silk tie with a gold-plated tie-pin, right down to the shoes that creak when she walks, an office clerk's shoes, always clean and shiny. Then there's the not very well sewn-up slit that makes her face look even tougher. Her behaviour is masculine too, but you can sense the effort under her rather unnatural habit of always checking the knot in her tie, the way she smokes, holding the cigarette inside her hand, and above all her obsession with always offering women a cigarette as if that were the height of masculinity. So much thoughtfulness is tiresome, and women often reproach her for it, though they also complain about the lack of gallantry of their men.

"Hey, are you scared of me or what?"

Marcel doesn't answer. He hopes she'll understand that yes, he's afraid of her, without his having to say so. But she gives him a smack on the rear and turns to go back to the kitchen.

"You were right, what you said, Thérèse, your brother's so shy it's unhealthy...."

They were talking about him before he got here!

What could they have been saying? He hates finding about that people were talking about him when he wasn't there, behind his back, when he couldn't hear and even more, when he couldn't defend himself.

"Don't just stand there till tomorrow, Marcel, honestly! The muffins will be dry as a bone...."

Summoning up his courage, Marcel walks cautiously across the few feet to the kitchen.

And it hits him in the face as he walks into the kitchen. In the nose, actually. He couldn't put a word to what he's feeling—actually, he *is* thinking about a word, but he rejects it because it's ridiculous to think that about his sister—but he's convinced that it's real, that it really happened—and not long ago besides, because it's nearly palpable in the air of the kitchen. He should have glanced inside Thérèse's bedroom when he passed it. Unless.... He turns away, races out of the kitchen.

"I'll take off my coat in your bedroom...."

And there it is, very real, in the atmosphere of the bedroom, floating like fog; it clings to your skin and it smells...it smells so good.

The odour of love.

Very slowly Marcel takes off his parka; he looks all around, sniffs, inhaling the musky fragrance coming from the unmade bed, he bends down to touch the sheets, brushing them with his hand. He'd like to throw himself headlong into this bouquet of powerful scents but if he were gone too long, Thérèse would worry and she'd come and fetch him by the scruff of his neck. In fact she's calling to him from the kitchen now:

"Marcel! Your muffin's on your plate!"

A laugh, a little too coarse, a little too quickly repressed.

They're making fun of him again! With dirty jokes, no less!

He goes back to the odour of love.

He's always found it very hard to imagine his family and friends making love. When he finally understood, late, what was involved and why, he checked out his family—beginning with his mother, of course—and what he imagined disgusted him because, he told himself, surely the people you know don't put themselves into situations like that: Albertine in the arms of the mysterious man he's been pursuing since childhood, in dreams that are always incomplete, doing things unworthy of a mother, grotesque things, and the same for his Auntie Nana with her Gabriel, especially given her size! The basic position itself was ridiculous, humiliating, the little animal cries between kisses too, and the sucking sounds of damp skin against damp skin were disgusting.

His sister was less surprising; he didn't see her with her husband, drab old Gérard, however, but with a multitude of partners, because of her long-compromised reputation, the countless squabbles between Albertine and Thérèse—on the phone, here, at his mother's house, and more recently the slander of Madame Saint-Aubin and the tenants at 410—faceless men quickly dispatched and soon replaced. His mother and his aunt had seemed to experience a certain pleasure; not her.

He wasn't interested in his Auntie Nana's three sons; they'd pissed him off too much when he was little, so he put them aside as unworthy of his attention, with sex lives that must be very ordinary and very uninteresting.

Just one thing had surprised him during these guilty daydreams in which his family and friends indulged in behaviour that was, if not reprehensible, then to say the least surprising: the absolutely irresistible odour it gave off. It was more than intoxicating, it was hypnotic—he still thinks "hympotic" of course, certain that it's the right word—it knocks you down, then it roots around in your guts and sticks to you for a long time after the dream is over. The smell was there before, during and after he took his bath; it was at the same time dirty and clean, with the dirty being more appealing, more exciting. And it came back whenever you wanted it, because it was unforgettable, imprinted forever on the retina of memory.

The odour of love.

He imagined, no, he used the odour of his sister's bedroom as a prototype for the fragrance of love, not knowing it really *was* the odour of love. Now that he has guessed everything, though, because he's old enough to guess that which he doesn't know, when he visits his sister he is often on the alert for that scent he's so fond of, he's on the alert for it in her bedroom and on her, on her clothes and on her skin. And today the odour is more pronounced, more present, more...more alive. The love that's just been made here isn't dead yet. It is continuing. *In the kitchen.* Marcel is beginning to suspect that he's on the brink of a great revelation. But he isn't ready. He turns his attention elsewhere.

His very first adolescent fantasies had taken place not in a bed but on the stage of a nightclub; at the time, the object of his affection was a singer with a superb body and a bewitching voice—that's how he thinks of it, he likes the word "bewitching," especially for a voice, a siren's voice that's as dangerous as it is beautiful—that sang for him and him alone about Chinese nights, about tangos from deep in the heart of the South, about the little fountain of Pigalle and the lower depths of Hamburg and Whitechapel. And when the appropriately named Mercedes Benz—"the limousine of nightclub singers" in the elegant words of the MC at the French Casino—when *his* Mercedes Benz died under tragic circumstances, Marcel had found himself without a fantasy. Because Mercedes was irreplaceable.

Now, nearly ten years later, his dreams still too frequently dip into that same past because he has never found a worthy replacement for Mercedes and, as a result, he is suffering.

In any case, his hastily dispatched foot-washing sessions in the bathroom don't lend themselves to long, elaborate erotic delights.

"If you don't get back here your fuckin' muffin goes in the garbage! So move it!"

He emerges from the bedroom, walks down the hallway and up to the door of the bathroom where he knows that his sister commits another kind of sin, uglier and more destructive, then he takes a seat at the kitchen table where a huge muffin sits surrounded by pats of butter and a cold glass of milk.

He tucks in right away, not looking up at the two women who are watching him. He is very careful not to make any noise as he chews because he knows that gets on Thérèse's nerves; he waits till he's swallowed before taking a sip of milk. It's good. An All Bran muffin with lots of butter. And a glass of milk.

He nearly forgets the strange atmosphere in the room. Not altogether, though. He listens to the silence that had settled in between Simone and his sister when he arrived and interprets it as a prelude to something not very nice, something that will be nearly violent.

And it happens as he sets his empty glass on the plastic tablecloth.

Thérèse has always had the outrageous habit of announcing bad news either in public or in front of at least one other person, to short-circuit those to whom she's telling it, to paralyze them, prevent them from reacting; she uses this ploy as a gag, relying on the effect of shock in front of witnesses to avoid reproaches, outbursts and run-ins. Marcel has seen her do it so often, he realizes right away that she's using his presence to give Simone some news that won't make her happy. Because, as usual in these cases, her sentence begins with "By the way...."

"By the way, sweetie, there's something I forgot to tell you...."

Harelip lifts a curious eyebrow and Marcel tells himself she seems to know Thérèse as well as he does.

"What is it this time...."

"Nothing! Quit judging me before I even open my mouth!"

Thérèse is aggressive; this is liable to be *very* bad news for Simone.

"Okay, shoot. But I don't like it when you start with 'By the way'...."

Simone and Marcel exchange a look. A wave of complicity passes between them, along with a little panic in Simone.

Thérèse is fiddling with her cold cup of tea.

"I can't go into all the details just now, and it's none of your business anyway, but.... I hope you'll understand.... My mother and brother and me are going to be moving in together pretty soon...."

Simone jumps up, livid with rage but held back by Marcel's presence; he claps both hands over his mouth to stop himself from howling with delight. She knew that what she had to say would be bad news for Harelip, but she also knew it was going to make Marcel deliriously happy! He'd love to get up and throw himself in her arms, hug her tight, kiss her on her cheeks and on her neck, but the sight of what seems to be going on between her and Simone stops him.

Simone is leaning against the table, hands flat in the muffin crumbs, and she's obviously having trouble breathing.

Before the storm breaks Thérèse continues:

"Listen, I had to do it, okay? I'm short of money. Everything costs so much.... We're all short of money, Momma, me...."

She purses her lips. Marcel is convinced that she intended to go on, that she was about to name someone else.... They're going to move in with somebody else!

Harelip's head is tilted slightly.

"You don't have to say anything else, I get the picture.... You're getting back together with your husband, right?"

Now Marcel stands up, pushing back his chair. Thérèse isn't looking at either of them.

"Is that it? At least look me in the eyes when you tell me, Thérèse! You can do that, can't you?"

Marcel stares at each of them in turn. A complicated game of which he doesn't understand all the stakes is being played before his eyes and it's keeping him from truly experiencing the euphoria he feels. He couldn't care less about Gérard, whom he thinks is a jerk, but he's going to be with Johanne again! The little niece he hardly ever sees, who mustn't be a baby any more! She must be a little girl, at least! If not a woman! No, not a woman.... How old is Johanne anyway? But the conversation in the kitchen is continuing and he concentrates on what his sister and her girlfriend are saying.

Harelip is speaking now, very softly, with her harsh smoker's voice.

"I know I can't talk in front of...of him.... I know I have to be careful what I say.... My God! Yelling and screaming would be so much easier. You could've said something before, you could've told me it was the last time...."

"It doesn't have to be the last time...."

"Where are we supposed to get together? It was so easy here: no witnesses, ever, a big apartment just for us...."

"Watch what you say...."

"He isn't a baby for Christ's sake, he's as big as an ox!"

"Watch out anyway, maybe he doesn't understand...."

"And maybe he does! He's old enough!"

"I'd just as soon not take any chances."

"You're such a coward, Thérèse, do you know that?"

Thérèse turns towards her brother.

"I'm all out of cigarettes, Marcel honey. Will you go get me some?"

A ridiculous attempt at a diversion—there's a nearly full package sitting right there on the table. Marcel shrugs.

"Don't treat me like a moron, Thérèse. Anyway, I understand everything. The sheets in your room weren't even dry!"

All at once he turns red. He said it! It's the first time he has broached this kind of subject with his sister and now, like when he was a child, he's afraid of getting smacked. He shields his face with his arm, and while he's doing that, Simone continues her diatribe. She points at him.

"Look at that, he's scared shitless of you! You may scare everybody else, Thérèse, but you don't scare me!"

"What's that supposed to mean?"

"What it means is, I don't intend to stand by and let you treat me like this!"

"And what can you do, would you mind telling me that?"

"When I'm in the mood I could turn up and ring the bell at your place! Your gorgeous Gérard sure as hell won't stop me from seeing you! I could knock him down with one flick of my finger. Your mother too. She's always hated me and she won't even look at me! If I don't exist for her there's no way she'd know I'm sleeping with her daughter, even if I do it right in front of her!"

This time, Thérèse stares at Simone. She hesitates before going on. She can see the pain on her friend's face, the humiliation, above all the disappointment caused by such a cowardly betrayal. So then, as she always does at the most difficult moments (Marcel thinks she isn't very subtle, it's too easy to see what her game is now, she's lost that lovely ease that has marked her entire life and made her so enticing), she opts for charm, for good old elementary seduction with its powerful smell of despair and of the last resort. She walks around the table, gesturing to Marcel to leave the kitchen, and puts her arms around Simone. Surely her friend won't let herself fall into such an obvious trap! At first Harelip resists and then, under Thérèse's sweet words and touches, lets herself go in her arms and cries.

Despite his adoration of his sister, his unshakable admiration for this woman who has always done exactly what she wanted, Marcel feels an irrepressible disgust rise in his throat. Is it because he is seeing two women caress one another? He's positive that's not it. What disgusts him is his sister's duplicity: just now she didn't want Simone to even talk about their relationship in front of him, and now she's ready to do anything, even feel up Harelip in front of him, to save her own skin. She's always been like that, so he tells himself, she's always been selfish and heartless, with no consideration for anything or anyone. He adores her, he still adores her, he'll go on adoring her till the end, but now he can see her as she is, a coward, yes, a coward, Simone was right, and even more, a hypocrite. And what's most unbearable for him is knowing that he'll still be glad to move in with her and that no doubt he too will succumb to the same kind of seduction when Thérèse decides it's time to treat him the way she's treating Simone now. She's going to wrap him around her little finger with sugary kisses and sweet words, she'll put him away in her pocket and wrap him in her handkerchief so she can use him again when she needs to. She has always manipulated them and she always will. All of them.

He leaves the kitchen nearly at a run and leans against his sister's bedroom door. He can hear her wheedling voice, he can smell her duplicity just as, earlier, he smelled the odour of love on the sheets; it's an acrid perfume, cloying, unpleasant and insistent.

He looks up at the ceiling. No plaster cherubs here, no garlands of flowers and fruit. No possible way out either, because of his vow. He has to come to terms with everything he's just found out, without resorting to....

A precise image comes to his mind. A book hidden at the back of the hall closet, behind the Christmas decorations, a huge volume stolen from the municipal library, with illustrations that have the capacity to soothe him when he feels anxiety coming on. And right now, he senses the onset of anxiety, a powerful attack he fears he won't be able to get through unless he uses his imagination. It's a terrible dilemma that he tries in vain to brush away. Racing out the side door of the Club Canadien, he wonders if the illustrations in the big book will be enough to ward off a serious attack.

If not....

***

He arrives in front of 410 at the same time as his mother, who acts as if she doesn't remember punishing him a few hours earlier. Amazed, he follows her like a silly dog, moving from her left to her right, opening doors for her, even the smaller one that goes to the cellar. All to avoid being yelled at and to hide his distress. Time is short, he knows an attack is coming on, and he has better things to do than listen to Albertine's complaints and recriminations.

"What're you so worked up about?"

"I went to see Thérèse...."

"So that's it. I suppose she couldn't wait to tell you the big news?"

"Yes."

"And I suppose you're glad?"

"I'll be glad to be back with her. And Johanne."

Albertine takes out the key to their apartment, fits it into the lock, pushes open the door, which creaks.

"Did she say where we're moving to?"

"No. Do you know?"

Stamping her feet on the worn doormat, his mother turns to face him.

"No, I don't. Anyway, she didn't tell me."

She thinks he's agitated enough already; he doesn't need to find out that they're going back to where they started out, to where he was born, to the apartment he's never been able to forget, that he misses so badly and talks about so often.

"Don't you want to know where I've been?"

"I'm sorry. I know you were at the hospital. How's Auntie Nana?"

"She's dying, is how she is."

Marcel sits on the sofa to pull off his heavy boots.

"But she won't die today. And I don't thinks she's going to die soon."

Albertine switches on the overhead light in the kitchen and turns to him.

"How can you know something like that?"

"I just know."

"You think you're smarter than everybody else, is that it?"

"I'm not smarter than everybody else."

"So how can you know something like that? Did a little bird tell you? Or an angel, is that it?"

"I've just got a feeling, that's all. And don't make fun of me."

Never would he admit to her that he really smelled, with his own nose, an odour emanating from his aunt, one that was unchanged, her very own odour, which he has known forever—a mixture of cheap perfume and skin washed with scented soap, nothing like the odour of death—which suggested to him that Nana would still be around for a while.

Albertine shrugs as she does whenever Marcel says something she can't understand. She's so used to his ramblings she doesn't even bother listening to the end.

"You can sit there while I fix supper, but no TV for you tonight! You're being punished, don't forget. And you disobeyed me for the *second* time when you went to your sister's! You thought I'd forgotten, didn't you? Well I've got a little surprise for you! I don't forget anything, ever, as you ought to know!"

"Yes, Momma."

He is wearing the sheepish look of a child who's been punished, but deep down he's very happy about the bargain: she has ordered him to stay there right next to the hall closet where he's hidden the book he wants to look at.

"Can I read?"

"You can do whatever you want, you can get bored, you can even stand there with your mouth hanging open, just don't watch any TV!"

Immediately he gets on his knees in the closet and rummages behind the box of Christmas decorations. His mother sticks her head out the kitchen door.

"What's all that racket about? What're you doing in the closet on your hands and knees, are you crazy or what?"

She purses her lips. Brother Stanislas told her never to use that word in front of him, it could bring on a fit because Marcel, like all crazy people, is probably convinced that he isn't.

"I left an old book in there.... Here it is, I can feel it. You can go back to making the supper."

She gives him a strange look before she disappears. He can hear her thinking:

"Don't start telling me what to do in my kitchen, young man! One more remark like that and you'll go without supper!"

But she says nothing, to avoid contradicting him. She has noticed how nervous he is, his choppy way of speaking, and in particular, the slight squint that afflicts him whenever there's a danger of a fit. She sighs as she takes a can of Campbell's tomato soup and a loaf of sliced bread from the cupboard.

"This will do for tonight. I don't feel like breaking my behind for somebody who maybe won't even touch what I make for his supper!"

Marcel hugs the big book before he really looks at it. It's a book about the Italian Renaissance, abundantly illustrated, which he stole a few months earlier. One of his finest achievements: no one saw him because he'd hidden the art book in a big bag of groceries he'd been careful to bring along. Carrot tops were sticking out of it. And a cabbage. He had waited till all the librarians were looking for books and the guard was chewing someone out for making too much noise before he slipped furtively out of the room where you could look at books you weren't allowed to borrow, then out of the library itself.

He remembers very clearly the exaltation he'd felt once he was out on Sherbrooke Street with his big book in the Tousignant's grocery bag, his heart pounding as if it were going to burst; he remembers the tears that came to his eyes, above all he remembers his excitement at the thought that now he could plunge into the Quattrocento whenever he wanted!

It was purely by chance that he'd discovered this book. One day when he had nothing better to do he'd gone into the municipal library to kill some time, and while he was looking at the books left out on the tables in the reading room he had landed on a word he'd never seen before, but that, amazingly, he'd thought he recognized. Printed in big letters on a huge illustrated volume: QUATTROCENTO. He thought it was the author's name. Then he'd sat down because the illustration on the cover—a Virgin and Child—was particularly beautiful, and started leafing through it, not paying much attention at first, but then with growing passion. And the entire Quattrocento had appeared to him in all its inexhaustible splendor. A distant memory, long since buried, came back to him: a little boy sitting on a livingroom floor next to a piano that was producing achingly beautiful music; the little boy was leafing through a book, this same book, exactly the same one, and someone, a lady who smelled of flowers, of all the flowers in the world, was explaining the pictures to him one by one, in detail, with many clear and informative explanations. And the little boy understood. Everything. Unfortunately though, he'd forgotten it all even as he was comprehending.

Marcel recognized these paintings; and being reunited with them gave him a keen but disturbing pleasure.

And he'd stolen it because he knew he had to have that book, forever.

He gets up, settles in on the hall sofa.

He smoothes the cover as he does every time he wants to look at this book. There is a great danger though that he'll drift into daydream or worse, into the delirium these paintings often provoke in him. Today, because he needs to punish himself, he has decided he'll only consult them, look at them the way you look at something beautiful that consoles you for the other things that are ugly, nothing more; he must not let himself go. He turns directly to page 471 and....

Later on, he will claim that it wasn't his fault, that he hadn't wanted to dream, that the painting had actually *sucked him in*.

It's the most famous fresco in the world, its colours faded by time and pollution, but its power and its beauty are incomparable. At the very moment he first sets eyes on it, Marcel is virtually *absorbed* by the page, he dives head first into the painting without even having the time to resist, and his imagination hurls him into his third adventure of the day, a motionless one because it's painted, yet even more alive than the others because of its many mysteries, its keys whose secrets he alone knows, all the facts about it too, because you need reference points when you're interpreting your life through a painting.

It is a fresco painted onto the wall in the nave of the most beautiful church in the world, it is blue and blood red and lemon yellow and gold and a beautiful sea green and a magnificent sienna; it is at once gaudy and discreet; the water from floods, the smoke from torches and modern-day pollution have dulled some of its brilliance, but still it is and will always remain more brilliant than real life, because the characters in it have been alive forever, they are living and suffering today and they will live eternally.

It is gigantic, sublime, a work of art that has marked the history of the world, and its title is....

The Last Judgment

So. Here I am. My name is Marcello del Plato Monte Royale, known simply as Marcello (1459-1548). I am a painter of the Quattrocento, one of the most representative, one of the most significant. In particular, one of the forerunners. After me, thanks to my frescoes and paintings and their undeniable influence on the two Renaissances, the talents of Raphaël, Leonardo da Vinci, Botticelli, Michelangelo Buonarotti (Michelangelo, the monster of plagiarism, the vampire, but I'll come back to him later), Titian, Correggio, Tintoretto, were able to develop and flourish as they pleased. All of them went into raptures over my paintings, all looked up at my frescoes hoping to be worthy of them one day; they lauded the beauty of my colours, the brilliance of my pigments, they wondered where I got my clay to produce the mortar, absolutely unique to me, that was known as "Marcello's fresh mortar;" all of them also helped themselves to parts of my production: Bronzino to the hands, Michelangelo to the musculature, the pitiful Piero della Francesca, at the end of his life, to the composition—he who would always ask: "How do you do it, Marcello, your perspective is always perfect, while my characters seem to be moving about in a hopelessly two-dimensional world?"—and Leonardo, the smile. Yes, even that was stolen from me! If you are one of those uncultivated individuals who swoons over the Mona Lisa—the ridiculous miniature that tries to be a great painting—run to your dictionaries, look under "Marcello" and probably you'll find a reproduction of my famous *Dark Lady Smiling*, from which Leonardo shamelessly took his inspiration for that bland and absolutely unenigmatic grimace. The woman is constipated, quite simply constipated!

It was claimed that I was paranoid during my final days, that my terrifying rages and my fits were provoked, apparently, by an unbalanced brain afflicted with the disease of disillusionment. Disillusioned I was, but sick? Only consider: at the end of my life I could go nowhere in either Rome or Florence without finding, on every bad painting I saw, in both the remotest churches in the roughest countryside and on the most prominent walls of the two great cities, a blue that belonged to me (the famous Florentine blue is mine!), the curve of a woman's shoulder that I had been the first to capture in all its vulnerability, all its unconscious eroticism, a proud expression on a manly face, a frown, a wrinkling of a nose lifted directly from my *Death of Hector* or my *Judgment of Paris*. What would you have done in my place? I protested, I screamed, I flew into rages that are still famous in the annals of the two Renaissances, until they finally shut me away for speaking too loudly in churches. Now you must understand: everywhere, I was seeing my works signed by other names than mine! Again, what would you have done in my place?

Little is known about me, aside from the escapades at the end of my life, because my treatment by the History of Art has been absolutely unfair. They've remembered my escapades and painted over my frescoes, and that's the truth! They say look in your Larousse, you'll be as astounded as I was, they say I was a minor master of the early Renaissance, that I left few works because I was notoriously lazy, and that, were it not for my *Dark Lady Smiling* mentioned above I would have been utterly forgotten. Me, forgotten! All the museums in the world, particularly the greatest, abound in facsimiles of my works! Scratch Botticelli's *Birth of Venus* or Mantegna's *Adoration of the Shepherds* or even the loathsome *Madonna of Victory* by Raphaël that you find so elegant, so inspired, and every time, as you glance at the setting of a ruined citadel or at the domed forehead of the Virgin, you will find the indelible mark, the indisputable signature of Marcello del Plato Monte Royale!

It is also said that it's not known what I looked like, that I was probably short, frail, ugly. Marcello, ugly? Nothing could be more false. People only say that because one day Leonardo wrote, backwards as usual, that "Marcello, poor thing, has just left, and his persistent squint is a sorry sight to see." It's true that I had a slight squint, especially during my most serious crises, but it is ridiculous to deduce from that, that I was ugly. And especially that I would have allowed myself to have a crisis in front of Leonardo da Vinci! Lay myself open to his legendary bitchiness? No thanks! I'd have left his place at the first symptoms and gone to hide where I'd have been sure he wouldn't find me! What is more, it's not known that I am the subject of a rather famous portrait by Bronzino. So if you want to know what Marcello looked like, run out and buy a book about Bronzino, look up the *Portrait of a Young Man*, and you'll see how unfairly I've been treated. Even where my looks are concerned.

They claim that the portrait is of the Duke of Urbino, a city where Bronzino worked. Which is false. That is.... Look. It's true that the Duke of Urbino, the father, commissioned that portrait of his youngest son from Bronzino, who didn't know how to say no and accepted every offer for fear that he'd run out of money. So there he was, a month before the date on which the painting was to be delivered, the work nearly complete—but *without a face* for the younger Urbino, whom he'd met only once, on the day he received the commission, and whom he'd forgotten to sketch! Just think about it. And he called himself a professional! One morning, then, when I'd come to give him a lesson in how to paint hands because his were always a mess, he gave me a long look and finally asked if I would pose for the unfinished painting because, he maintained: "There's something of Urbino about you: the oval of the face, perhaps, or the aristocratic nose, and...." He dared not utter the word squint, but I knew that the Urbino eyes avoided and even turned their backs on each other, so I said nothing and seated myself behind the easel, between the table and chair decorated with ridiculous carved heads, just as a favour to a friend! And so there I am in every book about the Renaissance, my face at any rate, perched on a body that's somewhat thin, true, because I was, shall we say, on the plump side, and decked out in a grotesque Florentine outfit I wouldn't have been caught dead in! Do a friend a favour and he'll paint a ridiculous portrait of you that others, especially your enemies, will be quick to see as authentic and faithful! Especially because, if you look more closely, you'll realize that young Urbino's very beautiful hands are not by Bronzino. Yes, I actually took my kindness that far! And look where it got me!

But if you think the face is handsome and intelligent, let me remind you that the face, especially the slightly peculiar eyes, brown verging on sienna, a colour I was so fond of, that that face and those eyes have seen, have studied, have judged all the beauty in the world and reproduced it in works of art of such clarity, such elegance, that the painters who came after couldn't help not only copying them, but—and this is the greatest tragedy—massacring them by *painting over them inferior works that are no more than the ghost of the original, sometimes flamboyantly ersatz, but never equal to and never worthy of it.*

Which brings me to my masterpiece, *The Last Judgment*, painted on the wall of the Sistine Chapel in Rome and massacred by the last of the plagiarists, the worst copier, the worst thief in the History of Art.

Oh, I know, you're educated and you've guessed who and what I'm talking about; you've just thought about that *Last Judgment*, the one you know, the crowd-pleaser, that vile copy, that pitiful travesty of what can be found underneath it: mine, the real one, the original, the one that frightened Pope Julius II so badly that he ordered Buonarotti to hide it from his sight, to cover it over with those ridiculous little caricatures that give only a vague idea of Life and above all, of my Great Work. There's been a good deal of gossip about the alleged squabbles between Michelangelo and Julius II, about their splits and reconciliations, but no one remembers a thing about my own humiliation when I saw, during my lifetime, a minor master burying my masterwork beneath a layer of gaudily coloured mortar that's unworthy of my own!

The two *Last Judgment*s are an example of the saddest, the most unjust palimpsest in human history.

Open your encyclopedia of art history or your scholarly study of Michelangelo, if he really is your idol, open it to the page devoted to the *Last Judgment*. Take a good look at the hodgepodge, at the confusion of bodies tangled together in affected and farcical postures, look at the unbalanced composition that makes it a string of different paintings instead of one complete whole from a single source; study the spongy sky that is totally without transparency but that looks, you might say, dusty, the instability of the left side compared with the right (you could swear that the whole wall is about to tilt to the right, the crowd is so compact, the characters impossible to differentiate and too numerous) and the little segment of hell in the lower right that has never frightened a soul. Is that what you call a great masterpiece? Now, close your book and forget all that. And let me describe to you what is underneath, what's been hidden, what's been killed.

First, some historical background.

It was from me that Julius II had commissioned a *Last Judgment*. The contacts were made through the Cotroni family (my sister Teresa was working for them) who had done some favours for the pope who one day, in some way or other had to, so to speak, "thank" them. He did so by bringing me from

Florence bag and baggage to cover the great altar wall in the Sistine Chapel. My reputation preceded me—Julius II already possessed some of my finest canvases—so my arrival in Rome did not go unnoticed.

Despite numerous invitations from Rome's most influential families, I took rooms in a discreet little hotel under the sign of "The Sucking Sow," at the end of a steeply sloping alley behind the Vatican. Having no time to waste, I toured Rome quickly, then I threw myself into my work almost at once, grateful, it's true, for the honour being paid me, but preoccupied by my art and overjoyed at the prospect of painting a wall that was reputedly impossible to decorate.

I spent months studying every nook and cranny of the wall (the end of that arch in the middle, at the top, presented incredible problems of equilibrium which, as a matter of fact, I alone was able to solve; what you saw just now is downright ridiculous: like a hat plunked onto the head of God!), measuring it, covering it with a primary coat of plaster, smearing it with charcoal sketches copied from drawings that I spent my nights finishing, undoing everything, redoing everything, choosing my ingredients for the mortar, my pigments for the colours; I burned my eyes from painting *in fresco*, in fear of seeing it all break away at any moment, of having slabs of poorly dried cement land on me, or seeing my work turn to powder if my measurements were off; unlike my successor who never in his life made any move unless he was surrounded by adorable slaves who did everything for him, I worked *on my own*, labouring day and night to produce—I have to say it, even though I'm the one who did it— an absolutely irresistible fresco that literally lit up the Sistine Chapel, bestowing on it the life, the lightness which it lacked, overwhelmed as it was by that ceiling over-decorated by the other one, that lunatic who couldn't leave the tiniest corner of a canvas alone but had to mess it up with oversize muscles and undersize penises. Atrophy—in every sense of the word—was Michelangelo's prerogative!

It has been said that Julius II covered his face when he first laid eyes on my *Last Judgment* and then spat in my face, telling me I was lucky to have contacts in the Cotroni family, that it was that which was saving my life, otherwise he'd have locked me up for the rest of my days or given me a taste of the Borgias' delights.

Nothing could be more false. As soon as he entered the Chapel—and may God strike me dead if I'm lying—the pope fell to his knees in ecstasy before the power emanating from my fresco. And then he uttered a verdict that would have been famous in the annals of painting had not everything surrounding that fateful day and the one that followed been erased:

"I shall be the only one to have gazed at this masterpiece, Marcello. It must be hidden from the sight of the common man. It is all too overwhelming in its very lightness, in its celestial light, for the plebeian who will come here seeking refuge and consolation, not terror and fear. For the sake of humankind it must be hidden and I hope you can forgive me for that."

And so it wasn't because he thought it hideous that he had my fresco covered over with the stammering, the gurgling, the drooling of Buonarotti, it was because he found it was too powerful! Like the Bible itself, which the ignorant were forbidden to read! It was sad and unjust, but the pope's argument was reasonable and I had to bow to it. In front of him, at any rate.

Now, let's concentrate on the work itself.

I don't know if I'll be able to find the words to describe my painting; for your part, think movement, colour, light, lightness and violence, and forgive the style of a poor painter who has been greatly wronged and whose specialty is not writing.

First of all, in the place of that wrathful and belligerent God who now dominates the altar wall of the Sistine Chapel, I had placed a God enthroned, magnanimous and tolerant, a Knight of Justice who did not threaten to strike everything that surrounded Him, but was stretching out his obviously merciful arms towards suffering humanity. Not only was He beautiful, He was kind, while those who surrounded Him were less so.

He was flanked by two women—Michelangelo's looks as if he's stomping on some poor weeping woman who just happened to be passing by, whom it's impossible to imagine being related to Him—two magnificent women whose names I had inscribed beneath their effigies, Albertina and Nana: the Mama, who was weeping too, but over herself, over her flaws and her shortcomings, not because of her ungrateful son, and the Zia, plump, even fat, jovial and above all—this you could sense from the laughter coming from her mouth that you could almost hear, from the joyous creases around her eyes, from the generosity of her physique—in radiant health! Both were pressing close to Him; one, the Mama, had placed a hand on her son's shoulder as if she were seeking consolation there; the other, Zia Nana, was looking at him as if hoping to find the strength to survive him because never, never would she consent to leave him to his fate, even if he was a Knight of Justice, a God. It was from him that she drew her health.

They loved him; the three of them formed a shield against the absolutely terrifying world around them.

Now here, I have to talk about the arrangement of the trio in relation to the rest of the fresco: it is placed much lower down than Michelangelo's God, precisely to avoid having the end of that arch, which suggested the foot of a column, look like a hat on them and in particular, to make room for another character, so small that, from a distance, you could mistake it for a nail, about whom I'll have more to say later.

The three figures—the Hero, the Mama, the Zia Nana—don't have their feet planted in a cloud that acts as the base of a pedestal to justify their presence in heaven; they're floating in the air! They are part of that sky whose blue I invented for the occasion: Marcello blue, Florentine blue transposed to the light of Rome, the *real* blue of the *real* sky! Forget Buonarotti's vaguely bluish grey and think about...I don't know, think royal blue, indigo, mauve, think about the colours adjacent to blue which are all contained in my blue! There, I think you've got it. Magnificent, isn't it? Now extend it over the entire fresco, even if you don't yet know all the components; brush the altar wall in the Sistine Chapel with the blue light that's so good for the soul, let yourself go, let it console you, steep yourself in it. There. Now you're ready for what comes next.

Have you been able to follow me so far? Do you see the trio, elegiac because this fresco is a poem, plunged into a sea of blue? Good. Let's continue.

To the Hero's left, and thus to our right, was a crouching figure whose face we cannot see, a man who had been humiliated and had just now fallen to his knees, a pariah who had earned some punishment and was waiting for it apprehensively, because he knew the Hero was uncompromising. Stooping, his hands at his sides, he dreaded a punishment too severe. Hell. But about that, about hell, we'll have more to say later on.

In Buonarotti's work the same character exists but the man is not so humble; he is self-glorifying, he dares to raise his head and even his forefinger towards the one who will punish him, practically provoking him with his hand, as if to say: "Go ahead, I'm not afraid of you!" But that man, we can sense it, is not the Hero's father, whereas in my work....

In my painting, you could tell that there was a serious conflict between these two characters, that an endurance contest, a battle of wills had been under way for some time now, whose dénouement had just taken place, showing the victorious Hero and his vanquished father. You knew they were father and son because their bodies were alike in every respect: the skin of both had the same pallor, while I'd found different tints for all the other characters (a darker one for Zia Nana, for instance, a more sallow one for Albertina, and so on), the same powerful bone structure, the same shade and length for the hair. Even crouching, the man resembled his son! Who seemed, though, not to be savouring his victory; no irony, no mockery, no joy showed on his face. He was there to mete out punishment and that's what he was doing. But fairly, without malice, and only to those who deserved it.

In the *Last Judgment* we're familiar with, the man to the left of God, as well as being decked out with a head-shaped excrescence on his right shoulder from being pressed so hard by a too-dense crowd, is holding an empty skin, a limp, deflated body that dangles over the void. True, it's a self-portrait of Michelangelo, that's obvious, but what isn't known is that it is a self-portrait dictated by guilt at having agreed to replace *me*, to wreak havoc with my work in order to cover it with his own and not, as has been assumed, a proof of humility and modesty before God's Grandeur. I who knew him well can assure you here that Michelangelo was a vain and arrogant man for whom God's Grandeur mattered very little! But he was also an artist who could make allowances, who could recognize talent when he met it, and I'm convinced that he could not, in all honesty, even unconfessed, have spattered my masterpiece without experiencing some guilt at doing so. Which he integrated into his own fresco, to confess his betrayal. And to gain my forgiveness. Ha!

But let's get back to the father of the Hero. My character was not shown surrounded by an intrusive crowd as in Michelangelo's work. No, I had instead isolated him in his corner of heaven. One's gaze was quickly drawn to him because his skin had the same luminosity as the Hero's; his abasement, however, called forth not pity but disgust, so much could one sense—it's a talent of mine—without even seeing his face, that the forthcoming punishment would be merited. One looked away from him then without remorse, gladly leaving him to his punishment. And once you'd left him, you forgot him. Totally.

To the Hero's right and set back slightly, almost at the very edge of the fresco on the left, was a group of four, an extremely bizarre composition, one of the strangest I ever executed in fact, in which the bodies of two women, a man, and a little girl were entangled in a pose I could not describe as erotic—never would I have dared display the erotic on a wall of the Sistine Chapel, to say nothing of involving a child—but shall we say, ambiguous.

The principal figure was a woman, the Hero's sister, Teresa— her name was embroidered at the bottom of her gown—who was more than beautiful, she was magnificent; plump, just plump enough, her face ravishing overall but in certain details so cruel, her body wrapped in a scarlet gauze that allowed viewers to distinguish her curvaceous feminine form. She stood perfectly erect, with her hands on the shoulders of a very proper little girl dressed in a sea green tunic and holding in her open hand what seemed to be a sweet or a small toy. The mother's hands were perhaps resting too heavily on her shoulders, because the little girl was grimacing slightly, as if she were feeling a slight pain. Something frozen about both the posture and the expression on the faces of both silhouettes bestowed upon the group a sense of discomfort, as if something surprising, if not abnormal, were going on around them. But one quickly realized that the discomfort one felt before this group came more from the two other characters standing behind them than from the mother and daughter themselves: on our right, a man, effeminate, too slender, too delicate; on our left, a man-woman, more virile than the man but, oddly enough, more sympathetic, the face crossed by a harelip that elicited pity and the eyes filled with such distress that, from the outset, it was to her that our benevolence was directed.

Dressed similarly, a yellow tunic for the man, a blue one for the woman-man, both were standing behind Teresa and both were clasping her by the waist, the right hand of the woman-man clutching at the scarlet gauze as if about to tear it, the left hand of the weak man resting on the sash. And each in his own way was claiming some right over her. The man had a ring on his finger so one could deduce he was her husband and the nature of his rights; as for the woman-man, she/he was looking at Teresa's profile so intently you might assume something else. But Teresa was quite obviously not responding to the signs of interest from either one; it was as if she were content to push her daughter towards us, entrusting her to us in such a way as to spare her the tragedies she saw as inevitable, that would come from the two figures who were behaving aggressively towards her. For one could sense more than interest on the part of these two who were infatuated with her, a certain form of aggression perpetrated against the beautiful woman that was not so much a struggle to win her over as an assault on her person that she couldn't steer clear of, that she was allowing to run its course while she feigned indifference.

All four were locked in an embrace then, but for different reasons which, while not fully visible, could be guessed at. They formed a complete tableau, that's the only thing for which I could reproach myself when I'd completed my fresco. True, they belonged in my *Last Judgment*, when you looked at the whole work they didn't jar, but they could have just as easily been cut out, isolated, and exhibited as they were, with no touch-ups or modifications.

I must confess that I made a second version some years later, one that was more tormented because of certain events that had occurred in the meantime, more powerful too, in garish colours, a large oil that I hid between two walls of my house in Florence and that may still be there today. If you should find it, I beg you, put it into the dictionaries and encyclopedias in place of my *Dark Lady Smiling*, which I can't stand the sight of, she's become such a cliché.

Just below these three principal groups the horror began.

In my work, the fine procession of bodies, those on the left rising up to heaven, those on the right being flung into hell that we see in Michelangelo did not exist in that form: everything that was underneath the Hero of Justice had been judged fit to be consumed by the flames, fit for eternal damnation, and those figures exuded terror. It was the only truly compact group in the fresco, a frieze that had nothing pretty about it, believe me, that sent shivers up your spine.

There were two hundred and nine of them. Two hundred and nine of the damned who were heading towards the mouth of Hell on the far right, where Beelzebub in person, depicted with the features of a tall man dressed in woman's clothes and outrageously made-up, was inscribing the name of each of the reprobates in a *Great Book of Fire*, as if he were checking reservations in a fashionable restaurant.

That grouping, which was smaller than the figures in the three main ones—I hadn't respected the laws of proportion—could be taken at first for an ornament, a coloured band of no great significance, but if your gaze lingered on them, if you undertook to read the faces depicted there, a terrible anxiety would overcome you as if you yourself were in the ranks, surrounded by the damned, about to be hurled into the everlasting flames; the true sense of the fresco appeared to you then in all its horror.

All were drawn towards the right, all of the crowd's energy was directed towards the gates of Hell and most of the crowd was resisting it. You could sense that from the position of the bodies, from the tensed muscles, from some of the heads turned towards the left as if calling out for help. Those at the beginning of the frieze were less aware of what lay ahead of them; some were even laughing, a wine glass in one hand and the other, in some cases, lingering in the vicinity of their crotch. They were together in the early morning hours after an eventful night, and their minds had not yet registered the signs that were accumulating around them, that should have alarmed them: the cries, the smell of panic, the sobs, the pleas, the grimacing faces. The further you read towards the right, however, the more panic-stricken the figures seemed. Some were trying to turn back, but, unbeknownst to them, those who came after were pushing them towards Eternal Death. Arms were raised, mouths hurled invective; violence was close at hand. Those closer to Beelzebub, who realized what was going on, reacted in two different ways: either they hunched their backs, lowered their heads, walked past their Lord, accepting their sentence without protest because they knew they deserved it, or else they fell to their knees to plead for mercy, begging forgiveness, promising the moon and more if they could be given one last chance. Some even dared to proclaim their innocence, but these were taunted by perverse little demons who burned the soles of their feet to give them a foretaste of what lay ahead of them. But it was too late, all their names were inscribed in the *Great Book of Fire* and, as soon as they had passed through the gates of Hell, they were flung into the Eternal Flames. The faces of those being pushed into the abyss were a gruesome sight; they showed physical suffering as much as fear of never-ending punishment. Never-ending. Their suffering would never end. Never. They were being punished. For all time.

They were being punished for the harm they had inflicted on the Hero.

So there were two hundred and nine of them. The Hero had counted them. One by one. By inscribing their names. In a little notebook he had then sold to the Devil.

It included the happy gang from Rome's lower depths who had laughed so hard at the Hero when, still a child, he would walk through the ill-famed streets holding onto his sister Teresa's hand: the painted women and the men-women who offered their charms for sale at street corners and in alleyways, the nightclub owners with their coarse laughter who called the Hero lamebrain or birdbrain while they groped his sister's behind, feckless petty thieves who took themselves for dangerous gangsters, talentless singers, unscrupulous jugglers, simple passersby with cruel eyes. People from his own neighbourhood, the Plato Monte Royale, were also depicted there, ordinary people, honest too, but who had been unfailingly mean to him, taking out on him their frustration at their own little problems because they knew he was defenseless. These were the people who lived across the street from him, next door, above. Some were very young, mere children, because even the children had laughed at him; classmates, so-called friends who played with him only to vilify and degrade him; everyone he knew, in fact, who had misjudged him, who had cruelly mocked him, found themselves in this frieze, waiting to be cast into Hell: his teachers as well as his neighbours, sellers of drinks as well as fishwives.

The men, as they landed in the fire, brought their hands to their faces, the women to their heads, because their hair burst into flame immediately. There were a dozen like that, open-mouthed, hair ablaze.

Once you had looked at this frieze you could never forget it, and that, I think, was why Julius II never forgave me, even while he had a connoisseur's admiration for the masterwork I had created. That irresistible movement towards the abyss was deemed to be too hideous, too final to be left within sight of the common herd. I had put into it, however, everything I had learned in my life: the ultimate teaching of the Catholic religion, *the irrevocable condemnation of unworthy Mankind* I had painted there with terrifying realism, but with great honesty and irrefutable sincerity as well.

Be patient, I am near the end and what follows is really quite beautiful, the hidden meaning of my fresco, the unseen signs, the dreamlike side that Julius II himself did not seek out. Luckily, or I might have ended up at the stake!

Take a look at the plate in your encyclopedia that shows Michelangelo's *Last Judgment*. At the far right, in the middle of the fresco where there's a cloud shaped like a pair of buttocks, can you see a spot that's darker, nearly black? That's all that remains of my fresco, the only thing dark enough to be seen through the dirty white of Buonarotti's clouds and the ridiculous blue of his sky. A living reproach, an accusation.

Looks like a nail, doesn't it?

Know that originally there were four. One in the centre of each edge of the painting. Not in the corners as you might have expected, but in the centre to suggest the compass points. Four nearly black nails that seemed to pin the fresco to the wall of the Sistine Chapel, as if the artist had considered his work unfinished, a sketch that at any moment he would take down from the wall and replace with the real painting. But they weren't nails. I had found this subterfuge, I had used this optical illusion to incorporate in the work some figures known only to me, figures that would have been highly inappropriate in a church fresco with a religious theme.

Follow me. Climb up on the ladder I've just propped against the wall, take a closer look at the bottom nail, the one under the sort of dark cave I'll have more to say about shortly, which also conceals a creature of mine that I alone know to be there. Come closer to the nail and squint. Can you see it? Is it not stunningly beautiful? In fact it is a woman in a violet tunic. With a sheet of music paper in her hand.

Each of the four nails represented a woman: the one on the left was dressed in rose, the one on the right in mauve, and the one at the top, their mother, whose name was that of my native city—

you knew she was the mother because she seemed older and she dominated the painting—was wearing a robe that combined all the colours, that took me ages to paint because no blend of pigments ever satisfied me. Those four nails are in fact what required the most work in that vast painting. Because of the miniaturization, of course, an insane way to paint if ever there was one, but above all for what they represented, which I wanted to be indecipherable and complete. I was well aware that one day, someone wanting to dust my painting or freshen it up, someone seeking to explain it, would look a little too closely at those nails and end up corrupting the mystery of my *Last Judgment*, but when that happened I would be long since dead and any suppositions by that particular specialist and those who followed his movement wouldn't matter to me in the least.

But let's come back to the four women. They had protected the Hero throughout a good part of his life, especially during his childhood, they had taught him everything he knew about Life and the Arts, and they delimited the painting of the apocalypse of his world to suggest—at least that's the meaning I gave to their presence—that as long as they were there, he risked nothing. They were watching over his head, over his two arms and under his feet, and he ran no risk of joining his contemporaries in the fires of Hell. Naïve? Perhaps. But so effective.

Need I add that I had painted them not only in minute detail but with love? I had made their mother the very opposite of the Hero's—I could almost say the antidote, so much did Albertina, despite the respect he showed her, seem to him at times to be an incurable disease that would disappear only when she died— gentle, calm, generous. And above all, understanding. And bearable. Her three daughters, guardians of the Arts, dispensers of Knowledge, were also at opposite poles from what had surrounded the Hero all his life. Those four women, the cardinal points of my fresco as I've already stated, kept the protagonists in the painting from escaping Punishment, at the same time promising Redemption and Salvation to the Hero.

This is the first time I've disclosed that secret and I feel relieved. Especially because I'm about to reveal the second one. Stay there, at the top of the ladder, and while you're there observe what looks like a grotto—which is still there in Michelangelo's work, incidentally, but he has turned it into some kind of absolutely ridiculous prompter's box or Christmas crèche—just above the south nail. Can you see the bit of wool in the background? Like a rag doll that seems to have been chewed at, mistreated, by someone too happy or too lively? And do you see the figures that live in the grotto? Yes, you're right, they all have cats' heads. If my fresco had survived Buonarotti's violation, it would have been assumed to be one of the sections of Hell where the damned were forced to serve as household pets; that section of the painting would have suffered simple-minded explanations by unimaginative specialists, as usual. But I want you to try to see further.

Come down from the ladder now. Step back from the painting. Now, look not at the details but at the entire picture. What do you see? Look again, you've nearly got it. Yes, that's right, you've got it! Simple enough, wasn't it? When you look at the grotto in its entirety you can see that it's a portrait of a cat asleep in his basket! This time, I used the very opposite of miniaturization; instead of making it smaller, I proceeded in such a way that every element in that corner of the fresco represents a fragment of something bigger: those two sleeping women are the eyes; the wineskin sitting on a wrinkled tablecloth, the muzzle and whiskers; the two women among the damned who are huddled around themselves, the ears, which are not exactly alike, one being perfect and whole, the other torn up, chewed off long ago by some aggressive dog. Once you've solved this mystery you can't forget it; as with the frieze of the damned, you can't see anything else: it's a cat, that's obvious, how could you not have seen it right away?

It too, the tiger-striped cat, was important in the Hero's life. It was his own Cerberus. His cat who served as his watchdog. It was unthinkable then that he not appear in the *Last Judgment*.

So there it is. I've finished describing my masterwork.

But there is another chapter to what the painting recounts, just as there should always be a follow-up to the fairytales that so often have unhappy endings and don't let us know what becomes of the protagonists.

When no one is left in the painting, when the story has been told, when all the damned have been cast into the flames, when Zia Nana is no more, when Albertina too has disappeared, when the quartet on the left have been consumed in a tragedy that verged on the ridiculous because, if you think about it, tragedy is always a little ridiculous, when, at last, the Hero's Father has paid the price of his cowardice and his abdication, all that will be left in this fresco will be the Hero in majesty, the four nails, and the cat's basket against the background of a sky so magnificent that no human gaze will be worthy of it. A sky nailed in place by four women with infinite knowledge and inhabited by the Hero and his cat.

Before leaving my *Last Judgment*, because I have nothing more to say about it, take a close look at the Hero's eyes. Yes, that's a squint. Because the Hero.... Because the Hero, to his dismay, is on the verge...on the verge of a fit!

"Stay with Momma. Stay with Momma now. Can you hear me, Marcel? Stay with Momma...."

She rocks her son gently, his big head resting against her bosom. It's not a severe fit, luckily; she didn't have to use the wooden spoon, which is still on the floor beside the hall sofa. Marcel had trouble breathing for a while, he brought his hands to his throat as he does whenever he has a seizure, he looked at her, his mother, with that pleading expression she's known all his life, that she can read—dear God, such distress!—and that upsets her so terribly.

"Was it the book that did it? Was it? It's just a picture book, Marcel, just reproductions of some things as old as Methuselah, I don't understand why it puts you in such a state!"

Marcel protests a little, shaking his head. He's still here, he hasn't taken refuge in a seizure; she feels slightly relieved. (When Brother Stanislas told her one day that Marcel *took refuge* in his seizures, she had asked: "But what from, for pete's sake? I look after him!" and he couldn't come up with an answer.) But Albertine believed him and she felt ten times more guilty: if her child needed refuge it was because she, his own mother, didn't know how to handle him. And every time he doesn't feel well, she curses herself, curses her ignorance and her helplessness.)

"Can you hear me now?"

A nod.

"I want you to do me a favour and put that book back where you got it."

A mild protest in the form of a groan. Some saliva has dribbled onto the collar of her dress but she doesn't dare wipe it away.

"Does this make any sense?"

And that's all. It's all she can think of to say. She wishes she could talk to him easily, console him with stories or sweet talk, take his mind off this seizure he's just emerged from with amusing repartee or anecdotes to make him laugh, but she can't think of anything. She never can. She contents herself with holding him, rocking him; she knows it soothes him because it always puts him to sleep, but she wishes she were more to him than the person who can put him to sleep when he's sick.

And now her back aches. She shifts her weight and Marcel, thinking she wants to get up, holds her more tightly.

"You aren't a child, Marcel, you're a grown man! And you're heavy! Let Momma move a little, just a little, Momma's back hurts."

He loosens his embrace, just enough to let her shift to the other cheek.

"Okay, that's better, Momma doesn't hurt now. Try and sleep...."

He speaks now for the first time. His voice is hoarse, as if it were coming from far away. She thinks that, actually, he is coming back from far away, that he may have fought very hard to ward off a serious fit, that this time he didn't feel an irresistible need to take refuge in that place where it doesn't hurt so much.

"I won't go to sleep, Momma. It's over."

And then oddly enough the words come out though she hasn't called them. All at once they are said, she hears them, but it doesn't seem to her as if she's spoken them, just that she'd formulated them in her mind.

"Is something bothering you, Marcel dear?"

He's as surprised as she is, because he has lifted his head a little. A thread of drool joins him to his mother's dress; he runs his hand over his mouth.

Never before has she asked if something's bothering him; the words can't take shape in her mouth and anyway, it's certain that she's afraid of the answer. She prefers a familiar guilt to confidences that would plunge her into confusion. Suddenly she thinks of her daughter, who also told her this morning that she preferred something that's bad but familiar over something better that she wouldn't know how to manage. She thinks:

"We're all alike in this family.... And we'll never change."

Marcel clears his throat.

"Don't you want to know what's bothering me, Momma?"

She knows that it's the exact truth, that she asked the question in spite of herself, and an intolerable lump of shame comes to her throat. Marcel straightens up a little more. Looks her squarely in the eyes.

"It's hard for you to breathe, Momma. Your heart's beating too fast. Go put on some perfume, you'll feel better."

He lets go of her, settles down beside her as if nothing has happened. She could get up if she wanted to. But she doesn't feel like getting up. Not because she lacks the strength or the will, no, it's simpler than that; she just doesn't feel like it, period. She would like to hold her child in her arms again, that's what she *does* feel like doing, and ask him to console her because she's the one who most needs consolation, but she knows that those words won't emerge from her mouth either. They sit there motionless for a few moments. Marcel looks at his mother who is looking...at what? At the floor? At the art book? No. At nothing. She is staring into space. She looks the way her son does a few seconds before his seizures, but she's not acquainted with that kind of refuge, there's no refuge for her, none, she has to put up with everything without losing sight of her unhappiness, of its devastating effect on her, she who is condemned for all eternity to be aware of and to tolerate a pain whose magnitude no one, no one will ever know....

All at once she's on her feet, heading for the bathroom. She got up automatically because she had to get up after all, she didn't need to think about it, it happened by itself. A simple reflex. She knows that her son is looking at her, she can feel his gaze on her shoulders. What is he thinking about? Is he still concentrating on the idea that his mother doesn't want to know what's bothering him because she wouldn't know how to respond to his appeal?

She shuts the bathroom door behind her, switches on the light, opens the medicine chest.

She has no idea why perfume makes her feel so much better. All her life, she has used perfume to pull her out of her rages, her dizzy spells, her fatigue, her letdowns. Once, a very long time ago, she had told her sister-in-law as she was leaving the bathroom: "A splash of perfume frees you from everything!" But that was the end of the confidence and Nana had to imagine the rest. And often, in the days when they were all living together in the apartment on Fabre Street, to lighten the atmosphere after a violent quarrel, her sister-in-law would smile and tell her: "I think you need a little *Libera me Domine*, Bartine!" And then she'd lock herself inside the bathroom as she's done just now, and open the medicine chest....

Four or five bottles of cheap perfume sit on the shelves. Today, it will be Yardley's Lotus. It's a man's perfume, a too peppery cologne her brother Gabriel has always used, that she'd brought along by mistake during the big move, but she tells herself that what she really needs is something violent that will wake her up. She opens the bottle. A healthy splash. That's it.... She feels better right away, and once again she's amazed. It goes to her head, it cleans out her insides, she can breathe more normally, her heart settles down. Nothing has been resolved, that she knows perfectly well, but everything is more tolerable at the heart of Yardley's Lotus.

She looks at herself in the little mirror. Circles under her eyes. Very dark circles. She shrugs. She calls it her tired spaniel look, in an attempt to make herself laugh, but it never works. She never laughs. Why should she? There's no reason to laugh. Nothing's funny.

She opens the door. Marcel is resting his head against the sofa cushion.

They speak in unison, in the same tone of voice, not even smiling because they've spoken at the same time.

"Feeling better now?"

Neither answers the other's question. What's the use?

Albertine goes to the stove, stirs something in a pot.

"Momma fixed you some Campbell's tomato soup, but since you were sick I can make you some nice Lipton's chicken noodle soup the way you like it. Would you like that?"

Marcel doesn't reply. He's frowning and seems to be thinking.

"For heaven's sake, Marcel, it doesn't take half an hour to answer! Do you want the goddamn Lipton's soup, yes or no?"

Her normal tone is back, her natural sharpness has appeared by itself, life can go on.

Marcel stops frowning, opens his eyes.

"Tomato's fine...."

"Okay, whatever you want. With sliced bread or soda biscuits?"

"Soda biscuits. Crumbled up in nice little crumbs."

"You can make your own crumbs! I don't intend to crumble your soda biscuits like you're a baby, believe me!"

Marcel gets up, crosses the hall to the kitchen table and sits down.

"It'll be good."

She stands in the middle of the kitchen, rooted to the spot, holding the saucepan and the soup spoon. She is observing her big child who in a few seconds will be slurping his soup as if he hadn't just been touched by a sort of little death. That's what Brother Stanislas called his sickness once. A little death. Marcel dies and is resurrected several times a month. She's beginning to envy him.

**

A few houses away, two women are in the same position Albertine and Marcel were in a few minutes ago: slumped on the deep livingroom sofa in the janitor's big apartment; Thérèse is holding Simone in her arms, trying to console her and reason with her, but as usual she's the one who finds herself in the middle of what she is saying.

"I can't stay here just because it's handy for you and me, Simone! Don't be so selfish! I'm the one that's stuck here cleaning up everybody's crap, not you!"

Simone has cried a lot after yelling a lot. She's used dozens of Kleenexes that now litter the worn old rug where they form new flowers, white and crumpled.

"You haven't got the faintest idea what it's like to be the janitor here! I matter to them about as much as that dirty Kleenex!"

"You don't matter any more to the customers on St. Lawrence!"

"That, my dear, is where you're wrong. I know them by name, I can talk to them and kid around with them and ask about their wives and the baby's scarlet fever. Here, even if I know their names and I know if they've got a little one or a big one, I practically have to bow and scrape because I'm the *janitor*, Simone, the *janitor!*"

"That's what you can't stand, eh, being a janitor! You never could deal with authority."

"I couldn't care less if I'm a janitor, as long as people respect me."

"Do they respect you on the Main?"

"I get respect when I make people respect me!"

"Come off it! You fight with everybody on the Main! You've always had a short fuse when you drink too much and you end up paying for it! You're better off here and you know it! You're getting paid more than you ever have in your life, you've got a big apartment that doesn't cost you a cent, you're probably the only janitor in the city of Montreal with such a big apartment, you can do whatever you want with your time when you finish your cleaning because the action doesn't start till late afternoon.... You won't be able to spend all day in boiling water back on Fabre Street, you know!"

"Are you trying to tell me I'm the happiest woman on earth?"

"I know some people who wouldn't mind being in your shoes."

"You do, do you? Who? Eh? You, I suppose. Right? Is that what you're trying to tell me?"

"Anyway, it isn't as depressing here as at my place...."

"So move! Anyway you've always liked walking behind other people to pick up their garbage.... It's as if you were born just to serve us, I don't know how you do it! You haven't got a drop of self-esteem!"

"If you'd let me move in with you, you wouldn't have to pick up their garbage...."

"Oh please, don't start that again! I thought that nonsense was over...."

"I'm not asking you to take me in, Thérèse, I know it's too late, I know you're going back to where we came from, the whole bunch of us, with your mother and your brother, as if you needed to start everything over! All I'm saying is...."

Thérèse has stopped listening. Simone has just brought up a delicate subject, something that had occurred to her a few days ago but that she pushes aside because she doesn't want to venture onto an avenue she knows is dangerous. She's right, why go back to Fabre Street? Is it really to take shelter in something bad that's familiar, as she told her mother just this morning? Or to make a fresh start, as Simone just suggested? The real reason.... To face up to what she's become, to contemplate that point of no return she's passed without realizing it and go back to the waking dream she's had so often, in which she's standing at her bathroom mirror with a bottle of sleeping pills in her hand, or stretched out in a scalding tub holding a razor blade against her wrist? To justify that morbid thought of suicide? Is she going back to Fabre Street to convince herself that any attempt to change would be pointless and that there's only one solution left?

This sudden dryness in her throat. Her tongue that's taking up too much room in her mouth. Simone is still talking. She hasn't heard a word.

"I'm thirsty!"

She pushes away Simone's head, gets to her feet. Her friend, interrupted in mid-sentence, is still lying there, her hand on her forehead.

"That's right. Whenever you don't know what to say, you drink."

Thérèse turns to face her before she strides out of the livingroom.

"When I drink, kiddo, it sure as hell isn't because I don't know what to say, it's because I know only too well!"

She goes to the kitchen, opens the refrigerator because she knows she's got just a few bottles of beer left and that it's too late to swipe something from the Club Canadien's well-stocked bar. The distinguished members are probably in the middle of some boring party to celebrate Madame Whatever's birthday or the Monsieur and Madame So-and-So's silver wedding anniversary. Evening gowns and three-piece suits.... Champagne, fake or real, depending on the means of the party's instigator.... Phony French accent, hearty laughter, discreet burps if the champagne isn't cold enough. She smiles at the thought of the tour of the red light district she could give those assholes.... Their amazement, their disgust, hers....

"Want a beer?"

The reply comes from far away, as if Simone were talking with her hand over her mouth.

"Sure, I'd rather keep you company than put up with you pissed...."

She opens a quart bottle, muttering.

"That's right, bawl, it's all you know how to do."

She takes two glasses, goes back to the livingroom. Leaning against the doorpost, she gazes at the woman-man stretched out on the sofa ridiculously disguised as an obsessively neat and tidy little gentleman.

"I hope you know, Harelip, the only reason I do it with you is because I swore that never again was any man going to get it on with me...."

Simone looks at her.

"You can say that when you're on your feet, but let me tell you, you don't give that impression when I'm between your legs!"

***

Gabriel came to spend a couple of hours with her. He hardly said a word, didn't even ask permission to smoke; he just stood there, arms dangling, head bent, until their two sons arrived, then he kissed her and left. She heard him blowing his nose in the corridor. As for her sons, to hide their consternation they talked too much, the older one complaining about how stupid his pupils are—he teaches French in a north-end high school; and the other one, the one she had wanted so badly, whom she over-protected and who is in the process of ruining his life very quietly, without making waves, buried in his books, his music and his dreams, apologizing because he can't stay any longer, because the smell of hospitals makes him sick to his stomach. He stayed till the end though. Till nine o'clock. And she heard him blow his nose, too.

She has played her part, as usual. She talked at length with Gabriel to reassure him and also to fill those long minutes that would have been unbearable in silence, then she let her two children fill the room with their meaningless chatter, concentrated on themselves as they were so they could forget that this room they were in was, perhaps, where their mother was going to die. Richard, the older one, hardly looked at her, a little like his father, and it was as if he were speaking to Parc Lafontaine across the street; the other one in contrast stared at her as he spoke, probably looking for a trace of relief on her features, in the hope, no matter how slim, of seeing her smile so he could think she was better. But the smile did not come; Nana didn't feel brave enough to give him the false hope that would let him escape from reality once again— not like Marcel, no, he didn't have Marcel's power to flee the world through seizures that worried everyone but him, no, he was simply a dreamer, one of those waking dreamers who slowly pine away, of whom people end up saying: "Funny, that one didn't do anything with his life.... Seems to me he had some talent though...." A little later her third son, Philippe, had phoned to say he couldn't come to see her that evening because his baby had scarlet fever, but he was thinking of her, he sent all his love. He'd be there tomorrow, he promised.

She lay back on the pillow, pretended she was looking at the little TV set that hung from the ceiling or at the pale green walls that had seen so many woes.

It was a private room, the only one available, and luckily no one had mentioned money. She would get some peace then after the bell rang to announce the end of visiting hours. No sick roommate spitting her lungs out without even excusing herself, no moans of pain in the middle of the night. In fact she was looking forward to being alone; the pain was coming back and she didn't dare put her hands on her belly because she didn't want to upset her three men. She wondered why she was acting this way now that she was in the hospital. At home, where she wished she were now, where she wanted to die, she didn't have that kind of modesty; when she was in pain she said so, she would move her legs under the sheet, reach out for the tube of 222s; when her sons asked how she was feeling, if she didn't feel well she would say so, but she'd also say she would rather feel bad in her own bedroom than feel better in a hospital room, drugged to the eyeballs. Here, though, in this big private room they couldn't really afford, she felt that the slightest complaint, the smallest frown would be misinterpreted and upset them terribly. Perhaps because they were going to be separated in a few minutes, while they were with her she wanted to reassure them. So why not smile at her youngest son? A few minutes before the end of visiting hours she had, she'd tried a little smile for him, and the relief she saw on his face had overwhelmed her; it had made her unhappy because she felt like a coward for having given him one more reason not to face up to things. She was sure he knew that too, because he'd left the room in tears.

Now it is half-past ten. Nurse Bouchard has just given her a shot; she knows she'll sleep well and she feels slightly guilty. Not so far away from here, in the apartment on Cartier Street with the beds unmade because she has always spoiled them and they've never learned to make their own beds, her three men will be worrying. And since they're incapable of communicating among themselves, they'll hold everything in, their sadness, their fear, even their apprehension at being without her tomorrow. Who'll make the coffee? The toast? Even that, they can't do. If she were there she would say: "Gabriel, you'll make the coffee tomorrow morning, it's in the tin by the stove..." or: "There's some pancakes left over from yesterday at the back of the fridge, and the maple syrup's on the bottom shelf.... Eat them before they go bad." They won't bend down to see if there are some leftover pancakes at the back of the refrigerator, she knows that; they'll get dressed, grumbling, and down some poison at the restaurant. Weak coffee, soggy toast, jam full of chemicals.

She tries to think about something else because she doesn't want to be crying when she falls asleep. She thinks back to the past, to the 1940s, and her last extended stay here at Notre Dame Hospital.

Twenty-one years earlier she had been in a room like this one, with a pain in almost the same part of her body, a totally different pain though because it was filled with happiness and hope. Her last child was presenting well—she knew it was the last because she was over forty—the doctor had said the head was in the right position, but she didn't know yet that it was a boy. She was expecting a girl. Two sons, one daughter, that would make a fine family. She had nearly died of grief when she lost her two oldest children, at the beginning of the war—her daughter, her only daughter, so beautiful, so bright, had died in her arms—and nine months before she had asked Gabriel to make her one last child, a daughter to replace the one who'd died, before it was too late.

Had she really been disappointed when that last child was a boy? She can't remember. Yes, probably. But she had wanted him, wanted that child so badly and she was going to love him so much.... On the morning of the delivery she had felt full of life and she'd sung—"Le Temps des cerises," as she always did—while waiting for them to come for her. The other pregnant women laughed as they listened to her, the nurses couldn't get over hearing a woman sing—and so well!—as she was about to give birth.

Today, she carries in her belly not life but death. She brings both hands to her pelvic area. She's not in pain, no, the drug has done its work, but she can tell that the pain is still there, she's reminded of it by an absence of pain that is questionable, hypocritical, that disturbs her. "Why doesn't it hurt when it ought to?"

She mustn't allow anxiety to slip into her solar plexus, to sneak its way into her heart, she needs to find a diversion.... What was that dream she used to have when she was expecting her child twenty-one years earlier, the beautiful dream she had developed over the long months she'd spent lying in bed because she couldn't move? It was such a wonderful dream! In it were the ocean, palm trees, mountains that disappeared into the clouds. A fabulous land, a journey she would never make because they'd never be able to afford to go any farther than Atlantic City, New Jersey.... That's right, it began with a bay! A vast bay opening onto the Pacific Ocean, but not directly.... Ah, yes, now she remembers....

Now she lets herself by lulled by her own words as she recalls them.

"It's not an open bay. It's not a bay that opens onto the ocean, no...it's a closed bay. When you look at what's in front of you, you don't see the ocean. The two arms of the bay are close together, nearly touching. To get there by boat you have to go between those two closed arms of the bay. It's the calmest bay in the world because the waves from the ocean don't come and stir everything up on the beach. The waves are quiet ones. Always. In back of you are the mountains. Mountains so high the clouds cling to them and never drift over the bay. It's never rained in winter on the bay because the mountains stop the clouds. It's never rained in the winter. I could sit in the water, just there, on the edge, and feel myself sink into the sand. Because when you sit in the sand on the edge of the water the waves dig a hole underneath you! I'd wear a bright-coloured house-dress and people would point to me and say: "See how happy that fat woman looks!" I'd lie on my back at the edge of the water and the waves would come and spread their foam all around my head! For the whole month of January. The whole month of February. The whole month of March. You'd read to me, *Notre-Dame de Paris* or maybe *Eugénie Grandet*, you'd read aloud and when the waves weren't in my ears, I'd listen.... I'd stay right there, nailed down in place by the sun and stroked by the ocean. And I'd give birth to as many children as I wanted! At noon you'd bring me pineapples and coconuts. We'd eat under the palm trees, laughing and kissing. All the children I'd had would be underfoot all the time, and we'd love it!"

She opens her eyes, turns to look out the window. Trees still covered with snow on the other side of Sherbrooke Street. So the room is at the front of the hospital. Like the one twenty-one years ago. Could it be the same one? The drug is making her happy, nearly euphoric, she feels like laughing and crying at the same time.

"There's nothing beautiful, though. Nothing!"

The palm trees come back, the waves, the wind and the red-pepper smell of the Brazilian pepper tree. Some saliva dribbles onto her pillow; she smiles. A word comes to her, a word filled with hope and exotic perfumes, a word that all her life has made her dream, a word whose real contents, whose real meaning she has never been able to verify, a word that helps her fall into a heavy dreamless sleep without the slightest little palm tree:

"Acapulco!"

***

Whenever she has insomnia, which is rare because she usually sleeps like a log, Albertine feels helpless at the prospect of the long hours ahead of her, at the darkness of the bedroom, the peace and quiet on Sherbrooke Street when all day long the sound of cars comes to her through the thick walls as a murmur. She dreads the interior soliloquy which she can't escape by going out to do her shopping or getting down on her hands and knees to scrub and wax the kitchen floor, which doesn't need it. And most of all, her inability to think of an answer till it's too late and her innate sense of exaggeration which take her to doors she wouldn't want to pass through and which always—or so she manages to believe—end up opening by themselves and swallowing her up. Just then she finds herself thrust into implausible situations, always tragic, stories in which she is the heroine, defeated and irremediably lost, that make her even more nervous and so drive away the sleep that she needs all the more as these midnight adventures are eventful and violent. Without knowing it, she spends these sleepless nights in a state of morbid exaltation not all that different from her son's when he invents the fantastic adventures of his Hero of Justice to help himself survive. But that is something she would never admit to herself.

She has always said to anyone who'd listen that she has no imagination, deliberately excising from her memory those dark nights when anything is possible for her—especially the worst. These delirious states that leave her at dawn exhausted, with dark circles under her eyes, she blames entirely on the night, which has an irresistible, disastrous effect on her, and she would never admit that she's brought them on herself because she needed them. So that she, like her son, can survive. So she can eliminate her excess sorrow or bitterness. Like her son. Like her crazy son.

That night Marcel, curled up at her side, is not snoring; she thinks to herself that he may not be sleeping either. They could chat a little, pass the time together, precisely so they wouldn't see it passing. She shifts her legs, plumps her pillow, taps it into a ball. Nothing. He didn't sigh, didn't turn over. He really is asleep. She would light a cigarette—a new vice that that has her in its grip, that soothes her anxiety a little, or so she thinks—but smoking at night makes her cough. And it would smell terrible in the already stuffy bedroom. She arranges her arms on either side of her body and casts a pleading look at the basement window, the little gray spot near the ceiling that gives her no hope of seeing the day break soon. What time is it? She doesn't dare to look. What if it were just half-past midnight? A hint of anxiety stabs at her heart. No, later, it has to be later, four or five or six a.m. No. It can't be six o'clock already. At this time of year the sky starts to turn pale by six.... No, it's the middle of the night, the worst time for getting back to sleep. What can she do during the long hours to come? Slip into the kitchen, make herself a weak cup of tea, stare into space while she blows on the cup? No. She's much better off in total darkness.

A door opens somewhere inside her, she hears it moving on its hinges, and she wishes she could avoid passing through it. Not tonight. She's too tired. This woman lying motionless in her bed in the middle of the night seems to be thinking of nothing, though she is waging a merciless struggle against a gap in her soul, a black knot of violence to which she refuses to surrender. Because she'd be lost there. This time, she feels that she could throw herself head first into this extremely ugly broth of blazing fury and get lost there forever.

To avoid going back to the apartment on Fabre Street. The eternal new beginning. With Marcel, whom she'd no longer be able to protect and the seriousness of whose illness would soon be revealed, especially by Thérèse who sees everything; Thérèse herself, of course, with her clinging, excessive acts of kindness when she's sober and her terrifying DTs when she's drunk—yes, yes, it's true, it is close to her brother's madness! Gérard, the stupid jerk she'd always loathed, who would go out of his way to drag his gimpy leg in front of her to exasperate her, Gérard with his goddamn beer always glued to his hand, his once handsome face now topped by unkempt hair that's not very clean, his smile that's supposed to be mischievous but that to her is idiotic, more idiotic than Marcel's worst grimaces in mid-seizure; Johanne, whom she eventually came to love but ignored for so long because Thérèse—my God, that was so long ago, so very long ago, like another lifetime—had concealed her existence for years. All that time she'd been a grandmother and didn't know it. A kind of punishment by Thérèse, a way of reproaching Albertine for not taking care of her when she was a child by robbing her now of her granddaughter's love. Another piece. Another piece in the big puzzle of her life, of which she doesn't understand a thing because, doomed to a peaceful little existence, she's been given a tremendous tragedy to live, one that's too heavy for her. That's it, she's found the right word. It's too heavy for her. Everything is too heavy. The house above her where she feels like a solitary rat shut up in the coal cellar, without food or water; the madness of her son which terrifies her because she's afraid it will turn into violence against her; her daughter's stupid mistakes, always the same ones, resulting from the same excesses; her own head, which feels as if it's going to burst.

There it is, it's coming. She's not going to succumb to one of those waking dreams that exhaust her. Not tonight. Because now the migraine she's been expecting all day is on its way. My God! The 222s! Are there enough to knock her out before it strikes full force? A glass of water. Four 222s. A cold washcloth.

No. Too late. A wave of pain washes over her just as she tries to get out of bed as carefully as possible. She brings both hands to her mouth. And collapses onto her back.

***

Maybe she should have. Said everything. Standing in the doorway she'd nearly unloaded it all to Simone, finally rid herself of the secret that has haunted her for so long, in which poor Harelip was, in a sense and unbeknownst to her, the officiant. Once again, she had held back. Out of modesty, of course, because it was so hideous she didn't even talk about it when she was drunk, but even more to avoid another endless scene and what was sure to be a permanent break. With her past. And her only chance for the future.

She lay down on top of the bedspread, amid the remains of a late-night snack—coffee, Mary Lee chocolate, jelly beans and cinnamon-flavored goldfish; she tried to watch television, to read an old *Paris-Match*, she even leafed through a porn magazine she'd found a few weeks earlier in the third-floor bathroom and which she kept for a particularly depressing evening. Nothing could distract her from what she could have told Harelip—she saw herself bending over her friend, the words coming spontaneously, herself speaking easily and to the point, it all came out with surprising ease; Harelip sitting glued to the sofa, wide-eyed and open-mouthed, and she, with a skill for snappy replies she'd never developed in spite of a reputation for always shooting her mouth off that she kept up from the depths of Plateau Mont-Royal all the way to the borders of Montreal's red-light district, she waxing lyrical, giving in to a verbal delirium as she did when she'd been drinking, but this time she hadn't been drinking, she was under control, she knew what she was saying, she was savouring it, she didn't want it to end, ever, it felt so good—then she switched off the TV, put down *Paris-Match* and the porn magazine, crossed her hands behind her head, and now she is gazing up at the ceiling, telling herself that when you get right down to it, she was right not to speak, you can't talk about things like that. Especially when you don't understand them yourself.

Harelip had finally left, after another stack of wet Kleenex had joined the ones already scattered on the rug. She had straightened her tie, slipped her feet into those ridiculous men's toe-rubbers that were too thin for the season, she'd donned her camel's hair coat that had cost her a fortune, her Tyrolean hat and her buttery leather gloves. A little man with a voice that was too soft, or a teenager trying to look older so he can get into a movie or a nightclub. They had exchanged the usual "talk to you tomorrow's," as if nothing had happened, as if Thérèse hadn't just come within a hair's breadth of a very, very dangerous confession that could have put her whole existence in peril. Because after such a revelation Simone, insulted and humiliated, would certainly have gone and told everybody that Thérèse, just imagine, you won't believe it but she told me herself, imagine, Thérèse is sicker than we think because....

If she only knew.

She had lied to Simone, telling her she did it with her because she'd sworn that never again was any man going to get it on with her.

"It's not that. Not by a long shot."

She has spoken out loud. She hates talking out loud, it makes her think of her brother and his tall tales. She stretches out her arm, grabs a cigarette, lights it. No ashtray. Tough.

When she's in Simone's arms.... How can she put it.... She never puts it into words, she usually contents herself with the sensations without formulating them clearly, she thinks in vague impressions, in disturbing feelings, in flustered emotions. Now, for once, she would like to see things clearly, express them to herself in complete sentences, without ambiguity or beating about the bush, even though she isn't brave enough to admit them to others.

When she does it with Harelip, whom she's known forever, who has been her friend all her life, she feels as if she's fucking her entire childhood. There, it's out. She is holding her entire childhood between her legs and it makes her come. She's making love with everyone she's ever known, with those she's barely met, with her family, yes, both the members of her own family and the neighbours or passing strangers, they're all there between her legs and she can finally love them. Or let herself be loved by them, she's not sure which. Simone of course, the weakest, the most delicate, who is trying to assume a man's role so she can assert herself and whom she, Thérèse, has chosen to officiate over the ceremony of life, but Pierrette too, who hasn't spoken to her for ages, ever since that stupid business with Maurice—it was just a meaningless quickie after they'd been drinking—Maurice himself, Simone's brother, future king of the Main who already behaves like a petty dictator, handing out rewards and punishments from behind his dark glasses, Maurice whom she'd known as a pimply-faced youth who drooled if she let him see too much of her milky skin or a budding breast. Her other girlfriends too, the ones from school, even fly-paper Lucienne, as well as those from Fabre Street, the Guérin sisters, older than her but so funny. The neighbours and their husbands, Marie-Louise Brassard and her hopeless Léopold, Charlotte Côté, Simone and Maurice's mother, Claire Lemieux, who had just found her son on the Main, as gay as pink ice and dreaming of making his living by dressing like a woman; Marie-Sylvia, the candy-seller—every single one, she opens herself to all of them because she claimed that she wanted to get rid of them too often for it to be true, because it's the only way she's found to prove her affection to them. The nuns at the École des Saints-Anges, those she hated and those she loved, the pupils in the boys' school as much as their teachers. And the members of her own family. That's trickier, her heart wavers, the images don't come so easily. She gives herself to all of them—her mother, the brother she adores but who is so often so irritating, her daughter whom she abandoned like a coward, her aunt who is so smart and who's always been able to read her like a book, her three boy cousins, her uncle Gabriel, even her uncle Édouard, at once the laughing-stock and the idol of the Main, the fat Duchess, vulgar enough to bring tears to your eyes but unavoidable because omnipresent—she gives herself *physically* to them all because she's convinced that she no longer has a soul, only a body. Which she leaves for them to devour. The only one who's not there is her own husband, obviously. Because he's not from the neighbourhood, but mainly because he nearly wrecked her childhood—she met him too early, under circumstances too dramatic—as well as her adult years. And so she is holding her entire childhood between her thighs. To find it again. So it can never get away from her again. Because as far as the present and the future are concerned....

Throughout her youth Thérèse was always complaining that she hated Fabre Street, that she wanted to leave, get rid of it once and for all—to forget it, yes, forget it forever, to be cured of it—and now she knows that it's all she has left. Which was why she jumped at the chance to go back. To see. To check and see if she really does still have a chance to survive. Once she's back on Fabre Street perhaps she won't need Harelip any more, the little girl who's as good as gold and too naïve to realize she's being manipulated, who can start anew on her own. By imagining that it's 1942 and the Corpus Christi procession is about to begin.

My God. A tear. It's been so long. Another one. She's going to cry. The lump in her throat is so big she's sure she'll choke to death if she holds it in. And what comes out is a cry of distress that fills not only the caretaker's apartment she soon will leave, but also every floor of the Club Canadien, deserted at this late hour, fortunately. Because she has read in the ceiling, like her brother, like her mother, that things aren't all that simple.

***

She has gotten back into bed. She has probably stuffed herself with 222s and in a few minutes she'll be snoring blissfully, arms outstretched, a cold washcloth on her forehead. The cloth will dry, Albertine will brush it off in her sleep, flinging it onto the floor or to his side of the bed where he'll find it in the morning, slightly stiff as if she'd used it to wipe up the residue of masturbation.

He hasn't fallen asleep yet. He listened to his mother move, sigh with exasperation, get up, bash around in the bathroom and tiptoe back to avoid making a sound, but coughing like a demon because whenever she takes a pill, she chokes. She cleared her throat, blew her nose, heaved some more sighs. He knows that she's lying on her back, that she's gazing up at the ceiling if the migraine isn't unbearable, that she has closed her eyes if, as she puts it so well herself, her head's about to split in two.

He dares not move in case she can tell he's not asleep and gets it into her head to start one of those empty conversations that are her specialty, long and repetitive, that would help her kill some time, help her get through the night. Marcel hates those endless monologues—he contents himself with monosyllabic replies to show that he's awake—in which Albertine keeps harping on the never-ending, boring stories he knows by heart, that don't possess the qualities of magic and transposition his own stories have because his mother, as she herself admits, has no imagination. She merely recounts what is—and what is, is deadly boring. Especially at night. In the dark. Underground.

Now that she's full of pills, she'll stop twitching and he can start the intimate little ceremony that helps him relax when, like tonight, he has trouble getting to sleep.

He squeezes his eyes shut, lets himself be lulled by the spots of colour floating in space, mainly red but blue as well, and some green too. Round spots, oval ones, globes with a luminous edge that shift when he moves his eyes beneath the lids. He tries to look everywhere, faster and faster, up, down, to the left, the right; a mad round spins in his head, a stunning ring of light encircles it, and when he stops moving his eyes, on the verge of dizziness, the globes continue to move, rushing at demented speed to the limit of his sight and then, with calm restored, as if a brake has been applied, the globes start slowing down, drifting lazily and finally halting in the middle of his field of vision, motionless planets in ceaselessly changing colours.

And that's when the music begins. It is strong and gentle, stirring and deeply moving, it emerges from him and from his instrument in cascades of unspeakable beauty, it is addressed to every human soul and to the entire universe, it is greater than everything, yet as intimate as a confession.

It puts him to sleep because it brings peace.

And its title is:

Loon Night Sonatina

The Hero is no longer a child in a man's body, he is now a mature man, a big strapping fellow, a little plump maybe, but not too much, handsome in spite of a slight squint that also makes him look intelligent. Over the past year he's become a concert pianist of international renown. Newspaper stories have talked about his dazzling rise. Tonight, he's been invited to inaugurate the brand new Salle Wilfrid-Pelletier at Place des Arts, and he's cancelled a recital at Carnegie Hall to come here and play Beethoven and Brahms and Mendelssohn for his fellow-Montrealers, whom he's been neglecting recently.

The curtain is already up but the lights are still on in the hall. An excited murmur rises from the crowd of three thousand who are packed in all the way to the stage, because they've come from all over Quebec, from Chicoutimi, Rouyn, Havre Saint-Pierre, from Gaspé, Saint-Georges de Beauce, Sherbrooke, La Malbaie to hear him—the little guy from Fabre Street who's been a success, the discovery of the year, the new international idol, the heir to...to...to all the great pianists with weird names who always come from somewhere else, who pass like comets then disappear forever after just one concert, whereas he, the prodigal son, is here to stay.

After the triumph he'll experience shortly, he'll step up to the edge of the stage, shield his eyes with one hand to block the strong lighting and tell his fellow citizens that he's back in Montreal to stay. That's not altogether true, he'll continue to travel, to give recitals all over the world, but instead of settling in Rome as he had originally planned to do, or in New York because of the exceptional musical life, he intends to settle down in Montreal. For good. Maybe even in the Plateau Mont-Royal. Maybe even in the Fabre Street apartment where he spent his childhood. He could invite his mother to live with him, to get her out of the damp hole where she's been stagnating for much too long, his sister too, yes, what a good idea, and his niece whom he hasn't seen for such a long time, even the brother-in-law he's not really crazy about. Generosity is the privilege of the great. He will take care of them, he'll spoil them, he'll tell them about his travels, his triumphs abroad, they'll have a fine summer together....

(No, no, avoid the summer that's approaching.)

The lights dim in Salle Wilfrid-Pelletier at Place des Arts. The murmuring dies down. The silence is impressive. The silence of a recording studio. From out of nowhere a voice rises up into the great dark vessel.

"And now, ladies and gentlemen, here he is, the man you've been waiting for...."

Before his name is even spoken, there's a roar from the delirious crowd. He counts slowly to ten to make them wait, to work up their excitement a little more, then he appears stage left, a timid little silhouette in this great storm of sound—he, the humble interpreter of the great geniuses of the 19th century.

Thunder is no more devastating. He wishes he could plug his ears, but it's love that is rising through these cries, this applause, these stamping feet that sound like stampeding buffalos....

(No, that's not a very attractive image....)

In any event, the ovation is gigantic and it doesn't stop till he lifts the two tails of his tailcoat to sit on the wooden bench he was careful earlier to place at the proper height so he wouldn't have to play the clown in front of his fans.

He doesn't look at anyone.

He is alone now with his Steinway. Until the final ovation. Which will be, tonight—so he has decided, because it's what he needs—the longest and most hysterical of his brief career.

He lifts his hands, gazes at them for a few seconds as if they were autonomous entities that are not part of his body, then brings them down with calculated slowness.

The music rises into a silence you could cut with a knife.

It is the first movement of the "Loon Night Sonatina."

As far back as he can remember, that's what he has always called this piece. He sees again the big upright piano with the rosewood carvings of roses, the fake cabled feet, the apron that tasted of varnish—sometimes he used to place his mouth against it to see if the music tasted as good as it sounded—the bench that was a different colour and contained hundreds and hundreds of scores covered with black spots that he never wanted to decipher because he preferred that the music remain a mystery to him. To play it by ear without understanding it. Someone bends over him, a woman. A ravishing smile, periwinkle blue eyes. She tells him: "Repeat after me: the moonlight sonata." Teasing—he knows he's going to make her laugh—he says, pronouncing each syllable very carefully to make it even funnier: "'Loon Night Sonatina.'" She laughs. So do the other three. "He'll never learn to say it properly, Mama!" "Come on, he can say it! He just does that to make us laugh." It's true, he does it just to make them laugh.

Tonight again, as the notes of the introduction rise up from under his fingers into Salle Wilfrid-Pelletier at Place des Arts which he has the honour of inaugurating, he says very softly, smiling beautifully: "'Loon Night Sonatina.' I'm playing it for you. Listen carefully. It's my own version and it's unlike any other, even if I play the same notes and I stick pretty close to the composer's instructions. You'll see, it's just a little slower, with a little more emphasis, I sustain the nostalgia in the places where other pianists—all other pianists—just race through it, playing legato so they don't have to get involved in what they're playing. I do though, I get involved. I always get involved, I never cheat, specially not tonight.... Because tonight I've discovered something absolutely wonderful. Something I thought I'd bungled this afternoon, but I just realized I'd succeeded. Partly, anyway. And I want to celebrate that. By giving the greatest performance of all time of the 'Loon Night Sonatina.'"

As the main theme is developed, everything around him disappears. First the audience—he won't need it till the very end, after the sound of his final note has been extinguished in the vastness of the cosmos and he'll need thunder again—then the stage, which is lit too strongly and finally the hall itself. Who needs a hall, a stage, an audience, for performing Beethoven? And he's back again, with his instrument, suspended in the sky above Montreal.

(No, he doesn't need that either; not the sky above Montreal, he doesn't need a sky at all.)

There he is then, suspended along with his instrument in the great universal void, in the original soup that goes back to the beginning of time and will go on till the end. He is head up, head down, it doesn't matter, in the void up and down don't exist. He is playing for the two gods who are watching him tenderly: the god of Music and the other, the one his whole family resents. Quite rightly.

She has to be there, of course: the loony moon is actually floating above the Sonatina, above his own highly unusual interpretation of her Sonatina; she's pregnant, of course, and reputedly a virgin...

(Like him, dear God, like him, but don't think about that, concentrate on the music. So as not to lose the thread. So tenuous. When he was very little...his great-uncle Josaphat...had told him...a story about the loony moon no, no, the music, get back to the music.)

...reputedly a virgin then, and cold. But this music that is dedicated to her is anything but cold. Ah! The syncopation here is so beautiful! It's his own, it doesn't appear in the score, but it's so beautiful. If He is really listening to it—God, that is, who composed this series of sounds that are almost unbearably beautiful, that look like nothing much scribbled onto lined paper, but that get inside you and transform your life when you hear it— will He forgive him?

He catches himself looking over his left shoulder. The two gods are still smiling. He can go on. Adding syncopation. But not too much.

The main theme opens out like a loony moon climbing towards her zenith; convolutions and detours form now and then, to complicate matters, to break the monotony of the musical phrase which is nevertheless so beautiful, but it's liable to become repetitious unless it's shaken up a little, until, inevitably, once she has gone past the zenith—at least that's how he sees it—the loony moon descends towards the horizon again, the music becomes uncomplicated and returns to the simplicity of the initial theme, so pure that once you've heard it, you think you've always known it. And when she goes out we think we've made a great discovery that will transform our lives.

Yes, the Hero made a great discovery a while ago, when his mother was tossing and turning in her bed.

(He can talk about these things now that the music is ending.)

He was mistaken this afternoon. At first he thought he hadn't been able to save his Auntie Nana from death. But that's wrong.

True, he didn't save her *definitively* from death, but he was able to *gain some time!* To save her *for the time being!* Had he not been there this afternoon, had the Hero not materialized during the brush fire to save them—to save her along with her mother and her sister—*she would be dead!* He'd done it! He'd gained some time. How much time he doesn't know, but he doesn't give a damn! One month, two, six maybe? Till September? Oh yes, please, till September! Six good long months! You never know what can happen in six months! Maybe in six months there will be another miracle!

In the middle of the cosmos that is revolving around him, the Hero is hunched over the keyboard of his Steinway. For the final notes. It's so small, so tenuous! It is transparent, fragile, it can spoil everything if it's played badly because the pianist has had enough, or because he has a cramp in his left hand. He must maintain the rhythm, the concentration, till the end. Until the end of the end of the very last note. And here it is. This is it. It is being played. It is played. It goes directly to the heart. Stretches out a little longer. Slowly dies away. And it's over.

He has celebrated his first true miracle, alone in the middle of the cosmos in the company of Beethoven.

His pillow is soaking wet, but a huge smile lights up his face. And at last he can go to sleep. Even before the ovation explodes. Because he doesn't need it any more.

Interlude in the Form of a Rotten Move

As he steps inside the Fabre Street apartment, Marcel realizes they've made the wrong decision. He had thought he'd be coming back to the place he'd left ten years before, the place where he had lived his childhood—sacred, inviolable, frozen in time and space, in the precise image of his own memories of it—but instead, everything is small, both the windows and the rooms, and dark, whereas in his mind everything is bright; it's lugubrious too, because the people who have just moved out didn't bother to clean up. The many layers of daydreams he has deposited over his childhood have conferred a mythic, a marvelous quality on this place, though in fact it's just a rather cramped apartment, despite the many rooms, that smells of the sticky humidity of the summer that's on the horizon. He is standing in the diningroom now, which has amazingly aggressive wallpaper with embossed flowers on a background of fake straw, and he stops moving. He has set his suitcase in front of the diagonal window, in the spot where he admired so many Christmas trees and unwrapped so many presents at birthdays, Christmas, Easter, he has stuffed his hands in his pockets and now he stands there, undecided, useless, planted there like a candle in the middle of the place. He will take root right here in the diningroom, he'll become a tree, pierce the ceiling of the second floor, the third, to carry his fruits up to heaven. That's it. That's what he will do. If they stay here, only stillness can save him.

His mother is pushing him a little, she actually shoved him aside just now because he was in the way of the movers who were sweating under the huge, brand new refrigerator Thérèse has had delivered from Dupuis Frères.

"Get a move on, Marcel! I've been telling you for half an hour! Put your suitcase in your room, you can do your inspection afterwards!"

"I'm not doing an inspection."

"That's true, you aren't. You're standing there as if you were putting down roots."

She knows!

He peers at her in her summer dress that's even more flowery than the wallpaper. She is avoiding his eyes, he can sense it, she contents herself with looking vaguely in his direction while she speaks to him. She pretends that she's busy but in fact she's going around in circles, trying to find a spot where she can settle in, or hide. He knows that, like him, she wants to hide, because she doesn't want to be there either. But surely she's not as disappointed as he is. Because *she* hasn't been dreaming about this moment for months.

What emerges from him now is not a sigh, but rather the grunt of an animal that's just been wakened and isn't sure where it is.

Albertine has tied an apron around her waist and now she's rummaging in the cardboard boxes, trying to find her white enamel teapot. She's banging around, muttering, on the verge of a curse. Sweat that she doesn't bother to wipe away runs down her face and she smells strong despite the perfume she splashed over her whole body before leaving 410. (Before they left, as she was returning the key to the basement apartment, she gave Madame Saint-Aubin a brand new dollar bill, saying: "This is for you, Madame Saint-Aubin, you've certainly earned it! Because everything you told me about Thérèse, the janitor at the Club Canadien, came in very handy! Because she's my daughter!" Madame Saint-Aubin, too proud to keel over in shame, merely gave a faint frozen smile in which Albertine could see all the dire thoughts of which a human being is capable.)

"Dammit, Marcel, you must've put my teapot in another box! Look around, it's clearly marked: kitchen things!"

"There's about twelve boxes of kitchen things, Momma!"

She of course isn't listening.

"Nothing like a good strong cup of tea to calm the nerves. But Jesus, I don't think I'll get even that little treat today!"

She finds the teapot, doesn't seem very happy about it, then disappears into the kitchen. A cry of rage explodes because the pilot light isn't lit.

"I'm afraid of gas! I don't know how to light a gas stove when the little flame is out! I'll have to drink Kik, for Christ's sake! When a day gets off to a bad start...."

He realizes then that everything in the apartment has changed except the sound. His mother's voice echoes in the kitchen exactly the same way it used to, and he claps his hand over his mouth to keep from crying out, because the leap back in time he's just taken makes his head spin.

Throughout his childhood Marcel slept in here, in the diningroom, on the old sofa that smelled of dust and the whole family's backsides, often unable to fall asleep till very late because this room was the heart of the apartment, it was where everything happened, both the tragedies and the happy events: there was as much yelling as talking and there were plenty of tears because conversations in this three-branched family headed by three strong women often turned into arguments, the arguments into battles, the battles into knockdown, drag-out fights. He heard it all from his improvised bed which was always in everybody's way: the terrifying night sounds—his grandmother, Victoire, limping across the whole apartment on her way to the bathroom behind the kitchen, a ghostly silhouette from the most terrifying fairy-tales; his uncle Gabriel, coming home after work and having trouble finding the lock because he'd been drinking and whom Marcel takes for a burglar every time; solemn events—his sister confiding to her mother and Auntie Nana that she has to get married, then yelling at them and telling them to go to hell because they're crying instead of encouraging her; his cousin Richard, Nana and Gabriel's oldest son, who finds out that his parents can't afford to send him to university and who, unlike Thérèse, retreats inside himself forever instead of reacting in a healthy way; his other cousin, Philippe, the night he had an attack of acute appendicitis, and the others, so many others, comical—his uncle Édouard standing at the window in the middle of the night, howling a love song to the full moon, or tragic—the same uncle Édouard who wants to jump out the same window because of a heartbreak nobody in the house will talk about—but always noisy. They disturbed the sleep and the mental balance of the oversensitive child that he was because, already, he was transforming everything in his head, exaggerating everything he saw or heard and turning it into material for his dreams, organic, living matter that he dipped into whenever he wanted to escape from reality, transforming it to make it bearable. His first flights into fantasy began right here, in this corner, he remembers these so clearly it's as if he were reliving them: he is still the terrified child who takes refuge in a waking dream, he has forgotten nothing, but suddenly he feels too tired to start all over again. And he wishes he could leave without even opening the suitcase he automatically set down here, in this corner from his childhood, even though he knew when he walked in that now he was going to have a room of his own.

"What's the point of going to all that trouble, will you tell me?"

Is she talking to him?

Without thinking, he heads for the kitchen door, even though he'd decided a few minutes earlier that he would never move again as long as he lives.

She is leaning against the cold stove, a glass of Kik Cola in her hand. She looks up when she senses he's there in the doorway. Yes, she was talking to him.

"Why go to all this trouble? It isn't going to work. Thérèse and I, we've never got along and we won't start now, you know that, you know us! I was fighting with her when she was five years old and I'll be fighting with her when she's fifty! Well, maybe not then. When she's fifty I'll be long since dead and buried...."

He ought to say something, encourage her, give her the support she needs to go on with her day, but he can't think of anything because she's right: relations between his mother and his sister have always been stormy and there's no reason for them to change now. So he responds to her last remark, the only thing that can't be verified:

"Come on, Momma, you won't be dead when Thérèse is fifty!"

"You think I don't know that? I just said that to give myself a lift, you know! I know perfectly well we'll end up like a pair of old lunatics locked in the same room, yelling at each other till we're both dead! When she's eighty I'll be a hundred, the age difference won't matter then, and we'll look like two crazy sisters who can't stand each other! But what people won't know is that it's been eighty years we haven't been able to stand each other, *eighty years!*"

She takes a big gulp of Kik.

"Ugh, this tastes terrible when it's warm. Want a sip?"

"Why offer it if it's so bad?"

"I just said that. I knew you wouldn't want any. And if you'd said yes, I'd've told you not to...."

"I can't figure out what you mean, Momma...."

"Don't worry about it, I can't either!"

She rinses the glass carefully, sets it in the sink. She bends over, sniffs, makes a face.

"Even the sink smells bad. If I see just one cockroach come out of that drain I'm moving back!"

"We never had cockroaches before, Momma...."

"Because we were clean! There were ten of us in the house but we were clean!"

"Maybe the people that lived here after us were clean too!"

"You think so? Did you see the crap on the walls? Eh? Did you see the steak fat on the ceiling?"

He looks up. In fact there's a big patch of grease on the ceiling above the stove.

"When we were living here, twice every year your aunt Nana and me would get one of the men to climb up on the ladder and scrub the ceiling.... Twice a year, and let me tell you, even that was none too often!"

Marcel remembers. During the first days of spring and fall, his uncle Gabriel or his uncle Édouard, armed with a bucket of soapy water and a rag, would climb up on the wooden ladder, cursing, to scrub away that brownish, oily, disgusting substance, a mixture of animal fat, burned butter and the strong tea that the women in the family had always used to make their gravy.

At 410 these past years, the ceiling was lower and they cleaned it more often—it was his job, in fact, and he tried to curse like his uncles in an attempt, vain of course, to get a laugh out of his mother—so the stains weren't as disgusting as the one that he's looking at now, which will take hours of elbow grease to get rid of.

Who will get up on the ladder here? Not his brother-in-law Gérard, who once again will hide behind that goddamn limp of his that nobody knows if it's real or made-up. As for him, Marcel, he's subject to vertigo and he'd never climb up so high.

His mother is definitely reading his mind today.

"You won't be cleaning it, right? You'd just spread the grease around! And don't even think about Gérard! He's as big a mess as that spot is, he'd be afraid it would swallow him up! Thérèse can do it! After all, she's the one that wanted to move back here!"

"What if she won't?"

She turns towards him. Her eyes are dark and she has that stubborn look she always gets when she's about to make one of those retorts that seem unplanned and that come to her lips almost in spite of herself:

"If she doesn't want to we'll leave it like that, and when it's so thick it falls into my hair, I'll tap on it to make it shake like Jell-O!"

A sound from the balcony at the other end of the house, a door opening.

"Momma! Marcel! Are you there?"

Stiletto heels running down the corridor, a package that's plunked down a little too hard.

"I guess you're in the kitchen! Have you started making us a yummy lunch, mummy darling?"

Albertine approaches her son.

"She's being too nice. Either she's been drinking or she wants to butter me up because she knows I'm pissed off to be back here. Whichever it is, she won't get me!"

Thérèse arrives in the diningroom, crosses it nearly at a run, and appears in the kitchen, nearly hopping up and down like a small child. Albertine sees a little slip of a girl of twelve or thirteen, already wearing too much makeup, who's just stolen a slice of ham from the fridge on her way to go dancing at the Palestre Nationale, and she feels a pang. The same room, the same doorway, the same light—only her daughter has changed. For the worse. As she's always known she would.

"I knew you'd be in here, both of you! Hi, little brother!"

She kisses him on both cheeks.

She's dressed to kill, in a white dress that's a little too tight, with patent leather shoes and a fake leopard purse. Marcel thinks she looks gorgeous, even if in his opinion it's a funny way to dress for moving. Especially because she's dyed her hair a beautiful red, like Rita Hayworth's on the posters for her movies.

Albertine takes one look at her, then turns away, wiping her hands on her apron.

"Instead of dressing up like a slut for moving you could've got here sooner to light the goddamn gas in this old stove of yours!"

***

The arrival of Gérard and Johanne is extremely sad.

It must be said that as soon as Thérèse arrived here, she took matters in hand—or at least she gave that impression. She exchanged what her mother called her slut's outfit for a pair of skin-tight tapered lime-green slacks and a little white lace top that didn't hide much. She didn't dare admit to her mother that she'd come straight from work. There had been a party at the French Casino where she'd gone back to work as a waitress a while before, the bar stayed open till dawn and after a long white night rich in tips, she'd ended up at Geracimo's for breakfast with her friends: Simone, Pierrette, Maurice, her uncle Édouard, pissed to the gills and a little too turbulent for her liking, others she didn't know so well, in particular a guy named Tooth Pick, an ugly, puny, malodorous individual reeking of hypocrisy who'd been introduced by Maurice as his new right-hand man and to whom she'd taken an instant dislike. She hadn't had time then to sleep or change. She had expected this though, and the night before she'd gone to work with a change of clothes in a little overnight case.

With a scarf knotted around her head and armed with a rag, she started rubbing here and there, in no particular order, while her mother merely shook her head and sighed.

Marcel had followed his sister wherever she went to reassure himself, to convince himself that he was still happy about coming to live with her. She told him some funny things as she dusted whatever her eye lit on, even cartons full of junk destined for the garbage, and he liked that.

(He hasn't been back to the Main since the death of his idol, Mercedes Benz, the singer he'd daydreamed about during his adolescence, but he loves it when his sister tells him what's going on there, what's coming up, events both funny and tragic, and since she's been back there, Thérèse brings home an endless store of incredible stories that make him miss the French Casino, its nightlife, its smells, the dancers' skin and the MC's dirty jokes.)

And so partway through her description of the costumes—or rather the absence of costumes of the performers from the two o'clock show, who were more in the crowd than on stage in fact—Thérèse is interrupted by the sound of a truck's brakes.

"That'll be my things coming from Gérard's."

No other mention of him or of their daughter. Her furniture is arriving, she's been separated from it for a long time and the rest doesn't matter much. She runs onto the balcony, waves at the two truckers who start to drool at the sight of her plunging neckline. Gérard and Johanne are following on foot, they're a few houses away, but she doesn't see them, going inside after she's assured herself that the two men, her type, are ogling her ample hips molded into the tight-fitting lime-green jersey.

From the livingroom window where she has posted herself, Albertine hasn't missed a thing.

"Momma was right. You can't be a slut by night and a mother by day. The night always wins!"

Gérard and Johanne have had to wait for the truckers to bring up the big oak diningroom table before they can edge their way onto the staircase.

Thérèse has come back to crouch against the wall in the middle of the corridor which used to be dominated by the big coal furnace that pumped its heat through a network of tin pipes running along the ceilings. She scrubs away, saying whatever comes into her mind, her neck craned in the direction of the movers. Marcel is leaning beside her, his back to the front door, listening to her blissfully.

As for Albertine, she sees it all but doesn't intervene.

The two truckers are in the diningroom, noisily setting up the oak table with its multiple leaves, taking their time, when two silhouettes appear in the front doorway.

For a few seconds nothing happens, then Gérard and Johanne react simultaneously: he coughs into his fist, she comes out with a timid: "Hi, Momma!"

Thérèse jumps to her feet with a little cry that is half-surprised, half-amused.

Marcel, glad to see his niece, not so glad to see his brother-in-law, would throw himself at them to greet them, but just then the two truckers go past and unintentionally break the semblance of intimacy that could have been getting under way among these five individuals who haven't been together in the same place for such a long time. An awkward feeling settles in then, because Gérard and Johanne have to walk out to let the movers go by. Thérèse, trailed by Marcel, goes up to them just as Albertine comes out of the livingroom. All at once there are five people in the tiny vestibule who are obliged to look at one another, and all of them, at the same moment, can read on the others' faces the absurdity of this situation.

So then they all start talking at once; Marcel, over-excited, talks too loud, Johanne says something he can't hear and he doesn't know what to say to her; Albertine awkwardly kisses her granddaughter, calls her "sweetheart" then notices Johanne is sporting huge round glasses she's never seen before—her granddaughter is blind, that's all they needed! Thérèse and Gérard exchange a half-hearted kiss along with a polite: "How's it going?" "Not bad, you?" then break apart as if they've had an electric shock.

But no one moves; they stand there, prisoners of the vestibule, looking at one another till the two movers, toting huge cardboard boxes, ask them to get out of the way. Gérard and Johanne leave the house for the second time while the other three take refuge in the livingroom.

Albertine thinks this is a very bad sign. She sits on the nearly new radiator that hasn't had time to get rusty since the old heating system was replaced.

"An eternal new beginning...."

Thérèse goes back to her corner to rub at a stain that she knows is indelible. Marcel doesn't know if he should follow her or look after the new arrivals.

He looks at Johanne because she doesn't intimidate him as much as his brother-in-law, whom he considers to be a world-class jerk he can never think of anything to say to.

"Feels funny to be back here, eh?"

It is Gérard who answers and his words startle Thérèse and Albertine.

"I never got to know this place very well. I never lived here. And Johanne doesn't know it at all! She was born on Dorion Street, and you moved out practically right after...."

Thérèse goes immediately to her daughter; she takes her by the waist and pushes her into the middle of the hallway.

"That's true, you've only heard about this apartment, haven't you? Here, I'll show you around, I'll show you where everybody's rooms used to be and where we'll all be now!"

Albertine comes back to the livingroom. She'd nearly forgotten that this double room had been her bedroom for twelve years! She leans against the door. Her huge bed, her "boat" as she used to call it, used to stand right there in the back, near one of the two plaster columns that separate the two parts of the room. It was here that she'd made Thérèse and Marcel, with the dumb animal she'd always loathed. It was here too that she lived her widowhood—if she'd had the slightest notion of the meaning of celebration she could say that it was here that she *celebrated* her widowhood—where she brought up her children in the midst of other people's children, her brother Gabriel and sister-in-law Nana's brood, it was here that she had finally realized, not by comparing them with her three nephews, no, simply because *it showed*, that they weren't normal.

For a long time Thérèse had slept here too, on a fold-out couch with her cousin Philippe. Till she got married, in fact. That's right, she and Philippe, as adolescents then as young adults, first cousins sleeping in the same bed because there was no room anywhere else. She has a crazy thought that makes her knees go weak: what if Johanne.... No, no, that would be too terrible.... But she knows now, she should have let Thérèse and Marcel, her two children, sleep on that couch.... Why didn't she? Ah, yes. Because of him. Because his nightmares would have kept Thérèse awake. In any case, she supposes that was why. She's no longer sure.

She feels something like a dizzy spell. Her memories are overpowering her. She's going to fall. No. It's passed. She has never fallen, *nothing has ever made her fall*, she's certainly not going to start going weak today.

She barely hears her daughter's explanations; in any case, Thérèse must be counting on her charm to mesmerize Johanne, to hide from her how terribly sad this all is, this attempt to go back to the beginning, this ridiculous backward leap that will yield nothing, absolutely nothing; everyone knows it and no one will have the courage to say so, as usual.

***

The space is allotted amid total confusion, though Thérèse had already assigned each of them the room they'd occupy.

"When we get there, Momma, you'll have grandma's double room and Marcel will be next door in Uncle Édouard's. That way you won't be separated. Johanne will take your old room in the double livingroom and Gérard and me, we'll take Auntie Nana's, off the diningroom."

There's no question of arguing. In any case it seemed logical, since none of them really wanted to return to their old places. Marcel thought he wouldn't be able to sleep in the diningroom at his age, Albertine didn't want to be confined to the stuffy atmosphere at the back of the double livingroom, and there was obviously no question of Gérard and Thérèse sleeping in the same room as her.

Once she's there, however, Albertine, who makes it a point of honour to criticize everything because she'd give anything not to be where she is now, begins to resist her daughter's initial plan and shifts her suitcase to her old bedroom.

"It doesn't make sense, the other double room isn't big enough for two people."

Thérèse, warned by Johanne who has no idea where to go, comes and stands there, her fists on her hips, red with anger.

"Momma, for Christ's sake! We talked it over dozens of times and you said it was fine with you!"

"We didn't talk about it dozens of times, we talked about it exactly once and you made all the decisions! You didn't ask us if it was all right, you only told us what to do! The other double room is too small for two people and that's that! I'd forgotten how small it was, I've got a right to forget, haven't I? It's narrow, it's dark.... I didn't leave one hole just to move into another one, that's for sure!"

"Grandma Victoire and Uncle Édouard slept there for years!"

"There were ten of us in those days! There was a war on and we were poor, so we had to squeeze in! There aren't as many of us now so we don't have to squeeze. We can arrange ourselves differently.... Marcel and me are going to sleep in here, it's big, there's room, there's light, we'll be able to breathe even though I can't say it brings back happy memories, and Johanne can sleep on the other side.... There's just one of her and she's small! I couldn't care less if you take Auntie Nana's old room, you're a couple, at least you're supposed to be, but I'm the one that decides what goes on on this side of the house! Let me have that at least!"

"You always have to get your own way with everything—you're still as stubborn as a mule, aren't you?"

"Everything, no! That, yes!"

"Just remember this: I'm the one that pays the rent and I'm the one that makes the decisions! Johanne will be a teenager soon, she'll need a place to entertain her boyfriends...."

"Johanne's still a child, for Christ's sake! Let her grow up a little before you start making plans for her boyfriends! When the time comes, four or five years from now maybe, we can talk about it again. Meanwhile, let's show some common sense!"

"*Your* common sense!"

"No, everybody's! What does it cost you, eh, what does it cost you to do like I say? How does it change your life? You made a mistake, it isn't serious! You just tell yourself, 'I made a mistake,' then you move on to something else, it's no big deal! But it sure is hard to make you admit you were wrong, you're so perfect!"

Marcel breaks in, his voice quiet, but they both hear and they turn to face him.

"I could go back to the diningroom, Momma, I wouldn't mind."

Albertine, furious, pinches his arm the way she used to when he was little. (A fleeting vision gives her a pang: the same place exactly, he is standing in the doorway, she's in her bedroom; he's three years old, he's just done something wrong—wet his bed again, maybe—and he's crying; she moves her hand towards his arm, spreads her thumb and index finger.... Oh, the poor little thing, hardly any skin even, just a tiny bone....)

"We'll settle this, Marcel, it doesn't concern you!"

"It does so, and I told you I don't mind sleeping where I used to!"

"Marcel, I said shut up!"

Thérèse, of course, adds her two cents' worth.

"Quit talking to him as if he was three years old!"

"And you quit thinking your daughter's old enough to have boyfriends!"

"When I was her age...."

"Oh sure, when you were her age you were already unbearable, you don't have to remind me! I know what was on your mind then! And it sure as hell wasn't your schoolbooks!"

"Just exactly what's that supposed to mean?"

"What that's supposed to mean is, you wouldn't have had a double room to yourself when you were just fifteen years old!"

And they're off, the infernal machine is up and running, a machine oiled by years of endless verbal battles that don't go anywhere. Outrageous remarks will be made by both parties, bitchy words exchanged in a strident tone, one thinking the other has gone too far, for the sole pleasure of outwitting her, and so on till one of them cracks or slams the door because of an impending migraine, fake or real.

Johanne has come to join her uncle and attend this prelude of what lies ahead for all of them in years to come. Marcel is overwhelmed, as usual, but she, surprisingly, takes it all in with a certain detachment, as if she were watching a show or a television screen. Beneath a fragile appearance, she is building a shell that's liable to cut her off from the real world too.

The argument continues, absurd, sometimes funny, because the protagonists are prepared to do anything, even the worst, to score a point. Which one will win? The one who's less tired, of course, who's more resilient. And the one who's more resilient this morning is Albertine, who slept fairly well last night, while Thérèse had a bad night.

So it's decided—Thérèse, fuming and cursing, goes back to the kitchen to scrub—that *for the time being* Albertine and Marcel will take the big double room and Johanne the small one. From the kitchen, Thérèse yells:

"When company comes we'll put them in your room!"

Albertine steps into the hallway to deliver her reply:

"Would you rather have them in your daughter's room and keep her awake? Isn't she nervous enough as it is? Besides, you know perfectly well we've never entertained anybody in the livingroom! When people come over they always end up in the diningroom, it's handier!"

She heaves a long exasperated sigh, then goes on:

"Besides, who's going to come here anyway, would you mind telling me? Do you think I'm going to ask people over?"

She lowers her voice, says to herself to keep from poisoning the discussion even more.

"I'd be way too ashamed...."

She goes back to her room, sits on her suitcase because her bed is still on the other side of the hallway, leaning against the wall. She gets up abruptly, leaves the room, makes her way to the diningroom where she yells at the top of her lungs:

"I don't want to sleep in the room where my mother died, can you understand that?"

They'd forgotten that Marcel would need a bed, so he ends up that night on the livingroom sofa, old and battered and smelling of dust, that had been covered with a clean sheet. (Another theme for a squabble: Albertine wanted to put her own sofa in the livingroom, which wasn't as worn as Thérèse's, now that she was in her own place, but her daughter stuck to her guns, insisting that hers was going in the livingroom and her mother's in the diningroom, where it used to be. Out of sheer fatigue, Albertine gave in. But she's determined to take advantage of Thérèse's absence to move them.) There's a prickly cushion by way of a pillow, an old coat for a blanket. But he doesn't need covers, he's hot.

He is also too dazed from fatigue to dream. In any case, the plaster moldings on the ceiling here are different. No chubby cherubs, just four scrawny strings of grapes, yellow from tobacco smoke, surrounding a frosted glass ceiling fixture spangled with gold stars and dirty with flyspecks, hideous. Nothing that will ever make him dream.

Never will he be able to launch himself into that ceiling to search for his father or to save his aunt from death. Or to draw the altar wall of the Sistine Chapel. Or to make music.

Wait, what if he were to try....

He lies on his back. Nothing. On his right side. Nothing again. He is about to turn onto his left side when a thought strikes him head-on; he jumps as he does when all his nerves let go at once as he first falls asleep, but he's not sleeping now, he knows he's not sleeping, knows he hasn't dozed off even for a second.

Why didn't he think about it before?

He gets up, being very careful not to wake up his mother—who is snoring, in fact, though she spent the evening claiming she was afraid of ending up, just like that, in the same place as ten years ago, it wasn't normal, it would bring on bad luck—then he slips out of the house.

It's a magnificent night in May, purple and vast. With no wind. Soon it will smell of lilacs. Just now though, there is the sweet smell of wet leaves. His mother's old rocking chair has already been moved onto the balcony, but he doesn't even give it a glance. He goes down the stairs, turns right, takes a few steps along the sidewalk, turns around.

That's where they used to live. All four of them. The four nails in the Last Judgment. He just had to go down the stairs, any time, at any hour of the day or night, in any weather, and they'd take him in, silent or eloquent depending on his needs, hilarious when that was what he wanted, serious and patient when he asked them to teach him things. And what he learned, as a child who was over-awed by all the beautiful things hidden under the universal ugliness, a model pupil because he was so passionate! With his big tiger cat in his arms, he learned that the stars arranged in the shape of a saucepan are called The Big Dipper, or the meaning of "Multi sunt vocati, pauci vero electi," which they maintained referred to him because he was unique, he had been chosen, and above all because he was a thing of beauty. When he was particularly depressed, he would tell them: "Tell me in words I don't understand that I'm a thing of beauty!" And then he would let himself be lulled by the juicy words, the rich tones, the rolled "r" in "vero" that sounded like the way Montrealers roll theirs.

They're gone now. They've been gone for a long time. They no longer answer when he calls to them. For a while they lived in the ceiling of the apartment at 410, but now he has replaced them with his own dreams, which correspond better to his current needs.... And yet they had sworn they would always protect the Hero, from the North, the South, the East, the West, promised they would serve as his compass and sextant. And that they would stay rooted in his heart forever.

An overwhelming longing catches in his throat and he can't stop himself from pushing the little metal gate that creaks just as it used to, exactly the same sound for the same time in the same key.

He climbs the few steps to the front porch, goes up to the door...and rings the bell.

***

Just opposite, on the other side of the street, a shadow crouches on the outside staircase in front of one of the windows in the apartment of Manon Brassard who, since the death of her parents, spends her nights in prayer in front of an electric vigil lamp. A small red glow seeps between the steps of the outside staircase, between the feet of the shadow, like the one that advertises Betty Bird's house on Sanguinet Street, but Marcel hasn't seen it. A woman-man encased in a suit that's too tight is observing the child in a man's body who rings five, six, seven times at the door of the apartment that's been empty for ten years before he gives up.

And while a sheepish Marcel is going back home, the glowing tip of a cigarette burns a hole in the May night.

PART TWO

The Autumn of Every Distress

"You have to watch out for women that talk too much
and look behind them too often...they're liable
to knock themselves out on a post!"

—*The Sayings of Victoire*

The summer was rough on everybody.

In the Fabre Street apartment the negative forces that had been reinstated after so many years of separation were steeped in latent violence every day, and every deed that was done, every word that was spoken was given a hidden meaning that was at the very least ironic if not downright disastrous, because everyone misinterpreted everyone else. All five were spying on one another in the heart of the heat wave, during electrical storms, at the table in the morning when there was a good smell of toast and strong coffee, and in the evening around a meal that was always too heavy for the season because Albertine had learned to cook from her mother who came from the country where the diet wasn't a lean one. During the wonderful August evenings too, which were cooler that summer and not so sticky and could have been oases of peace—the other balconies on the street testified to that, with the creaking sounds of their rocking chairs, their lovers' murmurs and laughter quickly repressed because you mustn't disturb the neighbours—instead you could have cut the tension with a knife and spread it on your bread. Everyone sat stiffly on their chairs, looking nowhere in particular, not speaking. Except to toss off insults. Or to say that Thérèse had left for work in a rotten mood which was a bad sign.

Albertine spent her days giving Gérard a hard time, calling him lazy and heartless—accurately, in fact, because he did absolutely nothing except drag his gimpy leg from one room to another or slump in front of the cartoons on TV, blandly sipping his lukewarm beer while Thérèse was trying to forget her hard nights in a sleep that was heavy and agitated. When he finally answered his mother-in-law, it was always to say something stupid so that she was even more deeply disappointed as a result. She'd never been able to stand him and now she was obliged to put up with him twenty-four hours a day, because he never went out except to cash his veteran's cheque and rarely changed out of his pyjamas. He was pale because he never saw the sun, he smelled bad because he didn't often wash, and he was still an idiot because he had no curiosity about anything. At forty-three he was the mere shadow of the good-looking guy he'd been, whom Thérèse had married on an impulse even though he had practically raped her in the spring of '42 when she was eleven and he was twenty-one. To Albertine, he'd always been a potential rapist and she paid obsessive attention to everything he said to his daughter Johanne and everything he did with her, which only made her even more neurotic.

Johanne, who ever since birth had served as a buffer between her father and mother, found herself caught in a spider-web that was even more complicated now, because things here were stated even less explicitly than in the apartment on Dorion Street, where her mother would materialize now and then to give her a kiss and heap insults on her father. The slurs her grandmother hurled at Gérard were nothing compared with what Thérèse was capable of when she showed up drunk, prancing around on her stiletto heels in the middle of the night after work to humiliate her husband. Johanne would wait apprehensively for things to blow up, while she listened, filtered, interpreted what was being said around her. She shut herself away inside herself more and more and was developing a facial tic that worried Albertine.

At the beginning of summer, Thérèse was adorable when she hadn't been drinking but, as always, a demon straight from hell when she'd let herself go at work and, even though it was forbidden, got drunk with the customers who were glad to treat her because she had a nice ass and didn't stop them from groping her skimpy black taffeta skirt. Alone in the diningroom because the others had scattered through the house to avoid her, she would let herself go in hysterics she'd been holding in, as if for the first time in her life she'd been afraid of giving in to her instincts. She must have been frustrated too, because she'd emerge exhausted, though a good outburst usually calmed her down, at least for a while. Her mood suffered as a result and as the days went by, she began to be not so adorable, even when she was sober.

Sometimes, when she sensed that her daughter was more vulnerable, usually after one of those rages that Thérèse hadn't carried through to the end, Albertine would take her aside and speak to her very softly. The others pricked up their ears but could hear nothing.

"Thérèse, you still haven't answered me. Why did you make us all come back here? There must be a reason! It's not just a coincidence, Thérèse, it can't be, it's not just a coincidence!"

Thérèse always made the same reply:

"It's a trip, Momma, you wouldn't understand...."

"Quit saying that and tell me or you'll drive me crazy!"

"I told you, you wouldn't understand...."

"I'm not stupid, Thérèse!"

"I didn't say you were. But I know you won't understand. Especially because it isn't working."

"What isn't working? Your trip?"

"Yes, my trip. I thought.... But it isn't working."

"Tell me! Tell me! You nearly did just then!"

But the conversation stopped there and Albertine, exhausted, would go to her room to lie down.

"Her and that goddamned trip of hers!"

She sometimes came close to the truth, however, to getting a glimpse from far away, as if through the small end of a telescope, of what her daughter meant when she talked about a trip. But unconsciously or not, she brushed aside the idea that was starting to take shape inside her so she wouldn't see all the ramifications and, even more, all the consequences. And she was left with an image that, to her dismay, she couldn't get rid of: five mice, five guinea-pigs shut up inside a box for too long, and the inevitable carnage that ensued.

Marcel for his part was alarmed. Nothing was working. The ceiling in his bedroom remained flat and uninhabited, the two lakes in Parc Lafontaine no longer acted as a movie screen, his book on the Italian Renaissance was of no use to him. His head stayed empty, woolly. And he knew that the four women next door were gone for good. Deprived of the marvellous, as the days passed he was declining, and an unbearable tension raced constantly through his nervous system, keeping him awake nights, leaving him every morning exhausted and demoralized at the thought of the long hours he'd have to get through to arrive at the next night, when maybe....

Sometimes, in the very middle of a sleepless night, he would raise his head and look in the direction of his mother's bed. An urge would come over him then to get up and tiptoe over to it, to slip between her sheets, cross his hands behind his head as if he were back at 410, and the chubby cherubs on the ceiling were about to whisper wonderful dreams. Or else, less often, it's true, but more and more present in his mind, a red glow would drift into the double livingroom, a magnificent shimmering whose cause he was aware of, and at the heart of which he was convinced he would find peace. Finally. A blaze. A tremendous blaze. He needed a tremendous blaze.

Across the street, still at her post, the shadow that had followed Thérèse from the French Casino was sometimes dozing but often awake, curled up in the dampness of early dawn. The neighbours who were early risers had finally got used to her. No one called the police because she seemed to be gentle and harmless. Someone even saw Rose Ouimet bring her a coffee one day, without asking what she was doing there, probably assuming she was some harmless lunatic, a kind of pet, even though she used to know her very well because she used to live there, just across the street, on the third floor. She'd gone to school with her sister Pierrette and there'd been a lot of talk about her after the half-successful operation for a harelip that had never disappeared completely. If she had stared at her a little when she offered her the coffee instead of just setting it down on a step without looking up, she would probably have exclaimed:

"Simone! My God, what are you doing here?"

A few streets away, in the apartment on Cartier Street, death, inexorably, added its grain of sand each day; the hourglass was full; the time had come.

Everything was in place, the apocalypse could begin.

***

"Aren't you asleep? Usually at this time of day we can hear you snore all the way to the kitchen!"

Thérèse pours herself a full cup of coffee without replying. Albertine goes on:

"Your cup's going to overflow and you won't have any room for milk and sugar...."

"For Christ's sake, get off my back!"

The other four are sitting over the remnants of a breakfast prepared in haste and hastily gulped down; toast crumbs are scattered over the red-and-white checked plastic tablecloth, cracked from use, the glasses that had held orange juice sit next to cups full of still steaming coffee, a jar of Raymond strawberry jam sits unsteadily on a stained and crumpled paper napkin, the plates are empty. The four of them were chatting peacefully—actually, Albertine was giving her orders for the day—when Thérèse, who never eats breakfast at home, appeared in the doorway. When she gets off work too late, she goes to Geracimo's or the Sélect with her friends and bolts too quickly a meal that's too heavy, that will give her heartburn a few hours later. A bottle of Phillip's Milk of Magnesia stands permanently on her bedside table and, when the burning starts, Thérèse reaches out, swigs a mouthful of the viscous white liquid and goes right back to sleep.

She takes a little sip from her brimming cup then sits down at the table with her mother.

"You can't have got much sleep...."

Sitting her cup on the plastic tablecloth she replies:

"I didn't sleep at all, you mean."

Marcel swallows his last bite of toast, a bit of cold, dry crust he's just filched from his mother's plate.

"You think I could still be hungry?"

Thérèse jumps to her feet.

"Want some more toast, little brother?"

Albertine, with the toaster still beside her on a varnished diningroom chair, gestures to Thérèse to sit down.

"Never mind! He's had enough!"

"For pete's sake, Momma, one slice of toast...."

"He's had four already, Thérèse! And he finished everybody else's. He's had enough."

Thérèse lowers her head, sips some coffee. She speaks to her brother without looking at him.

"She's right, you've had enough...."

Marcel ought to get up and leave the kitchen as he always does when he's finished eating—without asking permission and, even worse, without saying thanks, which often makes his mother howl about ingratitude—but something indefinable about his sister's behaviour, a new kind of vulnerability, the way she is holding her cup and taking tiny sips from it, keeps him there. It's Thérèse, yet it's not her. A small part of her has been subtly changed, but he can see it very clearly. She smells different too. It's like another version of her usual odour, more pronounced and more unpleasant. He suddenly realizes that something has happened and she wants to talk to them. She has something important to tell them and she doesn't know where to start. Maybe he should help her. But how? By asking her a question, but what?

He's about to open his mouth and say whatever comes into his head, just to fill the silence, when Johanne inadvertently gets things going.

She is fiddling with her fork, something that usually gets on her mother's nerves, but for once Thérèse doesn't say anything. Johanne, you can sense it, is talking just for the sake of talking, as her Auntie Nana would say.

"The nun at school said if you want to be healthy you're supposed to eat bacon and eggs *every day*. She says toast isn't enough. And neither is porridge."

At once Thérèse straightens up, nearly knocks over her cup.

"What nun told you that?"

"I don't know, one of them...."

"You don't know her name?"

"Well...umm...Sister Rose-du-Rosaire I guess...."

"Well you can tell Sister Rose-du-Rosaire she's a degenerate! They all are! The whole gang of them!"

"Come on, Momma, don't talk about the nuns like that!"

"I've had enough to do with them to know!"

"They aren't the same ones as in your day!"

"Maybe not, but they're all alike, believe me!"

Albertine steps in to protect Johanne, but she only makes matters worse.

"For heaven's sake, Thérèse, she just said that for something to say! And maybe the nun's right!"

"Since when have you been siding with the nuns? You always hated them!"

"I don't like them any more than I used to, but maybe it's true that you're supposed to eat bacon and eggs every day to stay healthy! The nun must've said so for a reason!"

"She only said it to make us spend more money!"

"Come off it, the nuns don't sell eggs or bacon, for Christ's sake! Why not give it a try? I'll buy some for tomorrow, I haven't had sunny-side-up eggs for ages! Our family's never got in the habit of eating eggs, we always liked porridge better and even that we aren't eating so much! It's funny though, eh? In the summer, with the windows open, we can smell bacon and eggs from other houses, but we.... So maybe the nun's right.... Maybe we should go back to it.... To stay healthy. I'll buy a dozen tomorrow. And a pound of bacon."

"Oh no you won't! You won't be buying anything for tomorrow! No eggs, no bacon, no oatmeal! You'll be lucky if you've got bread for toast tomorrow morning!"

"Come on, Thérèse, what's got into you? You have plenty of faults but you've never been cheap!"

"What's got into me is I lost my job, if you really want to know! Which means that as of now we're going to forget about the eggs and bacon and concentrate on the crusts of bread! The crumbs too! Because not many people in this house go to work except me, right? If we wait for Gérard to get a job to buy us bacon, we'll go to our graves skinny! And Johanne's too young.... And Marcel...."

The silence that settles into the kitchen is more eloquent than the worst row. Albertine, flabbergasted, brings her hand to her heart. Johanne puts down the fork she's been twirling between her fingers and lays her hand over her mouth where the first tic of the day has just blossomed. Gérard's shoulders—yes, he's been there all this time, doing his best to make himself invisible—Gérard's shoulders hunch over a little more. Marcel, who knows something's wrong, has trouble swallowing, because for a while now food has been all he has left. Or so he thinks.

"You got fired."

Albertine has said this out loud to make it register, as if to make it official. Because until she says it out loud, she won't believe it.

"That's right. I lost my job. And it isn't the first time, is it?"

"No, it isn't the first time."

Silence falls again, but not for long. A few seconds later Albertine gets up, leans both hands on the table and looks at her daughter over the remains of breakfast.

"You went out of your way to make it happen!"

Thérèse looks down, pretends to sip her coffee.

"To make what happen? I don't understand what you're trying to say...."

"Oh yes you do! You understand perfectly well! And that's why you didn't sleep last night!"

"I didn't sleep last night because I had a stomach ache!"

"And how come you had a stomach ache, eh?"

"Because I ate bacon and eggs before I went to bed, if you really want to know!"

Now Thérèse is facing her mother. She gets to her feet, leans across the kitchen table. Albertine lifts a lock of grey hair off her forehead.

"And you've got the nerve to joke about it! You promised us heaven and earth if we moved back here, you told us we were going to be happy, you said everything would be like it was before, that we'd be better off together than separate, and now you're telling us you haven't got a job and we'll have to start eating crusts!"

"What do you want me to tell you? I can't tell you I've got a job if I haven't!"

"You made one of your scenes again and they kicked you out!"

"Drop it, okay? It doesn't matter why they kicked me out...."

"No, and I don't want to know either!"

They look each other in the eye for a few seconds. It's rare and each of them notices the terrible colour of the other's eyes, reading there things she has never seen before, that terrify her. Hatred? Is that hatred in Albertine's dilated eyes; and the brand-new yellow in Thérèse's eyes, is it contempt?

Johanne stands up, trembling.

"Don't fight. Please don't fight. If you start fighting it'll never end...."

Albertine lowers her head, sits down again.

"I know it'll never end. It will never end. Never."

Thérèse grabs the cigarette her husband has just lit.

"If it's apologies you want, Momma, you won't get any, so forget it!"

Albertine is fiddling with her knife, her coffee spoon, her paper napkin; she moves the jam jar and the butter dish. She's keeping busy. She's keeping busy so she won't explode. She speaks as calmly as she can, but now and then her voice breaks and you can sense the depth of her anger and the havoc she could wreak if she let herself go.

"God knows I don't want apologies! What I want.... I don't know what I want. I knew goddamn well what I didn't want though. I didn't want to move! I didn't want to come back here! To be back with...back with the rest of you. I didn't want to be back with the rest of you, understand?"

"You'd rather have stayed in your hole?"

"You know something? That's right! Yes, I'd rather have stayed in my hole! It was peaceful in my hole! I can't say I was happy and neither was Marcel, but the two of us were peaceful in our hole! We didn't harm anybody and nobody harmed us either!"

"Don't start looking for sympathy, Momma! I didn't lose my job to hurt you!"

"I didn't say you did! I didn't! Don't always misinterpret what I say!"

"I suppose you never misinterpret what I say or what I do, eh?"

"I'm your mother, Thérèse! I'm the one that made you and I know what you're like! I've got a pretty good idea what you did to lose your job and I know where it's going to take us and I don't want that, understand, I don't want that, Thérèse, I don't want to start counting the beans in the soup and the corn in the shepherd's pie just because you got in a fight with a customer at the French Casino, or some bum on St. Lawrence Boulevard, because you were drunk and you couldn't stop yourself!"

"I didn't get in a fight with a customer or a bum, Momma, it was with a cop! A pig! A fucking pig that took me for a hooker and told me to keep moving! Nobody tells me to keep moving, Momma, nobody! So I bit him! One pig attacking another one! I practically tore his cheek off and if Maurice hadn't been there with his fat wallet, I'd be in the slammer right now! I'd be in the slammer and it would feel so good! So good! So much better than here! You're right! We should've stayed where we were before, me at the Club Canadien and you in your cellar! But what do you want, what's done is done, you can't turn back, you have to go on!"

Her mother can't hold in her anger; her voice becomes strident, hysterical, the veins stand out on her neck and she pounds the table with all her strength. It doesn't last long, but it's devastating.

"I'm fed up with carrying on, Thérèse! I'm fed up with always going on! I want to stop going on before it's too late!"

When Albertine is in this state there's just one thing to do. And they do it: all four leave the kitchen without further ado, like children who've been punished, like dogs who've been beaten.

They leave her alone.

***

As soon as she was awake she knew that today was the day.

She was not afraid. She didn't cry. She reached out to be sure the phone was on the bed beside her, then she took away the washcloth, which had had time to dry since Gabriel's departure. She thought:

"Bartine will be here in a few hours.... I just hope it doesn't happen before that...."

She hasn't prepared herself either. Why bother? Ever since.... She certainly hasn't had time during the six months that have just passed to commit any sins.

"Honestly! Sins at my age."

Some hours have passed. She hasn't slept. She allowed herself to fall into a kind of lethargy close to weakness, which surprised her. She thought about Gabriel, about her three sons, about her daughter-in-law, her grandson whom she hasn't seen for so long and misses but doesn't say so to his parents, who don't bring him over so they won't "disturb" her. She didn't feel like saying goodbye to them or rather, she said a silent goodbye, from a distance, in her imagination; kissing each one in turn, lavishing acts of kindness and advice out loud, as if they were there beside her, gathered around her bed one last time.

She took great comfort in imagining the scene without having to play it. It was more beautiful and, most important, not so sad.

To Gabriel she repeated her love, her admiration that he didn't always deserve, perhaps, but that over the years she'd been able to keep alive, as fresh as on the first day; to her sons, especially the last, she offered her advice because she knew their frailty, their fears at the prospect of a life that all three thought was harsh and unfair; she advised her daughter-in-law not to wait on her husband Philippe, her second son, so much, not to spoil him, and to find time for herself if she didn't want to end up like the women of earlier generations, like her mother-in-law, in fact; to her grandson, she administered endless cuddles, cuddles so brusque and passionate they almost hurt. She told him as she'd always told her own children when they were little:

"I love you so much, so, so much, I could bite you till you bleed!"

On her grandson's cheeks she left the traces of imaginary bites. Which didn't hurt.

Ah, that's it! She opens her eyes. So that's what has been bothering her for hours now, ever since she woke up and knew that today would be the day. She's not in pain any more! She knows it's the end because she's not in pain.

She puts her hand on her belly. No, no pain. Not here, not there. She presses harder. Nothing. She isn't thinking about a cure, no, she knows a miracle is impossible; she tells herself that she's started to die from her feet and that it's rising, slowly, inexorably, towards her head. Her cancer has been put to sleep for good.

And that is when the tears start, abundant and so pleasurable because they spring not from the pain that has been gnawing at her for so long, that makes her writhe on her bed and scream, but from an *absence of pain*, from relief born from the absence of pain. She had forgotten what it was like not to suffer and realizes she's that much happier because she thought she would die without experiencing again that blank space in her lower belly where for months the terrible fire that's consuming her has been raging.

She would like to leap up, to run to the kitchen, listen to the radio while she fixes herself a big breakfast, call all her acquaintances, all her relatives close and distant alike, to tell them that she's not in pain, she's not suffering at all, but she restrains herself from even trying to move. Because she knows that she has started to die. From the feet. If she tries to wiggle her toes and can't she'll be afraid whereas now, as she lies on her back, the fire in her belly extinguished, she feels nearly happy. Nearly. Not completely.

"At least I'm not all alone like a rat...."

No. Don't think about that. She would rather go all by herself, discreetly, with no mourners. Without her prostrate husband or her hysterical sister-in-law.

"That's not true. It's not true! I'd rather have them around me. All of them. Crying. Crying their eyes out. Because they're sad! Because they won't be able to manage without me. Because I'm irreplaceable! I wish there were people lined up in the hallway all the way to the door and down into the street, and around the corner of Mont-Royal all the way to Chabot! Crying! And screaming! And howling! I want mourners! Lots and lots of mourners!"

She looks for the washcloth. Which is too dry to give her any relief.

"But I mustn't think about that. I have to think about how this is better, I'd rather have it like this. Otherwise.... I don't want to get angry before I die. I mustn't die angry!"

She ought to think about something else, about someone else, otherwise she'll sink into despair.

Albertine, of course, she'd forgotten her. And Thérèse. And Marcel.

Marcel! A strange urge comes over her. A need, sudden and urgent, that she can't explain to herself: Marcel, she absolutely has to see him one last time! It's important!

Why Marcel? Why not her sons? Or her husband?

It doesn't matter why. She doesn't have time to explain to herself. Time is passing.

She reaches for the phone.

***

The few strollers who venture into Parc Lafontaine on this late morning, which the early autumn is already turning brown, witness a peculiar sight.

A heavy young man is pacing beside the lake, visibly nervous, gesticulating as if he were speaking to someone, though he's alone here and is not actually speaking. Actually, he sometimes lets out inarticulate sounds, more like grunts, but no one could make any sense of them in any language because they belong to an invented world, one that may be lost forever, that he has come here to mourn. Sometimes he leans over the water, as if he were presenting to someone at the bottom of the lake an extremely urgent petition: his movements become more abrupt, the sounds that emerge from his mouth more plaintive. No one answers him, of course, but it seems to surprise him or at any rate make him angry. He takes off in the direction of the municipal library, then rushes back towards the big restaurant which is closed till June, fulminating, gesticulating even more—very close, one might say, to a terrifying rage.

The passersby don't walk across the lawn, yellow and dry now, to stroll by the lake; when they spy the heavy young man, particularly when they see him carrying on, they assume that he's drunk, maybe dangerous, and simply continue on their way. After all, there's another lake on the other side of the concrete bridge that has very recently replaced the one made of fake wood and stone, so beautiful, that had been the pride of Parc Lafontaine during the blessed days when lunatics and drunks weren't allowed to walk along its shores. The passersby all end up around the second lake and all, without saying so, know they are there for the same reason, because they've been driven from the first lake by a lunatic who, without looking at them, without even being aware of their presence, has scared them off with his bizarre behaviour.

And so the heavy young man is all alone beside the phony lake rippled by an early breeze that heralds November more than October. He isn't speaking out loud but his interior monologue is a very violent one.

"I don't swear very often for fuck's sake, my mother always told me not to, goddammit to hell, but I can't take it any more! I just can't take any more, get it? Jesus fucking Christ! I can't take jerking around with my brain and nothing comes of it. I want something to happen goddammit! Understand? I want it to be like it was before! I want the fish to climb out of the water and talk to me if that's what I'm in the mood for, I want a fabulous battle to be fought down there at the bottom of the lake, with Joan of Arc kicking the goddamn English the hell out of France, and Robin Hood robbing the fucking rich to give to the poor, goddammit! With sound! And colour! And loads and loads of action to get rid of the bad! If I haven't got that to get rid of the bad, what the fuck's going to happen, will you tell me that? Will I have to turn bad? Eh? Will I have to get a whip and whip people for real and set fires so I can put them out? Is that what you want? For me to be a fucking criminal? But it used to be so goddamn easy! So easy! I just had to lean across a little, mainly in the winter, yes, but sometimes in the summer too, when I really needed it, I just had to lean over a little, think a little, dream a little and then...then all these beautiful things happened! It was so beautiful! So beautiful! It emptied out my head, it felt good, it relieved me! That's right, goddamn it to hell, it relieved me, and I could carry on pretty well normally! Now I need relief, right here, right now, and nothing's happening! I need relief! I'm calling you to help me, don't you get it? And all I can see is the fucking mud at the bottom of the goddamn lake and the corpses of the goddamn fish and dirty goddamn papers and empty goddamn bottles and old goddamn running shoes! That isn't what I want to see! That isn't what you got me used to! You got me used to.... You know what you got me used to, I don't have to tell you! It was more alive than life, more real than the real world, more beautiful than beauty! It was more beautiful than beauty, it came out of my own head, it exploded in colours that don't even fucking exist, in colours my own brain made up, and life.... Was life beautiful? I don't know, but anyway, I'm telling you things happened, things I couldn't see, like today, and that's what my father and mother let me in for when they made me! I could even imagine that my goddamn father didn't have anything to do with making me, that my mother was some kind of Blessed Virgin, Saint Albertine-of-Montreal or something, and she'd made me all by herself because she needed me so she could live and most of all, most of all, most of all, I was all-powerful, because I only had a mother; I was all-powerful and I was pretty goddamn close to being God Almighty! With no sister that always wrecks everything with her goddamn drinking and her yelling and her tantrums and her crazy ideas, no fucking brother-in-law that's the biggest jerk in the world...with no...with nothing at all, goddamn it to hell, nothing, all by myself, all by myself in the fucking world, but powerful, by Christ, POWERFUL! My power fell in the lake, it got drowned there with last summer's garbage, I can't find it and I can't take it any more! I can't take any more wishing I could take it!"

He is kneeling on the cement shore now, his face very close to the water's surface. He wants to talk into the water, wants his lips to touch the water, to marry the water, so his thoughts will be transmitted to it clearly, but the disgusting smell from the lake turns his stomach and he straightens up, his hand over his mouth, close to vomiting.

"And on top of everything else, you fucking stink! You stink to goddamn hell! So...if that's how it is...if that's how it is, I'll take care of everything myself! Never mind! Never mind, the whole gang of you! Don't come...I'll take care of everything.... Maybe there's some way.... It isn't far...I'll go right away.... We'll see.... And if it doesn't work.... If it doesn't fucking work I'll just jump in, I'll jump in this lake, I'll find the plug—there has to be a plug, you aren't a real lake—I'll find the plug and I'll pull it and I'll empty you out! I'LL EMPTY YOU OUT, GODDAMN YOU, do you hear me, so I won't be the only one that disappears!"

He's running now, he races up the divider, runs across Sherbrooke Street almost without looking to the left or right, he turns towards Amherst Street....

"If she isn't there I'll bang the door down!"

***

"He left before the fight was over."

"Do you know where he went?"

"No."

"And you don't know when he'll be back?"

"Hardly."

"I see."

"Did you want him to do an errand?"

"No, no. I would've liked it if he came with you, that's all...."

"I don't know if I would've brought him.... He's been acting funny for a while now.... I mean, he was always funny, that's for sure, but now, I don't know, it seems worse. So I pretty well let him do what he wants and I don't get involved."

"You sure that's the right thing to do?"

"No! I'm not sure it's the right thing to do! But there's nothing else I can do, so I do that!"

A brief silence. Nana frowns.

"Bartine? You still there?"

"Of course...."

"You weren't saying anything...."

"I didn't have anything to say...."

"Will you be here soon?"

"Sure. I won't be long.... I practically had my coat on. Is there anything you need in particular?"

"Oh no."

"You sounded strange when you said that...."

"No I didn't."

"And your voice sounds funny...."

"You think so?"

"Are you okay?"

"Bartine! I'm going to die, how do you expect me to be okay?"

"That's not what I meant...I mean.... Are you feeling worse?"

"I feel weak."

"And the...the pain?"

"Funny, but I can't feel it today."

"Maybe that's a good sign."

"Oh sure, that's right. Maybe it's a good sign."

Another silence. Nana doesn't want to hang up. Not right away.

"Did Thérèse go back to sleep?"

"Are you out of your mind? She got dressed and then she disappeared—her too! I saw her going up Fabre Street with.... Do you remember Simone Côté, the neighbour's girl?"

"The little girl with the harelip? Of course I remember her! Poor child, I used to feel so sorry for her...."

"You wouldn't feel sorry for her now, let me tell you, she's ugly! Thérèse was with her."

"Just now?"

"Yes. When she left. She ran into her here, across the street, I don't know.... She wears men's clothes now."

"Who? Thérèse?"

"Hardly. Simone Côté! Aren't you listening?"

"Of course I'm listening.... But I told you, I'm tired...."

"Anyway. I saw them walking arm-in-arm. And I felt ashamed...."

"How come?"

"Hard to say.... They were a strange looking couple.... A phony little man doing everything he can to hide the fact that he's a woman, and my big girl Thérèse standing a head taller.... What will the neighbours think.... Already they've been giving us funny looks ever since we moved back here...and women dressed up like men are going to be wandering around the house and taking off with Thérèse...."

"Do you think they...."

"Not Thérèse, that's for sure! She may have her flaws, but not that one! I knew she'd been seeing Harelip again since she went back to the Main but...."

"They were childhood friends, Bartine...."

"They're all childhood friends, that's the trouble! They make the rules on St. Lawrence Boulevard, they fight, they break up, they get back together again, it's the same thing over and over, it never stops! Just you wait and see if Thérèse doesn't turn up in a few days to tell us she's back at the French Casino!"

"If that's where she's happy!"

"You really must be tired to say a thing like that! That's where she ruined her life, you mean, it's where she did things she can't ever make up for, that we all have to pay for because otherwise, if she doesn't work, we're liable to starve to death!"

"That's true. You're right."

"I know I'm right!"

"We'll talk about all that later on...."

"Right, we'll talk about it later.... If I feel like it. Because I warn you, I may not feel like it!"

"Don't be too long, okay?"

"Of course I won't."

"Don't stop along the way."

"Course not. I haven't got any errands to do. And as of now, I sure as heck haven't got any money to waste on cream sodas or butterscotch sundaes!"

"I'll let you go now. I'm really tired."

"Want me to call the doctor?"

"No, no."

"You're sure?"

"I told you, don't bother...."

"Okay, fine...I'll be there soon."

"I'll be expecting you."

"Okay. So long."

"So long."

The fat woman waits a long moment before she hangs up. She wishes Albertine were here, right now; she feels as if she can't spend another hour by herself. An indescribable anguish wrenches her heart; she feels as if she's going to suffocate. She takes deep breaths, glances out the window. Maple leaves are turning red against a perfectly blue sky. It's very beautiful, but it brings her no relief. She needs a human presence, a hand in hers, two eyes to look at, a voice to listen to. She could call her husband, he'd be here in a minute. But she doesn't want to worry him. Even though she senses that she's about to die, she doesn't want to worry him.

Marcel, though, could.... She doesn't know why she is thinking about Marcel, why he's the one she'd like to have beside her while....

She quickly dials her sister-in-law's number again.

"Hello?"

"Bartine?"

"My God, you're really in a state...."

"Good thing you haven't left yet...."

"I was on the balcony when the phone rang...."

"Could you leave a message?"

"A message? Who for?"

"For Marcel, who do you think? Tell him to meet you here before it's too late...."

"Where am I supposed to leave the message, this house is so big...."

"Leave it on the fridge. You know the first thing he does when he comes in is look in the fridge...."

"Why do you want to see Marcel so badly?"

"I'd like to see him, that's all.... He hasn't been to see me for ages...."

"Okay, fine, I'll leave a message. But I can't make any promises!"

"I know. But do it for me anyway...."

"Okay."

"See you soon...."

"See you soon."

"Hurry, please. It's just a ten-minute walk...."

"I know, but if you want me to leave, hang up!"

"You're right. I'll hang up."

Anguish, again. Afraid of dying? No. Afraid of not having enough time to talk about it before it happens.

***

Simone leans across the red and yellow Arborite table and jabs her index finger in the vicinity of Thérèse's heart.

"Is there anything there?"

Thérèse immediately brushes an imaginary crumb off her plunging neckline.

"What? What is it? Is there a spot?"

Simone sighs, lights her cigarette with a wooden Eddy match from the box she always has on her, that in certain circles has earned her the nickname "the little match boy."

"That's not what I asked you...."

An ashtray full of butts that are more or less extinguished, some crumpled paper napkins and two cold cups of coffee sit between them. The waitress asked if they wanted a third, they said yes but she hasn't brought it yet, she's busy with customers having a real meal.

"She sure is taking her time!"

"Don't change the subject, Thérèse, you know perfectly well what I'm talking about!"

Thérèse butts a half-smoked cigarette in the ashtray, looks towards the counter where the waitress is bustling about but still hasn't brought them their coffee.

"Mademoiselle! We're still waiting!"

She brings her attention back to Simone, as if she hadn't said a word.

"If I was her boss, let me tell you...."

Simone sighs again, rolls her eyes, drums the table with her fingertips.

"For the love of Christ, Thérèse, I'm talking to you!"

Her friend's face is transformed all at once. She blanches, her mouth shrinks into a nasty sneer, her eyes shine with hostility; she in turn leans across the table, slapping it with her hand and creating an unpleasant little splash because she inadvertently put her fingers in a puddle of coffee that hasn't dried yet.

"What is it you want to know? If I've got any heart? Eh? If I've got *a* heart? Is that it? Actually no, as a matter of fact, I haven't! Sorry, Harelip, but I haven't got a heart!"

"Don't *you* call me that. My name's Simone."

In reply, Thérèse uses her most insulting, mocking and patronizing tone.

"My goodness, I'm *so* sorry! What thin skin you've got! Am I supposed to call you Mademoiselle Côté too?"

She sips some coffee, curses because it's cold.

"You want to know if I've got anything there? Underneath my sweater? Under my skin? Under my tits? No, Simone, there's nothing. Hasn't been for ages either! I tore it out a long time ago because it was useless!"

"If it was useless you could've hung on to it!"

"That's not what I mean! What I mean is...."

The waitress arrives with two steaming cups, sets them down on the Arborite without a word and walks away.

Thérèse watches her go.

"About time! If you'd waited a while longer you could've brought the Thanksgiving turkey too!"

She pours in two packages of sugar and half of a third, letting her spoon scrape the bottom of the cup as she stirs it.

"There was too much of a heart before, that's the problem. For too many people! And it beat too hard! And pumped too much blood! It was always about to break and I'd end up all alone and crying...."

Simone breaks in before she can finish her sentence.

"When was that? Eh? When was it? I've always known you like you are now, Thérèse! I didn't ask till today but I've always known you didn't have a heart! I just wanted to hear you say it! You've always only thought about yourself, so don't start looking for sympathy!"

"Is that what you really think about me?"

"It's what everybody thinks about you, honey!"

"So what are you doing with me? Eh? If I'm not worth the trouble! If you know I haven't got a heart! Why did you spend all summer huddled under a staircase waiting for me if I haven't got anything to give you?"

"You've got something to give me besides a heart...."

Thérèse bursts out laughing, wipes her eyes.

"But it's not enough to put up with everything I make you put up with, *Simone*! Anyway, let me tell you it's been a long time since anybody made me put up with anything at all because of that!"

"Your mother's right, nobody can say a word to you, you know that?"

"That's right. They can't. I'd rather have a reputation for being someone you can't talk to than put up with your sentimental crap!"

"You can be sentimental too, you know, when you're drinking!"

"I'm a different person when I'm drinking!"

"Has it ever occurred to you that maybe that's when you're really yourself? Has it? A monster! But one with a heart!"

Thérèse doesn't reply right away. She fiddles with her cup, lights another cigarette, seems to dislike the taste, butts it, wipes her lips on a napkin that's already soiled. And then she smiles. She's finally thought of a reply that satisfies her.

"Could be, but the next day I've forgotten! I don't remember that I've been a monster and I don't remember that I had a heart! So it's as if I never had one! If I had a heart, Simone, I'd care about leaving a good job at the Club Canadien, forcing my mother and my husband and my child and my brother to move because I thought it would be good for us, for all of us, to turn back the clock and try starting all over again! It didn't work, it got screwed up like it always does whenever anybody in my goddamn family tries to do anything, but since I haven't got a heart, not any more, it doesn't hurt me! I could even say it doesn't affect me at all! I'll check out the want ads, I'll walk down Mont-Royal Street because apparently that's the only place where people can stand me, I'm going to get myself a crummy little job in some crummy hole like this place, with lousy pay for hard work, maybe I'll even try to go back to the barbecue joint I got the hell out of years ago, swearing I'd never set foot in there again, and everything will go on like before.... I know it and you know it. And then when I'm naïve enough and dumb enough to think that the Main's forgotten all my stupid mistakes, I'll go back and throw myself at your brother Maurice's feet and beg him to let me come back to the fold! And it will work! And I'll start over! With a heart or without one!"

She takes her coat from the seat beside her.

"Okay, enough about my heart or lack of one, I've got more important things to do.... I've got people to feed, I'm a head of a household! And I've never let anybody go hungry, never!"

"What're you going to do?"

"What do you mean?"

"With the rest of your life? What're you going to do? Go on like that? Like you just said?"

Thérèse gets up, pulls on her coat.

"Listen, you aren't my mother, okay? And even her, I don't let her talk to me like that! So forget about the rest of my life! I can take care of that on my own!"

"If you'd let me come and stay with you at the Club Canadien maybe it wouldn't've ended up like this...."

"Will you quit talking about that! And quit daydreaming! If you'd stayed with me at the Club Canadien, kiddo, in two days we'd've killed each other! I'm unbearable! And you are too, as far as that's concerned!"

"I'm unbearable?"

"That's right, *Simone*, you're unbearable! Slinking around like a beaten dog and pissing and moaning and *always* wanting to be useful and *always* making people feel sorry for you! You're worse than my mother!"

"Thérèse, don't you dare...."

"You're worse than my mother, Simone Côté, and never, *never*, do you hear, would I want to get stuck with somebody like you!"

"Not so loud! People are listening!"

"See? You sound just like her! That's exactly what she'd say! The very same words! The very same tone of voice! I know you inside out, Simone Côté, we've been stuck together since the day we were born! I'm leaving now, I'm going to walk out of this restaurant, and *you're going to follow me!* Even after what I just said, even after what I've been saying and what I've been doing to you since we moved, you're going to follow me like a little dog, you're going to sit up and beg and jump up and down so I'll give you some sugar!"

She storms off and heads for the cash register, her stiletto heels clicking across the floor. She tosses a five-dollar bill at the cashier.

"Here, give the waitress the change! That'll show her to be a little generous!"

Laughing, she emerges onto a sunlit Mont-Royal Street.

Followed by Simone, who comes and stands on her right.

And the two walk away, arm in arm.

***

"I told you ten times, I just want to look at the ceiling!"

"And *I* told *you* ten times, people live there and there's no way you're going inside that apartment when they're out! I'm a janitor, not a snoop!"

"Can I wait till they come home?"

"I'd love to hear what they'd say to you! A stranger that knocks at the door and asks to look at the ceiling! Honestly! What's so interesting about that ceiling anyway, will you tell me?"

"Never mind, you wouldn't understand!"

"That's right, call me stupid!"

"Okay, you're stupid!"

Marcel has raised his voice; Madame Saint-Aubin moves back a step, involuntarily bringing her hand to her throat.

"Don't you dare talk to me in that tone of voice! Who do you think you are, talking to me like that?"

When she opened the door to her janitor's apartment and recognized him, she was glad to see him in a way. True, she'd always thought he was peculiar, there were even times when she worried, if she saw him in a corner or crouched on a staircase, dreaming, but he was always polite and she sensed a gentleness in him, surprising in a man, that reassured her. She knew he wasn't dangerous. Odd maybe, but harmless. As much as she couldn't stand his mother who was always complaining, she had a soft spot for Marcel and took pity on him, though she still gave him a hard time when he went too far.

Curiosity, too, had a lot to do with her happiness at seeing him again: maybe she'd finally learn what had become of him, his mother, and the slut who used to work next door at the Club Canadien, about whom Madame Saint-Aubin had found out too late that she was Albertine's daughter. Had they all moved in together? Did the slut entertain her clients at home? Was Marcel mixed up in all that? And where was it? Where was it going on? Word had got around that they'd gone back to where Thérèse was born....

He struck her as nervous though and when he asked straight out, with the door hardly open, the greetings quickly dealt with, if he could look at the ceiling in the bedroom of the apartment he'd shared with his mother for so long (he'd asked: "Can I look at the ceiling in my old bedroom please? It's really really important!"), it took her a few seconds to reply, surprised by his tone of voice and by something new (aggressiveness?) that she could read on his chubby face. And Marcel's plea, repeated several times after she turned him down, only intensified her discomfort. The conversation quickly started going in circles and she could sense that she wouldn't see the end of it unless she shut the door in Marcel's face. Who now repeated for the nth time:

"I'm sorry. But I told you, it's really important for me and...."

"Don't start that again! I said no and I mean no! Anyway, it doesn't make any sense! I've never heard of such a thing, never!"

"It would just take five minutes!"

"Five minutes? Are you crazy? It doesn't take five minutes to look at a ceiling! It isn't covered with gold!"

"No, it's more than that.... If you only knew, Madame Saint-Aubin! If you only knew how beautiful it is!"

His tone has changed again. And the expression on his face. This time, Madame Saint-Aubin thinks she sees there a kind of fervor close to ecstasy, that you only see on religious statues or holy pictures. All at once she thinks that Marcel looks like a big saint or somebody who has just witnessed a miracle and now is trying to recount it to a skeptical crowd. A child at Fatima. He looks like a fat child of Fatima!

Still, there are no miracles going on in the ceiling of apartment number two! She makes as if to shut the door, saying nothing more, but Marcel, insistent, leans against the doorway, a heavy, threatening mass with folded arms and pursed lips. And very red cheeks.

"I'm not leaving here till you let me see my ceiling!"

"Move it, Marcel, right now, or I'll call the police! Do you hear me? There's a limit, you know!"

With no transition, Marcel is once again a pleading, whining little boy. The janitor is surprised at the speed of the change, as if a different person had suddenly taken a standing jump into Marcel's body to stamp it with another personality. Now she's getting scared.

Marcel has even folded his hands as if he were praying:

"No, no, not the police! Not the pigs! Please! I'm not asking for the moon! Just five minutes! Five minutes of your time! And I'll never come back after that! I swear! On my mother's head!"

"No. If I say yes once you *will* come back and there'll be no end to it.... I'm not getting mixed up in your little game.... Now move!"

She tries to shut the door, pushes as hard as she can, but Marcel does not move; he has even pressed his shoulder against the door and he's starting to push back.

"You've got no right to do that! You've got no right! It's too important!"

And suddenly the other one is there. Because their faces are very close to one another, Madame Saint-Aubin sees him materialize on Marcel's features, hateful, vindictive, unforgiving. And amazingly ugly, whereas Marcel is actually quite good-looking.

The Hero is back, but this time he has intruded on the real world, he's no longer the invented creature, proud and upright, who helps Marcel survive through cleansing dreams, but a demon from hell come to destroy everything.

"I'll whip you, goddamn you, I'll whip you till you bleed, I'll tear your eyes out, I'll break every bone in your body, I'll set fire to your hair!"

Madame Saint-Aubin pleads, calls for help, screams; Marcel is laughing and crying at the same time.

"You'll burn like a torch, you old hag! Like a torch, you old hag! Like a torch, you old hag!"

He has managed to take a box of matches from his pocket and he shows it to her through the half-open door.

"Look at this! Eddy matches! They're the best! They light fast and they smell good!"

Taking advantage of the fact that he's now holding the door with just one hand, Madame Saint-Aubin pushes with all the energy of despair and, with a great cry of victory, succeeds in shutting it.

Marcel can hear her sobbing over his own shouts, oaths and anathema in which fire, *fire* plays the leading role.

"Open up or I'll burn you down!"

He sees a great pyre in the middle of Parc Lafontaine, he sees a woman—her, the goddamn janitor—who swears and curses the world while she burns; he sees the Hero triumphant too, but a Hero who's totally black, as if charred, a Hero who has gone to the depths of the depths of hell and has not returned until he's reassured himself that all his enemies have long since been reduced to greasy ashes and nothing exists of them any more, no spark of life, no coal, no embers—only ashes! All that remains is her and she's in flames! All of Parc Lafontaine is burning and blazing red as well, and Plateau Mont-Royal and the city of Montreal and the whole world! The whole world is burning inside Marcel's head and he feels a migraine coming on, behind his left eye, the family scourge and his own punishment too, perhaps. He can sense that he's being punished for this dream that is too beautiful—but still it's a dream! at last!—and he greets the punishment joyously. For the ability to dream, no price is too high.

He lashes out at the door with his feet and fists, he pleads and curses, he calls for help and condemns without mercy. He feels weak because he hasn't expended so much energy for a long time, yet he goes on; his head is exploding, his hands hurt, he may have broken something, he has *certainly* broken something....

Suddenly he realizes that Madame Saint-Aubin hasn't been yelling for a while now; he understands that she really has gone to call the police and ten seconds later he's gone.

He climbs the stairs, opens the door of 410 Sherbrooke Street East, goes out into the afternoon sun. Slowly, he takes his dark glasses from his coat pocket and slips them on. And suddenly he no longer exists.

A siren howls in the cold air. Marcel shrugs, smiles. Then brings his hand to his temples. The pain, alas, doesn't know that he no longer exists or at least that he has disappeared, swallowed up by the bricks of 410 and blending into them perfectly.

***

As she always does when she enters the Cartier Street apartment, Albertine announces herself to her sister-in-law so the latter won't take fright if she hears any noise:

"It's me, Nana...."

No response.

She tells herself Nana must be sleeping, her pain relieved at last by the medication she finally agreed to take a while ago, and she undresses in silence. First she takes off the rainboots she'd pulled on without thinking, there was no sign of rain, then her coat which she hangs from one of the six hooks in the hallway, and finally her hat, the same one she's been wearing for years and can't give up, despite the fact that hats are no longer in style and the impression she has now and then that she's being laughed at when she has it on her head.

She thinks about her mother, Victoire, who always used to say:

"The day when women stop wearing hats to Mass, it won't be worth going to Mass!"

She has to cross the kitchen, then the second stretch of hallway that leads to her brother and sister-in-law's room and then, at the end, to that of her two nephews. But she just stands rooted there in front of the little wrought-iron table on which the telephone sits. Something, she doesn't know what, is holding her back. A feeling of apprehension maybe. Yes, that's it, she feels a sort of apprehension, as if the mere fact of walking through the kitchen would suddenly place her inside knowledge of a reality she doesn't want to share, an incontrovertible fact that will change her life, one that she feels the need to resist for another few minutes because she isn't ready to accept it.

This silence is too oppressive, too strange; something has happened since they spoke.

And suddenly it hits her.

Nana is dead.

She brings her hand to her heart, leans against the wall, then drops onto the chair by the telephone. She puts her hand on it, then takes it away. She can't call Gabriel, after all, before she goes and looks!

She doubts that she'll be able to. To walk across the kitchen and down the hallway, to stick her head inside the bedroom door would demand courage she doesn't have.... What will she find there? Her sister-in-law lying on her back, mouth open, eyes staring at the ceiling, hands crossed on her stomach in a caricature of peace? Or a bed disheveled from Nana's terrible suffering and the poor woman spread out in a ridiculous, humiliating posture, maybe even on the floor, on the linoleum, she who was always so clean, so elegant, so refined, so sensitive....

Albertine doesn't want to see that.

An icy hand squeezes her heart, she has trouble breathing, sweat stands out under the tight pincurls from which she's forgotten to remove the bobby pins.

She stays there for another few minutes, trying to get her breath back and even more, trying to find the courage to stand up and go...and go....

"What do they say? To certify the decease. I'll have to go and certify the decease. The decease.... The decease...."

She repeats the word. Decease. Decease. Decease. Breaks it into syllables. De-cease. De-cease. De-cease. Repeats them endlessly. Then, by dint of repeating them, she mixes up the syllables and, again mentally, starts to pronounce the word backwards until she can no longer understand its meaning: ce-dease, ce-dease, ce-dease, and then mixes it up some more until it stops making sense altogether: cease-dec, cease-dec, cease-dec....

"What is this! Have I lost my mind? My sister-in-law's lying dead in her bed at the other end of the house, and I just stand here saying a word over and over till I feel sick...."

She jumps to her feet without thinking, walks partway across the kitchen and then, when she gets to the gas stove, she feels herself weaken again. She leans against the big Bélanger stove.

"Tea. That's what I need, a hot cup of tea."

She then performs one of the most absurd actions of her life. She sincerely believes that her sister-in-law is lying dead in her bed a few feet away, yet she's fixing herself a pot of tea. She fills the kettle, sets it on the burner, takes down the box of green tea, adds a big spoonful to the moss-green metal teapot. She looks in the cupboard for a cup, sets it on the diningroom table, and sits down to wait.

And not once does she think about her dead sister-in-law. Without really being aware of it, she has made her mind go blank and she sincerely believes that she's making herself a cup of late afternoon tea, as she did the day before, as she'll do again the day after. She even gets up to dig around in the tin of Champagne wafers Nana always has in the house, because she adores them.

Time passes. The water boils, the tea brews, she pours herself a cup and then another. She hardly moves, only her arm changes position to bring to her lips the cup or a cookie, which she nibbles without realizing it.

When she has finished the light has changed, the sun is beginning to set. Soon it will be dark. And all at once she comes back to reality: she's not going to stay in a dark house with a dead woman in the next room!

She pours herself one last cup of tea, gets up, cup in hand, and finally makes her way to her brother and sister-in-law's bedroom.

The door isn't shut.

Albertine takes a step, sideways first because she doesn't want to confront right away what she thinks she's going to find in the room, takes a deep breath, then turns around.

Nana is looking at her, her eyes wild with pain, mouth slightly twisted.

All this time her sister-in-law was suffering and she'd done nothing to help her because of a ridiculous foreboding! She approaches the bed, puts down her cup, straightens up.

"I'm sorry. I've been here for ages.... I thought.... I thought you were asleep. I didn't want to wake you...."

Now on top of everything else, she's lying!

Nana pats the mattress beside her. Albertine doesn't understand what it means.

"Do you need something?"

The fat woman shakes her head, goes on patting.

"Is the pain back?"

Nana nods. But the patting continues.

Finally understanding, Albertine picks up her cup.

"You want me to sit there beside you?"

Nana nods again.

Albertine sits very erect beside her sister-in-law, in the place her brother has occupied for nearly forty years. She holds herself stiffly, taking little sips of cold tea as she tries to put on a bold front. She knows Nana is watching her but she still can't face her. She's annoyed with herself again, but her fear of confronting a dying woman's last look is stronger than anything else and she goes on drinking her tea, a little ridiculous in her stiffness, ashamed of her behaviour. Then she realizes that she can see her sister-in-law in the big mirror above the chest of drawers. She can study her without her knowing it. Albertine feels as if she is spying on Nana, who she thinks looks thinner, different, pale, but she tells herself it's better than nothing, at least she's looking at her.

But Nana wants something else and Albertine still doesn't understand what it is. The dying woman stops patting the mattress, she raises her arm, holds out her hand. Finally Albertine understands. She sets her cup on the bedside table, then takes her sister-in-law's dry hand in hers, though she still doesn't look at her.

Albertine feels like a coward because she can't help wishing that she weren't there, that she'd give everything she has, even though it's not much, to be able to stand up, leave the room, race out of the house and go home to wait for someone to call and tell her that her sister-in-law, poor woman, has just passed away, how sad, but it's better this way, she's been suffering so terribly for so long....

Nana's hand, though dry and rather cool, burns her, and she needs all her courage not to pull her own hand away.

She forgot to switch on a light when she came in and now darkness is slowly seeping into the room. Ah! she's found a way to take her hand away from her sister-in-law's....

"Want me to turn on the light? It'll be dark soon...."

But Nana tightens her grip. Albertine feels like a prisoner, she's hot, she'd like to undo the top of her dress. She tries to reach for the cup of tea she knows is empty, can't do it, then all at once she realizes that her sister-in-law has stopped fidgeting, that these may be her final moments and that she, Albertine, who lived with her for so many years, who's gone through so much, through experiences both beautiful and ugly, in the company of this fat woman who's so wonderful, now must accept her role with...with gratitude. That's the word which comes to her—gratitude—and suddenly, through that word, everything changes.

Albertine leans against the head of the bed, takes a deep breath. She's not quite so warm now. She relaxes. Her warmth blends with that of her sister-in-law, their hands, joined now for the first time in their lives, are communicating in silence. And there is peace. Albertine senses the arrival of this thing she's not familiar with as if it were a person coming to visit her; it is physical, palpable, and the good it does her is immeasurable. She won't cry, though, because she rarely can, but later on, when she thinks about this privileged moment, she will tell herself these were the only genuine moments of peace in her entire life.

She thinks she has fallen asleep, realizes she has just mentally reviewed the years when they lived together in the apartment on Fabre Street: the births of children, sometimes welcome (Nana's), sometimes unwelcome (hers), because she never, *never* loved her husband and even less had she wanted to give him descendants; her mother's death; the departure of her brother Édouard—whom even today she still condemns—for a wild life; her daughter's marriage to...to him, she prefers not to think about; the daily dramas, abundant and intense, during the war; the good times, the time when her husband was in Europe, hunting Nazis, when the bad things that happened had to do with her own temper and not his brutish nature.... She knows she's transforming it all in her head, that she is making choices, erasing some memories and covering them with others.... She doesn't know the meaning of selective memory but she has been using it during these long moments as she holds her sister-in-law's hand to help her die, because she does realize, all the same, that she is helping her to die.

Then it comes out by itself, it's more than a confession, it's a genuine declaration, one she didn't foresee but that has to be made.

"You know, Nana, I've always loved you...."

And the voice that comes to her from far away, from so far away there's hardly anything human about it, brings her at last to the verge of tears:

"Me too, Bartine, I've always loved you too...."

***

He managed to get away from them.

In the time it takes the police to park their blue car with its blinking lights, to enter 410, ask Madame Saint-Aubin a few questions, and calm her down because she's on the brink of hysteria, Marcel is already far away.

Going back out onto Sherbrooke Street five minutes later, they have a good idea of the appearance of the man they're looking for, they even have his name, but they don't know where to look or in what direction to go because Madame Saint-Aubin doesn't have an address for her attacker—a former tenant, apparently—and lazily, they let the matter drop, telling themselves this might be just another nut case taking her fears (and maybe even, in a confused way, her desires) for reality. They prefer to think of it as a false alarm, a nightmare invented by a crazy woman suffering from loneliness who makes up stories to pass the time. They drive away with the siren blaring, to reassure her.

Further east along Sherbrooke Street, the sun has started to set when Marcel climbs up the imposing staircase of the municipal library.

His heart is still beating very hard, adrenaline is still sharpening his sensations, his hands, still aching, tremble in his pockets even though he thinks he's invisible. The migraine won't be as severe as he'd first thought; he knows that a good half-hour's rest over a book opened at random will calm him and drive away the headache that's pounding at his temples.

When he walks into the huge building he takes off his dark glasses so he won't attract attention. He looks to the left to see if there are many people in the reading room. No. Hardly anybody. That's good. He slips inside rather slowly, like someone who's going there because he has nothing better to do, not knowing what learned book he'll consult today, says hello to the guard whom he knows by sight because he has outsmarted him more than once by hiding books that are small enough under his sweater or his winter coat, and makes his way to an empty table. He knows the guard is keeping an eye on him, as he does with every newcomer, so he steps up his prudence and false innocence. He takes off his coat, lays it on a chair, sits down, pretends to be thinking. One minute. Two. Then he gets up, as if he's finally remembered what he was looking for, goes over to the hundreds of boxes that hold hundreds of thousands of index cards that contain everything mankind knows about mankind since Creation.

He discovered a new painter a while ago. Two painters, actually. Two names that are practically twins which he still confuses, because he never remembers which of them painted the *Water Lilies* he fell in love with last summer. The other one he likes a lot too, he's spent a lot of time gazing at his *Bar at the Folies Bergères* which he thinks is full of life, but his favourite is the *Water Lilies* and they're reproduced on large fold-out pages, in soothing colours, shown from a mysterious perspective, and he needs to dive into them, to drown in them after his unsuccessful trip to Madame Saint-Aubin's. He pulls out the drawer for the Ms, quickly runs his finger through the cards.

Ah! there it is, *Mo*net, not *Ma*net. He knows the code nearly by heart. He knows the librarian will give him a strange look because she'll recognize him and know right away which book it is, she'll know its size and weight and that she'll have to look for it, sighing. He takes advantage of the chief librarian's absence then, a dried-up old lady with her glasses hanging from a fake gold chain around her neck, who didn't hide her displeasure the last time he asked for the *Water Lilies*, and holds out his form to a very young woman he doesn't know who perhaps doesn't know anything about the big book.

He waits for five long minutes. The old librarian has time to come back to her customer, a little girl in glasses, visibly shy, and hand her the three Agatha Christies she'd asked for, telling her sarcastically that there are other things to read in the Montreal Municipal Library besides murder mysteries. The girl takes it in without a word and walks away, red as a tomato, her shoulders hunched. Marcel feels his anger coming back, he wants to yell at the old woman the way he yelled at Madame Saint-Aubin fifteen minutes earlier, but he restrains himself. What's the point? And he wouldn't be able to look at the *Water Lilies* in peace.

The young librarian comes back, out of breath, with beads of sweat on her forehead. She sets the book on the counter. A terrible racket starts up in the library and the shrew, whose back had been turned, stares at the two of them as if, together, they had just committed a particularly perverse mortal sin. She moves closer to Marcel, glances at the book.

"Again! If it was a novel I'd think you were learning it by heart!"

Marcel has a ready answer which he tosses off proudly:

"You can learn paintings by heart too, you know!"

The book is *really* heavy, it's the biggest one he's ever seen. He drops the form in front of the guard and goes back to his table.

He takes a few seconds to get a grip on himself—his joints hurt, his arms ache—then slowly he opens the book that contains those plates, those beautiful plates that, when they're opened out to their full size, almost cover the table.

These sublime paintings full of colours that you're never sure, when you examine them closely, if they depict flowers or water or even the air, that divulge their treasures of beauty and calm when you step back from them, these paintings don't make him dream, no, nothing has been able to make him dream since they moved back to Fabre Street, but he has found in them a haven of peace, a place, a real place, that he's come to know perfectly by studying them from side to side and from top to bottom, a garden that has become his own garden, where he likes to stroll, with his nose in the corolla of a water lily or his head resting against the back of his chair, the book standing up in front of him, forming a screen between the real world and the Hero who has not been able to survive, gliding above stagnant ponds and the branches of weeping willows.

While his mother is brewing herself a pot of tea on the other side of Parc Lafontaine, sipping it slowly, letting it get cold, Marcel is plunged into a world of colours that envelop him, enchant him, soothe him and calm his migraine.

***

He wakes with a start when the guard comes and shakes him by the shoulder. He no longer knows where he is, what time it is, whether it's day or night. He has a bad taste in his mouth that he tries to get rid of by coughing into his fist.

"Seventeen years I've been working here and you're the first person I've ever heard snoring!"

Marcel spies the *Water Lilies* on the table, vaguely recalling that he dreamed he was sailing along in a gondola and picking water lilies, then he shuts the book and gets to his feet.

"Excuse me...have you got the time?"

"Ten past seven...."

"My God! Supper!"

The man laughs.

"It's true what they say, eh, you can't live on art!"

Marcel doesn't understand why the man said that. He shrugs, picks up his coat, dons it as he makes his way to the door of the reading room.

"Hey, didn't anybody teach you to put back the books you look at in here?"

Marcel makes a turn, almost a pirouette, slips on the floor, nearly falls.

"Sorry.... I haven't got time.... My mother's going to kill me!"

He tears down the outside steps four at a time, stands dazed, still not fully awake, on Sherbrooke Street which is glistening with rain. The dead leaves already strewn on the ground are wet and slippery; Marcel knows he mustn't run if he doesn't want to end up on all fours, with skinned knees and bloody hands. He looks everywhere, desperate, like someone who doesn't know the way. There's not enough time to walk, it would never occur to him to take a taxi—in any case, he has no money—but he spots a bus coming from the west and races as fast as he can to the stop at the next corner. He has no scarf, he hasn't bothered buttoning his coat, water is running down his neck, and when he drops his ticket into the box his hair is soaking wet.

It's a short distance to Papineau and, luckily, there too he is able to jump on board a northbound bus.

He is at his house in less than twenty minutes. Outside it, actually, because he doesn't dare go upstairs, already terrified at the prospect of the welcome his mother will give him. Never in his entire life has he ever skipped a meal. At eight a.m., at noon, at six p.m., he's the first at the table, he sniffs the air and most of the time looks forward to everything Albertine puts on his plate. When he eats somewhere else, at his Auntie Nana's for instance, he phones to let her know. Always. This time, though, even if he'd been awake would he have had the courage to call and tell his mother he'd be late because he was riding a gondola through the water lilies in "Monsieur Monette's" garden? He tries to laugh, laugh at himself, but he can't. This is a serious moment.

A profile stands out in the front door of the apartment, behind the lace curtain. He hides. He knows it's ridiculous: the later he is, the worse the outburst will be, but he can't convince himself to climb up the sixteen steps of the outside staircase, cross the balcony, push the door that's never locked because there are no thieves on Fabre Street and, in any case, as Albertine says, they have nothing to steal.

But he has to make up his mind, he's not going to stand outside in the rain all evening, he's already as wet as the dead leaves. He sneezes, once, twice, three times. Takes his handkerchief from his pocket. It's soaking wet too. He looks up at the balcony, takes a deep breath, musters his courage, starts up the stairs.

No sooner is his hand on the knob than the door flies open and his mother grabs him by the wrist and pulls him into the vestibule.

"Where were you? We looked all over! You couldn't have picked a worse time to be goofing off. I thought you were sick! Or dead! Your Auntie Nana died this afternoon. The visitation's tomorrow at two."

This is much too much information, he doesn't immediately grasp all the details. Especially not the terrible message hidden at the heart of what his mother has just announced. He stands rooted there in his wet clothes, eyes wide, mouth open, nose dripping. A small child. In a man's body.

And then the truth hits home. What he's been dreading for so long has come to pass. The six months are up. The reprieve is over! And the Hero, the heartless, no, the helpless Hero!—couldn't do anything this time. While he was sailing among the water lilies. Without suspecting anything. Without *feeling* anything. *Without feeling anything!* No punch in the stomach, no sharper pain in his head; he wasn't aware of anything; on the contrary his migraine even went away on its own, lost, drowned in the colours unfurled on the table in the reading room.... While he was running from the police, while he was consoling himself with Monet, his Auntie Nana, his idol, the kindest, the most understanding person he'd ever known, was dying, perhaps all by herself, and *he didn't know! There was no sign from on high! He didn't hear a cry for help!* The Hero, the Knight of Justice, is dead. Is also dead.

Marcel doesn't cry, but Albertine sees that his shoulders are rounded, as if he's become hunchbacked all at once; he becomes round-shouldered, his head slumps into his shoulders, he brings up his elbows like a helpless child. He seems to be shrinking. He opens his mouth to speak but nothing comes out. Albertine tries to pull him towards her but he pushes her away, not aggressively, no, he pushes her away just like that, like some perfectly useless negligible quantity.

She doesn't dare bawl him out, she's afraid it would bring on a seizure. She tries to talk to him gently, but what emerges from her mouth is still abrupt, because the concern she was feeling barely two minutes ago is still there: she's not sure he really is standing there in front of her, that it's him and not someone else disguised as Marcel to reassure her, that he hasn't gotten lost, hasn't been hit by a car or run over by a bus, hasn't died all alone like a rat, calling to her for help—she, his mother—and that she hasn't on the same day lost the two beacons in her life, her sister-in-law and her son.

"Come on. Come on inside. Momma's going to get you undressed. You're soaking wet. Momma's going to run you a nice hot bath. And while you take your bath, Momma's going to fix you a delicious supper. All right? All right, Marcel?"

He moans slightly. A puppy deprived of its mother. It's very very small, nearly inaudible, and so sad, so terribly sad.

***

Someone has to pay.

He did his best one last time to invoke the Knight of Justice, his whip and his sword, but the Knight of Justice is just a memory now, a burning pain in his heart which is now barren. If the Hero had been able to show himself one last time in his armour of light, sitting very erect on his caparisoned steed, handsomer than handsome, blonder than blond under his golden helmet, and all-powerful behind his dark glasses, someone, anyone, his father who died in the war or a particularly dangerous dragon, some insignificant person or another Hero, black of heart and black of hair, would have paid for the death of his aunt and for the definitive disappearance of his gift. But the ceiling stayed empty, of course; so did his head and, above all, his heart. He quickly realized that his heart was empty. He searched deep inside himself where it was usually aswarm with unfulfilled desires, inarticulate thoughts, a world abounding in emotions, needs, nameless riches, but he found nothing. With the tip of his index finger he touched what had been his heart, a thing now grey and tough, and there was no sensation. (The winter before, when he had a tooth pulled, his gums had been frozen, and now, deep down in his heart, what he feels is strangely like that total absence of sensation, the certainty that you can scratch, pierce, burn, butcher—and feel nothing at all.) His heart no longer feels anything. It is frozen. And Marcel thinks it could be extracted like a rotten tooth and he wouldn't even notice.

And so he cannot pay for the death of his aunt, because he wouldn't feel anything. It would be a pointless sacrifice.

He is moving around almost non-stop on his sofa, which has suddenly become uncomfortable. Sleep won't come, he's sure of that, until he has found the person, man or woman, who must pay. Not just for his Auntie Nana's death. For all the rest. He's not too sure what that means but he thinks he knows that it's within his rights to demand a sacrifice for all the *rest*, though he doesn't really know what that consists of except, vaguely, that it's a summary of his own life.

Johanne is too innocent, her father too asinine, Thérèse.... He thinks about Thérèse for a while, about her relationship with Harelip which he doesn't understand altogether, about the monster she becomes when she's been drinking; but selfishly, he also remembers that she's the one who feeds them all and that you don't sacrifice the head of a household just like that, there's too big a risk that everyone will pay. Which of course leaves his mother. He knew he'd get around to her eventually, but he's been putting off the moment, he was trying to distract himself by thinking about the other members of his family who were less important, less *responsible*. Isn't she the one when all's said and done who is mainly responsible for everything? Not for his aunt's death, of course, he knows it was a woman's cancer that took her away, but for all the rest. Ah, he's getting there. For all the rest. For his own condition, that of being the eternal child in a man's body, too long a prisoner of such beautiful dreams to be able now to do without them; for his sister's mental imbalance he's never been able to prevent, even encouraging it in the heat of quarrels and verbal battles that leave them both exhausted and helpless, and in a sense like victims of a drug because they know they'll begin again at the slightest opportunity; for the coldness of Albertine herself who's never been able to show the slightest affection for her two children, who's always been cold and dry, so much so that for a long time he thought she had a stone in place of a heart? Yes, she is the one who's responsible. Especially because she stole his aunt's death from him, she was present at it while he, who deserved so much to be there, was asleep in the overheated reading room of a public library.

He turns around, tries to see into the darkness that stands between him and his mother's bed. He sees nothing. When he gets up and slowly approaches her, taking hesitant little steps like in church when he has to go to the confessional to accuse himself of sins he doesn't understand. All he can see of her is her greying hair, lank from the rain she got caught in on her way home from the apartment on Cartier Street.

The apartment on Cartier Street.

His Auntie Nana.

The punishment.

He goes back to the livingroom, rummages in his pockets and comes back to his mother's bed with the box of Eddy matches.

Purification by fire. A torch. A living torch. A beautiful big fire that blazes for a long time. A sacrifice that will surely be accepted.... Where? By whom? It doesn't matter.

A little voice, far away, perhaps a vestige of a heart or feelings, shouts at him to go back to bed, saying everything will be better tomorrow, or at any rate not so bad. He shakes his head briskly, opens the matchbox, strikes one on the sandpaper edge.

It smells of sulphur. It smells of hell. It smells of punishment.

He brings the match close to the grey hair that's sticking out of the covers.

It happens so fast that he stands there, stupefied.

It doesn't even last for a second, it's yellow and blue, it climbs up to his mother's head, and when she starts to yell it's already finished. Besides, it smells like singed pig. (When she buys pigs' feet to make stew, Albertine singes the bristles first and that's what it smells like now, with his mother howling and holding her head.) He'd been expecting a huge blaze, a pyre on which the woman who is responsible for all the ills in the World would burn for a long time, he'd thought he had enough time to explain everything, to beg her forgiveness, to make her understand the inexorability of his act, of his Act, of his Quest, while she would pay for everything she'd done, but it was all over before it even began.

He stands unmoving in the middle of the bedroom while all around him is pandemonium. Albertine howls, slaps him, insults him, Johanne runs in and starts to cry, Thérèse and Gérard burst in still half-asleep and they too start hurling insults at him. Everybody is yelling. Everybody's yelling! He gets pushed, gets slapped around; his mother, who has never hit him, hits him. They're yelling too loud! It smells terrible! His mother no longer smells like his mother! He has a brief flash of awareness. It didn't work! Nothing worked. As usual.

And then he begins to howl. He opens his mouth wide and his immeasurable pain is manifested in a single cry, on one note, barely interrupted by his breathing, a lament so desperate that everyone freezes there in Albertine's bedroom. A tragic mask is howling before them; the mouth is perfectly round, the bulging eyes stare insanely, the forehead is creased. And what emerges from this mask of pain tears out your soul.

Now, suddenly, they realize that it will never stop. Even when Marcel is calm, even when they've put him back to bed in a little while, or the next morning at breakfast, and in the evening at supper, the cry will go on and nothing and no one, ever, will be able to break it off. A cry of eternal despair has just taken hold of Marcel's soul.

Then Albertine does what has to be done. For the time being. She says, still rubbing her half-charred hair:

"Leave me alone with him."

They protest, claim Marcel may be dangerous, but it's no use, she kicks them out, gently but firmly, and shuts the door behind them.

Then she takes Marcel by the waist.

"Come lie down next to Momma, Marcel dear. Come and lie down next to Momma."

EPILOGUE

Letter from Brother Stanislas to Albertine

Dear Madame,

Following our recent telephone conversation, I am pleased to confirm by this letter that we have found a place in our institution for our Marcel. You can bring him to us whenever you wish, we will be expecting you.

Rest assured as I have often told you that we will take very good care of him and we are convinced he'll be happy here with us. He will be well fed—I know that's important to him—the air of the Laurentians will do him the greatest good, and our community work program may help him to return to society.

You already know I believe that visits are authorized every Sunday afternoon and that you will always be welcome. Our Marcel will be spoiled during the week and your presence on the Lord's day will, I am certain, be a source of joy for him.

Looking forward to seeing you soon, I remain,

Yours very truly,

Brother Stanislas-de-Kostka

Brother of Charity

Key West

8 December 1996

—17 April 1997